a POSSIBILITY
OF WHALES

ALSO BY KAREN RIVERS

The Girl in the Well Is Me
Love, Ish

A POSSIBILITY OF WHALES

KAREN RIVERS

ALGONQUIN YOUNG READERS
2018

Published by
Algonquin Young Readers
an imprint of Algonquin Books of Chapel Hill
Post Office Box 2225
Chapel Hill, North Carolina 27515-2225

a division of
Workman Publishing
225 Varick Street
New York, New York 10014

Printed in the United States of America.
Published simultaneously in Canada by Thomas Allen & Son Limited.
Design by Carla Weise.

LIBRARY OF CONGRESS CATALOGING-IN-PUBLICATION DATA

Names: Rivers, Karen, 1970- author.
Title: A possibility of whales / Karen Rivers.
Description: First edition. | Chapel Hill, North Carolina : Algonquin
Young Readers, 2018. | Summary: Twelve-year-old Natalia Rose Baleine
Gallagher dreams of seeing whales on the beach near her new home,
and is consumed with the prospect that her mother who abandoned
her as a child loves and misses her, and wants Nat to find her.
Identifiers: LCCN 2017042935 (print) | LCCN 2017046757 (ebook) | ISBN
9781616208318 (ebook) | ISBN 9781616207236 (hardcover : alk. paper)
Subjects: | CYAC: Abandoned children—Fiction. | Mothers
and daughters—Fiction. | Whales—Fiction.
Classification: LCC PZ7.R5224 (ebook) | LCC PZ7.R5224 Po 2018 (print) | DDC
[Fic]—dc23
LC record available at https://lccn.loc.gov/2017042935

10 9 8 7 6 5 4 3 2 1
First Edition

FOR LINDEN AND LOLA.
Os quiero mucho.

Part One

CANADA

OH, CANADA . . .

On her fourth day at the new place, Natalia Rose Baleine Gallagher walked down the long, lumpy trail to the beach that lay at the bottom of the slope.

The "Baleine" was silent, was what she told people when they asked, which was pretty much only when she was registering at a new school or had to show her passport. *Baleine* was the French word for "whale." Nat loved the fact that it was there, hiding inside her perfectly normal name. She pictured the whale swimming past the *Natalia Rose* on her passport, surfacing when no one was looking to take a long huffing breath of air before disappearing again, under the *Gallagher.*

"Baleine" was the heart of her name. (When Nat had to do an "All About Me" poster in first grade, she drew a whale where most kids put a heart.)

"Baleine" was also a secret between Nat and her mother, who named her.

Her mother, who named her, and then *left*.

Nat did not know her mother. She had never met her, except for the few fleeting minutes after she was born. *You can come out of someone's body*, she thought, *and not have that count as meeting them.*

Not knowing her mother was the most defining *everything* about Nat's life, which was more complicated than she'd like. Purposely not asking about her mother was Nat's way of minimizing the complications.

Nat knew she could easily find her mother's identity by searching "XAN GALLAGHER daughter mother" (or some other combination of those words) on Google, but she didn't. She mainly used the Internet to look up untranslatable words, which were words that existed in other languages but not in English. Her goal was to learn every language in the world until she found the right one for herself. English was too limiting.

There is a word in Hindi, for example, *viraag*, which means the pain you feel when you are separated from someone you love. Nat had felt *viraag* about her mother for her whole life.

See?

It was complicated.

Sometimes, Nat thought that she liked not knowing. Who doesn't like a mystery? She rubbed the *not knowing* around in her brain like a pebble that was getting smoother and shinier and more beautiful over time.

Nat thought she knew a few things about her mother, whether she wanted to or not. She guessed her mother was French, for example, because the name Baleine was French. And that her mother liked whales for the same reason. Once she made those assumptions, they became true in her head, as real and solid as stone.

Nat also had a sneaking suspicion that her mother was "in the industry." After all, famous people—and Nat's dad was *extremely* famous—tended to fall in love with and marry only other famous people, although there were always exceptions to that rule.

Sometimes they fell in love with and married their makeup artist.

And as soon as Nat thought that, it became as true a fact about her mother as "French" and "liking whales."

Nat's dad and Nat's mom *must* have loved each other, but they did not get married. Nat was born and then her mother left. Those were the facts. No matter how Nat arranged the facts in her head, she couldn't really make them add up to something that was OK.

It wasn't.

Over the years, her brain—almost without her permission—had even formed a pretty complete image of what her mother looked like (beautiful, blond, pale, freckled). The whole portrait was pleasantly blurry, as though someone had put a glowing Instagram filter on it and turned it up so high you couldn't really make out the specific features of her mother's face.

When Nat thought about it too much—which she did, all the time, without being able to help it—she sometimes decided that her mother must have been a terrible person who wasn't worth knowing. Other times, she figured there was probably a really good reason for everything and so her mother, whoever she was, had had a good reason to go.

It was a lot to carry around inside her head—her dad clearly didn't want to talk about it, or at least, he never had so far—and she never brought it up with Solly, who was (in theory anyway) her best friend.

But . . .

But!

But Nat was a person who loved *possibilities*, and when it came to her mysterious missing mother, there were a lot of possibilities.

It was possible Nat just didn't *want* to know who she was.

It was possible she would *never* want to know.

And, at the same time, it was possible she *did* want to know.

It was even possible she wanted her dad to just *tell* her already, without waiting to be asked.

It was *also* possible she was glad he continued to pretend he didn't know that she sometimes did, and sometimes did not, want to know.

Life was like that: a lot of thin layers all stacked together to make something whole, like a puff pastry. Thinking about puff pastry made Nat hungry, but thinking about her mother was more like poking a bruise. Except the bruise was her heart and the poke was just metaphorical, not literal. (People who said "literally" when they meant the opposite drove Nat crazy.)

In addition to all the above possibilities, a new possibility Nat was considering—the most exciting one—was that it was *possible* that if her mother were to meet her now that Nat was twelve years old and not a purple-faced crying baby, maybe she would like her. Maybe even *love* her. (Some people were just not baby people.) And Nat might love her back.

It was a huge *What if?* that hung over Nat perpetually, like a thought cloud in a graphic novel.

But . . .

But!

But there was no changing the enormous and unforgivable fact that Nat was born and her mother up and left without even giving her a chance.

And apparently did not look back.

Nat loved her (whoever she was) because she couldn't help it.

Nat hated her (whoever she was) because she couldn't help it.

See?

It was complicated.

NAT MADE HER WAY down the trail, parts of which were muddier and steeper than they looked from up top. It wasn't much of a path. Nature was a lot messier when you were in it than it looked on postcards, and Canada was very nature-y and messy. This beach was called French Beach even though it was nowhere near the French part of Canada, which was on the other side of the country. It was, at least, a beach. And Nat liked the name. It was *très bien*.

She liked everything French, no matter what.

"*Je t'aime,*" she said out loud. That means "I love you" in French.

Her French was pretty good. It was one of her favorite languages to memorize. It made her think of bunches of flowers tied together with soft, pretty ribbons.

Nat kicked a big broken branch out of her way. Her shoelace got caught and came undone. She leaned down and tied it up. She tried not to make eye contact with her sneaker. Solly had drawn pictures of hearts with eyes all over the sides of her shoes. The pictures made her sad now. She closed her eyes and tied the lace blind.

When she had told Solly she was moving from San Francisco to Canada, Solly lay down on the ground like they had to do during earthquake drills. She curled up into a ball. "I'm in shock," she kept saying. "I can't stand it. Do people live in Canada? Why?"

"Don't be crazy," said Nat. "Get up. Plenty of people live in Canada. Millions."

"But they're Canadians," said Solly.

"Canadians are famous for being nice," said Nat. "I like nice people."

"You like Canadians better than you like me," said Solly. "I will miss you forever."

"Don't be weird," said Nat. She doubted that Solly even meant what she'd said. "I'll see you again. You can come and visit."

Solly had squinted at her dubiously from the ground. "I guess." She sighed. "It seems too far though."

Solly just didn't know, Nat thought now. Canada wasn't far at all. She had been to places much farther away, and to places that felt much farther away even though they weren't. Places that were so different it was hard to believe they shared the same planet with America. Canada actually felt a lot like America. She took a big lungful of Canadian air and let it out slowly in a long whistle. It was summer, so the air smelled good. Was it different from American air? She couldn't tell. It was oceany and warm and damp all at once. And clean. It seemed very clean.

A squirrel scolded her from a tree and Nat looked up, still walking, and tripped over a fat tree root that was lying across the path like a gnarly, bloated snake. She hit the dirt hard, knees first, because she leaned forward so she wouldn't land on her backside and break her phone. Her denim shorts offered nothing in the way of knee protection.

It hurt so much that she couldn't at first manage to make more of a sound than a gasping click in her throat. When she finally caught her breath, she tried, "Help!" but she knew no one would hear her. Her dad was the only one nearby, and he was impossible to wake up, even if she were standing right next to him, shouting directly into his gigantic ear.

Nat crab-crawled over to a rock that was half covered with soft green moss and freckled with tiny ants. From somewhere in the shrubbery and trees, she could hear birds chirping and the rustle of leaves and needles being jostled by the breeze. There was no sign of the squirrel who had caused the problem in the first place. "Jerk," she yelled at the tree where it had been. She sat on the rock, which was cool and solid, and hoped the ants did not bite. The sun burned down on the top of her head. Nat's hair got as hot as a black cat's fur in the sun.

Her knee, on close inspection, was as white and tattered as old tissue paper. The blood trickled slowly down her leg. She stared at it for as long as she dared, a familiar fainty feeling tugging at her. When she couldn't stand it for another second, she stretched her white T-shirt away from her body, leaned forward, and pressed it really really hard against the wound to make the bleeding stop.

She felt extremely, achingly sad. Not because it hurt (which it did) or because blood made her feel light-headed (which it did), but because she was too old to burst into tears when she skinned her knee. Being too old for anything made her *saudade*.

Saudade is a Portuguese word that describes a yearning for something you can never have again, like your childhood. It was a better word than plain old "sad."

"I am *saudade*," Nat told the snakelike tree root. The ants marched across the top of her white sneaker with great determination. The hearts-with-eyes that Solly had drawn looked up at Nat like they wanted something important from her.

"Solly," she said to her shoe. Her voice sounded very small compared to the enormous trees. She would write Solly a postcard about the trees, her knee, and the squirrel. That was good postcard material. She had promised Solly one postcard a week, minimum. They were going to call it the Great Postcard Project. So far, all Nat had done was to buy ten identical postcards at the gas station. They had Canadian flags on them. It was the only postcard the gas station sold. She hadn't gotten any postcards from Solly because she hadn't given Solly her address. She wasn't sure if she wanted to.

Nat looked up the hill. The Airstream looked very far away and very out of place. It was parked at a strange-looking angle to maximize its view of the sunrise. Nat was never even awake at sunrise. She was just not a morning person. Mornings were for sleeping, period. From where she was sitting, the trailer looked like a crooked silver tooth jutting out of a yawning mouth with tree-teeth. She held up her fingers, pinched the trailer between them, and pretended to shift it over to the right, where it would be in the middle of the clearing and make more sense.

At that exact moment, which was midafternoon on a Tuesday, her dad was inside, taking a nap. He slept sprawled out like a body that needed a chalk outline drawn around it. He took up more room than most people no matter what he was doing. She had left the door open, so she hoped nobody dropped in for a visit. But nobody would, because nobody knew they were there.

At least, not yet.

Nat knew it wouldn't take long. Eventually, someone would recognize her dad—XAN GALLAGHER—and that person would tell two friends, and one of them would post it on Facebook and the other on Instagram. And some other person seeing one of those posts would tweet it. Then the paparazzi would appear out of the Canadian fog like one of those jack-in-the-box toys where you turn the handle, and even though you know it's coming, you nearly have a heart attack when the clown doll jumps out.

There was one paparazzo Nat hoped to never see again. Nat and her dad called him the Lion because of his ridiculous hair and beard and because he was always sneaking up on them, stalking them through the savanna and/or the streets of San Francisco or Butte or even, one time, Bali. He was the worst one.

The only thing Nat liked about paparazzi was the word "paparazzi" itself.

Nat got up from the ant rock, brushed the ants off, and stretched her knee. The bleeding had stopped. She walked more carefully down the last part of the trail: The muddy path led to a gravelly area and then to a log the sea had tossed so far up that grass was growing on it. Nat walked along the log, balance-beam style, and then jumped off, landing with both feet in the smooth, wave-worn rocks, some of which slipped into her shoes. Her knee hurt in a sort of stretchy, sting-y way.

She sat down and took off her shoes, burying her bare feet in the cool stones. She could feel her phone pressing into her back pocket. She took it out and balanced it on the log so she didn't drop it or lose it by mistake. She could call Solly, but talking to Solly on the phone was too hard. It made her absence three-dimensional, an actual Solly-sized hole in Nat's life.

She thought about calling the Bird, and then decided not to. When big things happened, like moving, she both desperately wanted to tell the Bird and wanted not to tell the Bird, because sometimes acknowledging change out loud made it more permanent.

Her relationship with the Bird was complicated, too.

"We live in Canada now," Nat told the Pacific Ocean, which lay in front of her all vast and dark and gray. "We live here."

The wind picked up a bit and blew salt spray onto Nat's face and into her hair. The waves curled up and splattered in white foam along the tide line. There were seagulls circling around and calling out. Nat could smell rotting seaweed and the fresh ocean and the hot-from-the-sun rotting log. She scooped up a handful of smallish pebbles and put them into one shoe, and then started methodically sorting through them for a perfect one that she would take back up with her. It had to be a very good, very smooth, very beautiful pebble in order to be the One. So her head was bent and her eyes were on the pebbles when she heard the first loud, huffing exhalation of the whale.

BIRD (MOM)

The Bird was a person, or really, a *situation* that began because of Solly, even though Solly didn't know it.

Solly was accidentally responsible for a lot of things, and on-purpose responsible for even bigger things, like why Nat and XAN GALLAGHER had moved suddenly to Canada the week before. But that was something Nat preferred to not think about directly. It was too much like staring right at a solar eclipse and accidentally burning your retinas to a crisp.

The phone was not entirely Solly's fault either, but it also was.

Nat found the phone on the way to her first day of school the previous September. She was walking alone, having practiced the route already a million times with her dad. It wasn't far.

"No big whoop," she'd told him. She didn't want him to come. Walking down the street with her dad was like waving a giant neon sign that said, "Please stare at us and take our picture!" XAN GALLAGHER was unmistakably XAN GALLAGHER no matter what he was wearing or how much he thought he blended in. Sometimes (a lot), Nat just wanted to be Nat, not XAN GALLAGHER'S DAUGHTER NATALIA ROSE, all-caps.

That day, Nat was a medium amount nervous (to be alone) and a medium amount excited (to see what was going to happen). She knew she would be at this school for only one year, tops. Even if it was bad, it would be bad for only a few months, and then it would be a fading memory, so no matter what happened, it had a feeling of impermanence, like it couldn't possibly matter that much.

The new school was private, so Nat was wearing the requisite plaid skirt—she didn't usually wear skirts in her normal life, but this one swished around her legs in a not-unpleasant way—a crisp white shirt and a dark green tie, with a dark green blazer over the whole ensemble. Wearing it, she became just another girl. A regular person. Her hair was getting a little bit long, long enough to pull it into a very small ponytail if she wanted to, which she didn't. She liked how it made a curtain she could hide behind. (When the world doesn't offer you hiding places, sometimes you have to create your own.)

Nat was considering whether or not Mika—her last year's BFF—was missing her today, if this was her first day back, too, and if she had already mostly forgotten about Nat, when her eye was caught by a glint.

The glint was the sun reflecting off a cell phone.

The phone was just lying there: It was half on the sidewalk, half hanging over the edge above the sewer grate. It was also perilously close to dropping into the sewer. Obviously,

Nat *had* to take two steps to the right, to bend over, and to pick it up.

So she did.

The phone was pleasantly warm from the sun. She pressed it to her cheek.

Nat's dad never wanted her to have a phone. "Who are you going to call?" he'd always say. "*I* don't have a phone." He tapped his temple. "Yep yep." He'd read something once that said phones caused brain tumors, and even after Nat pointed out that phones have speakers and you don't have to hold them next to your ear like people did back in the 1990s, he still refused to consider it.

"Yep yep" could have meant almost anything when her dad said it, but in this case Nat knew it meant "nope nope," in the same way that, to other people, "yeah no" means no and "no yeah" means yes.

"Yep yep" was Nat's dad's first—and most famous—thing.

He said it a lot: In the press. In his life. Sometimes even in his sleep.

Now other people said it, too, when they were mimicking him.

Sometimes even when they weren't.

Famous people always have a *thing*. Her dad had a whole bunch. Nat couldn't even think of what they all were, but she knew when she saw them: the "yep yep," the Eyebrow Raise, the Table Slap, the Huge Laugh, the Save-the-World sayings that sounded like mantras. Everything about XAN GALLAGHER was larger than life, all-caps, but mostly only when he was being XAN GALLAGHER.

When he was being Nat's dad, he was just Nat's dad.

But some things snuck in.

Like the "yep yep."

And the eyebrow.

XAN GALLAGHER's Oscar-winning movie, the movie that changed him from being an action star to being a Real Movie Star, was called *Tumbleweed*. It came out the winter before Nat was born. In the movie, her dad played a man with only one eye who walked, ran, rode, and belly-crawled from one side of America to the other to save his sweet angel daughter from a kidnapper. It took place in olden times. There were storms, and there were bears that he fought off with his bare hands. His movie daughter had extremely long blond hair, coughed up blood inexplicably, and had skin as pale as chalk. She was played by twins who were named Kate and Cait in real life, which was pretty much the dumbest thing Nat had ever heard, and she'd heard a lot of dumb things. *Spelling a name differently does not make it a different name!*

Even though *Tumbleweed* was ancient in movie terms, XAN GALLAGHER managed to stay famous and on the covers of magazines and was frequently featured on gossipy websites. Since she was born, he hadn't done any huge movies like *Tumbleweed*. He only filmed things in the summertime, and a lot of them were animated movies where he just had to do the voice. This year, he hadn't done anything.

But the paparazzi never went away.

They never stopped.

It got so bad in New York, which is where they were before San Francisco, that frequently the long lens of a camera would poke out from behind a display in Whole Foods, and a couple of days later, Nat's own wide-eyed, startled image would show up on the Internet or on the front cover of one of those crummy newspapers in the checkout line. Her friends at school would show her the pictures.

Friends. Ha.

Her *frenemies.*

In the photos, her dad was never wide-eyed or startled. His eyes were always half shut, as though the effort of opening eyes all the way was the work of people who were not as famous as he was.

"Cellular phones are brain fryers. And I like your brain," Nat's dad had continued the last time they'd had this conversation, one which they liked to repeat with slightly different versions of the same script each time. "I like your brain too much to radiate it like popcorn in the microwave."

They also did not have a microwave.

"But Dad—" she'd started, and he'd held up his gigantic hand.

"No way," he'd said. "Never. Over my dead body."

"Don't be weird, Dad," she'd said. "*Everyone* has a phone. And no one says stuff like 'over my dead body' anymore. It makes you sound old-timey."

"*I* say it," he'd said, and raised his left eyebrow all the way up to the top of his forehead.

Nat had laughed, because she couldn't help it, not because not having a phone was funny in any way. It wasn't funny.

It was embarrassing, not to mention inconvenient. Her dad conducted all of his business using email on a Toshiba laptop that weighed about twenty pounds. He took photos for Instagram with an actual camera. He had a Hotmail account from the Dark Ages. As often as not, his manager had to appear in person at the door of the Airstream, clutching contracts or a script and wearing the exhausted expression of someone who has had to fly across the country when a phone call and an email would have been just fine.

A microwave would also have been pretty handy, too, not that they ever had any leftovers. Nat's dad was a big believer in eating everything on your plate, everything in the fridge, everything in the whole farmers' market. He'd probably eat the entire world if he could, as long as the entire world did not have any carcinogenic additives.

Nat thought about her dad's potential reaction while she inspected the found phone.

He wouldn't let her have it.

He would definitely make her return it.

Which she should do. It was the *right* thing to do.

But . . .

But.

But the phone was silver, but a lot of the silver was chipped off, like it was just a coating over plastic and not real metal. It looked like a toy, but Nat knew that it wasn't. It had too much heft. The display was lit up with the time (8:17 a.m.) and an icon that indicated it was sunny, which she thought was dumb. It was obviously sunny. Why would you need your phone to tell you it was sunny? The closest store to where she was standing was not open yet, so she couldn't place the phone on the counter and ask them to put it in their lost and found. She hesitated in front of the *CLOSED* sign, thinking she should maybe put it through the mail slot. Instead, she turned the phone off and slipped it into the pocket of her blazer. It felt reassuringly heavy, weighing down the left side of her jacket by just the right amount.

It felt like it belonged there.

All day, through the "New kids check in at the office!"

part and the "This is your locker!" part and the "First day assembly!" part, Nat kept feeling for the phone. She felt safer knowing that it was there. She felt *connected*, even though she knew literally nobody's phone number and had no one to call. But if anything went wrong, she could call 911. That phone could save a life!

Nothing went wrong.

The school was pretty and pleasant and smelled better and less schooly than most schools. She even had her eye on two or three girls who might turn out to be her new BFF. (The first day was for scouting. She'd learned not to make any real moves until day two.)

By the time the school day ended, she'd almost forgotten that the phone wasn't just part of her blazer, a familiar weight, like an old friend. She made one stop on the way home, which was to buy a charger that fit the phone. It was a hard thing to rationalize, so she made herself not think about it. She didn't make eye contact with the clerk, and after she paid, she slipped it into her other pocket without looking at it either.

Who am I? she wondered. *What am I doing?*

When she got home and hung up her blazer in the tiny Airstream closet, she didn't even take the phone out. She left the charger in its package. If she didn't plug it in, it wasn't intentional. It was all still just a misunderstanding. A mistake.

She definitely didn't tell her dad about it.

The next day when she went to school, it was still in her pocket.

She thought she might just carry it around for one more day, or until she didn't feel like calling 911 might be a possibility. It couldn't hurt. She would give it back eventually to the dum-dum who owned it, who needed to be told by the screen what the weather was doing.

On the second day of school, everyone was nice and everything was fine. But no one was too friendly to her. They weren't *unfriendly* either. But she felt uneasy, like she didn't quite fit. Then the gym teacher shouted at her because her socks were the wrong color, which was embarrassing. She'd never been to a school before that required you to change your socks for gym class. She had to do a plank for three full minutes as punishment.

By the end of the day, there was only one person who seemed like a good candidate for friendship, and that was the other girl in gym class who had also worn the wrong socks. That girl ate alone at lunch, in the corner, reading a book and laughing out loud to herself. When Ms. H had forced them to plank, the girl had made eye contact with Nat a few times, and the last time, she had crossed her eyes, and Nat had collapsed from her plank, in a fit of giggles. It was close enough to a connection to count.

The girl's name was Solly. She had purple hair with blue tips.

Nat could tell that Solly was someone who didn't care about rules. She overheard the gym teacher telling the homeroom teacher that Solly was asked by the principal to dye her hair back to a "normal" color and Solly had suggested that the entire school dye their hair purple, since wearing a shirt, tie, and blazer was not "normal" but became "normal" when everyone did it. The gym teacher was laughing when she told the story.

"She makes a good point," the homeroom teacher had

conceded. "What kind of normal kid would wear a tie if they didn't have to?"

Nat hated the color purple, but she liked Solly's toughness, her ability to read and laugh alone in the cafeteria, her carefree take-it-or-leave-it vibe. Nat's dad had once told her that you make friends with people who remind you of yourself *or* who have some quality that you're missing, to balance you out. Solly had a lot of what Nat thought she was missing. Nat had very little, if any, ferocity. She preferred to disappear, rather than stand out. She was, she figured, Solly's opposite in almost every way.

After school, Nat had looked all over for Solly but couldn't find her anywhere. She was about to give up, when she spotted her purple hair. Solly was on the boys' playground—the whole school was segregated like that, boys in one classroom, girls in another—leaning against the basketball hoop's post. Solly was talking on the phone while a group of boys with loose, flapping ties tried to shoot baskets and shouted at her to move. Nat watched for a few minutes. Eventually the boys gave up and wandered off, jostling and pushing. Nat had never really understood how boys knew how to do that fake punch-playing. They looked like puppies tumbling over each other.

When Solly finally looked up and noticed Nat, she frowned. "What?" she said. "Can I help you?" She rolled her eyes.

The only thing for Nat to do was to take her own phone out of her pocket (*Act natural!* she told herself) and say, "Did you get a signal? I can never get a signal on this dumb thing."

Solly looked suspicious. "Let me see," she said. She took Nat's not-her-phone and flipped it open. She pressed a few buttons. "My brother has a phone like this," she said. "Why are you using a burner phone? Did you drop yours in the toilet?"

"I don't know," said Nat, truthfully. She made a note to herself to Google "burner phone" next time she was at the library. She hoped it was nothing bad. "I mean, I didn't drop anything into the toilet. This is just my phone." The lie felt like the truth once she'd said it out loud.

"It's not very good," said Solly. "You should get an iPhone."

"OK," said Nat.

"They're expensive though. If you're poor, you can't afford it. That's why my brother doesn't have one."

"I'm not poor," said Nat. She stepped back. Maybe she didn't want to be friends with this person, after all. Her words felt like jabs. Nat rubbed her arm.

"I didn't mean anything by it," said Solly. "People are poor. Sometimes. It's all relative. We're poor. I get a scholarship to this rich school. Mom bought me this phone when we weren't poor for about six months. She sang a gross Christmas song that got popular three years ago." Solly looked thoughtful, then added, "She thought it was so good, but it was popular because everyone couldn't believe how seriously bad it was. It got a lot of radio play so that the announcers could make fun of it. She's embarrassing. *And* she's bad with money. The money was gone like that." Solly snapped her fingers. "Are you calling your mom?"

Nat blinked. "Um," she said.

She could have said, "I'm calling my dad."

She could have said anything.

She could even have said, "I don't have a mom."

Instead Nat said, "Yeah. I am. Calling my mom. I have to call my mom and tell her how school went. Because it's a new school. First day. And she isn't here." She rolled her eyes in a way that she hoped looked as cool as it had when Solly had done it, and not like she was having some kind of weird fit. "Mom just *has* to know everything. She's away for work." The word "mom" felt funny in her mouth. She ran her tongue over her teeth. "My mom," she repeated.

"What kind of work does she do?" Solly asked.

"She's a makeup artist," Nat answered.

"Huh. Cooooool," said Solly. She looked like she was trying not to laugh.

"What's so funny?" said Nat.

"Nothing." Solly squinted like the sun was in her eyes, which it wasn't. It was behind her. "Is she in LA, then?"

"Yes," said Nat, softly, relieved that her lie at least now had some distance between her and itself. "She's working on a movie." She imagined this distance to be like a calm, turquoise blue sea stretching between the boys' playground and LA, where her imaginary mother was just then dabbing imaginary concealer on an imaginary movie star's invisible pimple.

"You can try her again now that your phone works," said Solly. There was something in her voice that was challenging. "Do it."

Solly handed Nat's phone back and tipped her face up, like she needed some warmth on her skin. She moved around to the other side of the pole so the sun was right on her face, and she closed her eyes. She looked like someone in a spotlight, glowy and surreal.

"OK," said Nat. "Thanks." She flipped the phone open.

She thought about what to do. This was the last moment where she could fix this, where she could correct the misunderstanding. *Or* she could go with the lie and have to carry it around forever, or at least for the school year.

What if? she thought.

Nat took a deep breath and stared at the keypad on the stranger's phone. Then she dialed. She hoped the phone worked. She crossed her fingers on the hand that Solly couldn't see.

She dialed the area code for LA.

Then she added her favorite number, followed by her locker number, and her birthdate.

She didn't have a lot of time to think about it.

"Why isn't your mom's number already in your phone?" said Solly. "What's up with that?"

Nat shrugged. She held up her finger, like she was listening, which she was.

The phone was ringing.

"Hello?" chirped a woman's voice.

"Hi . . . Mom," Nat said, weakly. She wasn't optimistic about how this would go, but she was in it now. "Um. It's me. I'm at school. Well, on the playground. I'm with my new friend Solly." She immediately regretted saying that. What if Solly thought that was weird? "My new friend Solly" *sounded* weird. They weren't even friends yet. They just met! "Anyway, Dad said I had to call you."

"Oh, honey." The woman's voice reminded Nat of a tiny bird. "I'm not your mom, you've dialed the wrong number."

"No, I didn't," said Nat. She had to make this work. She spoke quickly and in a hushed voice. "It's just a thing. Trust me. Please, Mom."

"What kind of thing? Is this a prank call?" The lady didn't sound mad, only slightly amused.

"Not quite," said Nat. "I'm sure it sounds like that, but it isn't like that. Thank you. It's OK. I promise, it's OK. Do you have time to talk for a minute?" Solly opened one eye and gave her a funny look. "Like, I know you're busy at work."

"I'm going to hang up," said the lady. "I don't know what's happening."

"It's just . . . please don't. Um, the boys' playground and the girls' playground here are different places. Everything is separated. It's pretty weird."

"Is this a cry for help? Have you been kidnapped?"

"Not exactly," said Nat. "I mean, not at all. No! Definitely not. Not even close. I'm just calling because Dad said I should. You know how he is, Mom."

"If this is an emergency, say 'peanut butter sandwich,'" said the bird-voiced lady. She sounded quite happy now. "I can call the police for you. Tell me where you are?"

"It's not like that," said Nat. "MOM. You're so funny! Yes, I had a good day! It was fine. But I hate gym. And I need new socks. Gym socks have to be white."

"That sounds like a fancy place," the lady said. "White socks!"

"What else? Well, my homeroom teacher's name is Mr. Knox. He's from Texas. He reminds me of Uncle Bill. Like, with the big hat? But he wasn't wearing a hat. He just seemed like a person who probably would. His head just begs to be hatted." The lying was getting out of control, although it was true there was a Mr. Knox. But Nat didn't even *have* an Uncle Bill. She was a terrible person. Her mother probably was a liar, too, lying to everyone and saying that she'd never had a baby named Natalia Rose Baleine Gallagher. Liars sucked. Nat swallowed hard. "I miss you," she added. She had lost sight of what was a lie and what was the truth now.

Oh boy, she thought.

The bird lady made a laughing, chirpy noise. "This is the strangest conversation I've ever had with a prank caller," she said. "You're very funny. Uncle Bill!"

"Uncle Bill," Nat repeated. "Remember when he fell out of his chair at that wedding?"

"It was very funny," the voice agreed. "So funny. The way he fell right into the cake. But why was the cake on the floor? That cake was awful. No one should ever put raisins in cake."

Nat laughed. "Raisins are gross," she agreed. Then she didn't know what to say. The sun was very bright and hurting her eyes. "Um," she said.

"Should I hang up?" the lady said. "Is this prank call over?"

Solly made a face at her and rolled her eyes, so Nat rolled her eyes, too. The eye rolling was starting to be a thing. Having a thing was good, but she wouldn't have picked eye rolling necessarily. Eye rolling made her think of cows. Cows with flies buzzing around their eyes.

"Hello?" said the lady. "Goodbye!"

"No, don't go! I just, well, is there anything else you just *have* to know, Mom? You know how you are, how you like to know all the dumb details. Ha ha." She said those words, "ha" and "ha," separated like that. Who did that? Who was she turning into? A liar who *ha* and *ha*'d? She cleared her throat.

"I *definitely* know how I am," the bird lady said. "Dumb

details are my favorite things. I'm glad you called me. This is odd but it's making my day. I do wonder why you are calling me, a stranger, and not your actual mother though."

"I don't have one," said Nat. "At least, if I do, I don't know her."

"What?" Solly mouthed. "Who?"

Nat made a gesture that was somewhere between a shrug and wave, then she turned it into a point. She pointed somewhere behind Solly.

Solly turned around. "What?" Solly said. "Is there something there? Is it those dumb boys? Like they *own* this basketball court."

"I should go," said Nat. "I'm on a basketball court. I told you that, right?"

"I didn't know my mother either," said the bird lady. "She died when I was born. Can I tell you something?"

"Sure," said Nat.

"When I was little, I thought that everyone's mom died when they were born, and then I went to school and I found out other people had living moms. I somehow hadn't noticed all the moms before. I guess my dad kept me mostly at home. I felt so ripped off when I realized. When I came home from school, I punched my dad right in the nose. He got a nose-bleed! After that, he always called me Muhammad Ali. He was a boxer. Not my dad, but Muhammad Ali."

"That's terrible!" said Nat. "About, you know." She glanced at Solly. "The first part," she whispered.

"I know," the bird lady whispered back. Then, in a normal voice, she added, "But it might be worse to not know who she was. I have to think about that. If you prank call me again, ask me, and I'll have thought of an answer. I like to think about my answers. I have lots of time for thinking. I think about my mother a lot."

"I do, too," said Nat. "Mine, I mean."

"This call is taking *forever*," said Solly. "You and your mom have totally weird convos." She put her hand on the pole and twirled around it a couple of times, her purple hair streaming behind her in the sun like an ad for hair dye. Nat had a monkey on a stick toy that spun around just like that until it landed at the bottom. Then you turned it over and it raced back up to the top. It was the one toy her dad had let her keep from when she was little. It lived in the box she kept under her bunk in the trailer. In general, he didn't believe in "things"—he was a minimalist—but he kept his Oscar, so she was allowed to keep Stick Monkey.

"I kind of do have to go now," said Nat to the bird-voiced lady. "Thank you. It was really nice of you to . . ." She squinted directly at the sun. Her eyes were watering. It was probably because the sun was so bright. "I love you, Mom. Have fun in LA." She had never said the words "I love you, Mom" out loud before. Her throat had a huge lump in it now. The lump was the size of a basketball. She swallowed.

The bird lady laughed. "Love is a big deal," she said. "And you're welcome."

Nat hung up the call and saved the number.

She wrote "Bird" in the blank that asked for the name. Then, in parentheses, she wrote "(Mom)." She tilted the screen so that Solly couldn't read it. "Glitchy," she said to Solly. "It keeps deleting it. I keep putting it in."

"Huh," said Solly. "Those phones are junk."

"I guess."

"What's your mom like?" said Solly. "*My* mom is a freak."

"Oh. My mom is . . . pretty. She's nice. I don't know. She's a mom. A normal mom. You know, chirpy." Nat was really growing the lie now. After all, what kind of *normal* mother would abandon their purple-faced baby? Even in nature, when animals were faced with actual danger, mother animals stuck by their babies. Usually. Not always. Nat and her dad once found a baby harbor seal on the beach, and when they called the Ocean Rescue Center, the guy who came said it happened all the time. "I think some of them are just really dumb," he said. "I think they just forget they even have a baby."

But Nat's mother wasn't a harbor seal, so she had no excuse.

"Helllloooooooooo. I said, 'Where are you going now?'" Solly asked. "What are you doing?"

"Home," said Nat. "Do you want to come over? I'm not doing anything." She didn't really think about it before she asked, but she regretted it immediately. If Solly came over, she would know Nat's dad was XAN GALLAGHER, and then everyone would know. Not that a secret could last very long in a city like San Francisco, which Nat had thought was a terrible choice from the get-go. Her dad had insisted on it because of his great friendship with the director of his last movie, whose backyard the Airstream was currently parked in. Her dad did that. He became GREAT FRIENDS with everyone. It was like the whole world—everyone he met—got swept up into his XAN GALLAGHER embrace, which was a world of its own. The director wasn't even there. He was in the desert somewhere filming a movie about Mars. They'd probably never see him again. The movie would take months to make. But that's how her dad's friendships worked: They were super intense and then they just faded away to nothing, like an Etch A Sketch that was shaken clear, leaving only a faint trace of what had been there, a memory of a friend. If her dad saw the director again, they'd hug and stuff, but it would never be the same as when they were on set, when they were soul mates.

Anyway, her dad had already been recognized in Rite Aid buying ChapStick, so it probably didn't matter that much. He really liked to keep his lips moisturized, much to the detriment of their plan to stay "under the radar."

"Sure," said Solly. "I'll come over. I'll just text my mom." She typed something rapidly on her iPhone with her thumbs. Her phone beeped in response. She laughed and typed again. "LOL," she said out loud. Then she looked up. "My mom is super famous. You can be famous and poor, you know."

"Sure," said Nat.

"You didn't ask me who she is," said Solly. "I'm deciding if that's weird."

"Who is she?"

"Gracie," said Solly, triumphantly.

Nat tried to arrange her face in a happily surprised way that she hoped wouldn't let on that she had never heard of Gracie. "Cool!" she said.

"You've never heard of her," said Solly.

"Not really," admitted Nat.

"Forget it," said Solly. "It doesn't matter."

"I'll Google her!"

"Don't bother. Seriously. I'm so tired of people being friends with me for having a famous mom. It's so tiresome."

"My dad is a little famous, too," offered Nat.

"I already know that, stupid," said Solly. "You're Natalia Rose. Your dad is XAN GALLAGHER. Duh. He's overrated.

That 'yep yep' thing is lame. But he was funny in that movie with the spiders. Did he really used to wrestle? I love wrestling."

"Yeah, that spider movie is a good one," Nat lied. "He doesn't wrestle anymore."

She hated that movie. Spiders were her one big fear. But it was true that her dad no longer wrestled. She was stacking truths against the lies to justify them. *This is going to end badly*, she thought. She didn't even understand where all these lies were coming from. It was like she'd rejected the truth now and had forgotten how to get it back.

Nat forged ahead. "He was a wrestler a really long time ago. He's still friends with some of those guys. Sometimes we go for dinner with them, and they're all, like, ENORMOUS." She did not respond to the part where Solly had said her dad was overrated. Maybe it was a good thing. If Solly thought he was overrated, she wouldn't narc them out to the Lion.

The "yep yep" part was just mean.

The hair on the back of Nat's neck prickled.

She reached up and rubbed it with her hand.

Solly had turned her into a huge liar.

It wasn't Nat's fault.

Solly laughed. "I might be a wrestler when I grow up, but I don't want to get fake boobs. Like *all* the girl wrestlers seem to have those." She looked down at her chest and then put her fists under the flaps of her blazer. "Nope," she said. She took her hands out again. "I want regular ones though. Like, yesterday."

"I would *never* do that," said Nat. "Get fake ones. That's gross."

"My mom did it," said Solly. "It looks ridic. Like her

boobs have nothing to do with her body, they are just stuck on there." She puffed out her cheeks.

They both giggled.

The phone stayed where it was, still just the right heaviness, in Nat's blazer pocket. When she got home, she put it under her pillow and then attached the charger to the outlet where her lamp was plugged in—a place her dad would have to crawl onto her bed to see.

Eventually, Nat sort of forgot that the phone wasn't hers in the first place. It became hers, *de facto*, which is a Latin phrase that means "whether it is right or wrong."

It *was* wrong, and she knew it.

But the person who owned it would have replaced it by then probably. And no one needed the phone more than she did.

It was meant to be.

THE ITCH

On the beach, Nat put the pebbles back in her shoe.

She was holding her breath.

She stood up, slowly. She felt as though if she were to move too quickly, this thing that was happening would stop happening.

"This thing that was happening" was whales.

Whales were happening.

Rising out of the water, only about twenty feet offshore, there was an impossibly tall black dorsal fin. She didn't know how tall it was, but it was definitely taller than her.

"Oh!" Nat said.

The orca surfaced and exhaled loudly, slowly blowing a misty spray of water. She could tell it was an orca because of its huge fin and distinctive black-and-white markings. She had seen orcas before, in Alaska, but that was different. That was from a boat.

The whale's exhalation made a rainbow between Nat and the sun that hung in the air like something magical was happening. Nat sat back down on the pebbly stones, and then she stood up again. She didn't know what to do with her hands.

"OMG," she said.

A wave of energy, like electricity, passed through her. She jumped up and down a couple of times, her feet rattling the pebbles. She felt like she might explode. "Wow." The whale was in only about three feet of water. He was so close to her. She stepped closer to the shoreline. The water was really clear. She could see the big white patch on his face. She could see his eye.

Then a second fin appeared a few feet behind the first fin. It was smaller.

Then, farther out, a third one, even smaller than that.

She could hardly breathe.

Papa, Mama, and baby, like the three bears: a family.

The fins were all lined up now, aiming right at the shore, as though they were going to beach themselves and then maybe grow legs and walk right out of there. *Which would actually be terrifying, come to think of it*, Nat thought. Her heart was going to beat right out of her chest any second. She wondered if the whales would eat her.

Were they *hunting* her?

Calm down, she told herself. The whales were just bobbing there now, huffing, like they were making a plan.

Nat thought about nature documentaries that she'd seen where orcas chased seals up onto the beach and then hurled themselves after them, only to drag the seals back into the water and eat them. But there was no seal here. She certainly hoped they didn't think *she* was one.

What if they did?

"I am not a seal!" she called. "Person, not seal. I'm Nat."

She looked around. There was still no one else there, nowhere in sight. A seagull flew across the horizon, but that was it as far as signs of life were concerned.

It was only her.

And the whales were *right there*. Right in front of her!

She wondered if she should run back up into the trees, in case they were confused and hunting her. But she couldn't stop looking at them. "This is crazy! This is totally crazy. What are you *doing*? What is happening? I mean, don't eat me! You're amazing. You are so amazing."

The wind took her words and whipped them up into the trees behind her. It was really picking up, blowing her hair all around her face and into her mouth, and pushing the salt spray toward her. She thought she could even smell the whales' terrible breath. Whales had bad breath. That was just a fact. Everyone knew that.

The huffing sound was so loud, it vibrated in the air. She kept looking over her shoulder, as though maybe somebody else would (should) materialize there, and then she could say, "Can you believe this? Look at this! Look at these whales!"

She turned around and picked up her phone from the log. She *would* call her dad to come down here, but he still stubbornly refused to have a phone. "DAD!" she yelled instead, just so she could say that she tried to call him. He would be super disappointed to miss out on this.

She wished her phone weren't a burner phone. She wished it had a camera.

This was unbelievable.

"Unbelievable!" she shouted.

Probably, afterward, no one *would* actually believe her. But she didn't care.

It was *real*.

It was *happening*.

Maybe it was even some kind of a sign, though of what, Nat didn't know.

She took three big steps closer to the whales, who were swishing around in the shallow water. Her ankles twisted precariously on the uneven ground, and the stones slid noisily toward the water, because the beach was very sloped. She got as close as she dared. Then the big whale made a whistling sound and did a wiggle that sent sprays of water everywhere.

It looked almost exactly like he was scratching his belly.

"Are you *itchy*?" Nat said. "Is that what you're doing? Scratching?" Just saying the word "itchy" made her own belly itch. She scratched and watched, watched and scratched.

All three whales were wriggling now, bellies against the rocks and pebbles. It made an amazing noise, a rattle and grind and splash all at once, the rocks all rubbing against each other. It was beautiful and terrible at the same time.

Nat crouched down. She wanted to tell the whales about how they were connected: Nat and her mysterious mother and those three whales and this place, French Beach, but she couldn't find the words. She just held her hands out, fingers spread. Maybe they would know what that meant. She had no idea.

"Baleine," she whispered.

The whales slid back into the sea and then heaved themselves up again, all in a row. Then the little one swished away and swam back and forth, parallel to the shore, as if he were bored. He was probably saying, "Mom, Dad, let's goooooooooooooo," in whale language.

The baby slapped his tail against the water. It made a sound as loud as a thunderclap. "Can you be done already?" he seemed to be asking. You didn't need to understand whale to understand what he meant.

Or she.

It's not like you could tell if a whale was a he or she just by looking.

Nat got a boy-vibe though. At least, she thought she did.

Her heart was slowing down now. She sat on the log. The beach was still deserted. The gulls were still playing in the wind. The two larger whales were still rubbing; the rocks were still rattling.

Nat hoped the tide didn't go out and leave them beached.

They were *huge*. There was no way she'd be able to push them back out to sea. Not alone. Her dad probably couldn't even do it. The fin on the biggest one was taller than even he was, she was sure of it. She felt tiny, like a marble in a bin of basketballs.

The whales flicked their mighty tails and then shifted back into the deeper water again. This time, they didn't heave themselves back in her direction. They hesitated there, a few feet offshore. Nat wasn't sure if they could see her or not, but she waved anyway. Then all three sank and rose in unison, exhaling in loud puffs. They swam out a little way and then back, like they were saying goodbye or like they didn't want to go.

Nat kept her hand raised, as though she were saluting them. "Goodbye," she said. "Thank you!" She felt weird talking to them, but she also felt like she had to say *something*. It wasn't enough to just let them swim away.

The trio of dorsal fins disappeared under the surface, one by one. Nat put her hand over her eyes to shield them from the sun. The whales were out a little way now. Then the smallest one jumped clear out of the water and slapped down again, belly first, the sound echoing around Nat like applause.

"Wow," called Nat. "All the wows. Wow forever."

The sun was starting to move lower in the sky. She'd lost track of how long she'd been there. Her dad was probably awake now and wondering when she was coming back, and where she had gone. She slowly dumped the pebbles out of her shoes and put the shoes back on her feet. She didn't even want to take a pebble back up with her. She just wanted to hold the picture of the whales in her mind, to keep looking at it again and again.

Nat picked up the phone to put back in her pocket, but then she changed her mind. She flipped it open, hesitated for a minute, and dialed.

"Hi," Nat said. "It's me. Guess what I just saw?"

"Hmm," said the Bird. She sounded like she'd been asleep. She cleared her throat. "Well, in order to guess, I need to know where you are."

"I'm at the beach," said Nat. "We moved. I should have told you that. There's a beach here. We are in Canada."

"I love beaches everywhere in the world. I can hear the wind on your beach through the phone. Canada is lovely. Aren't you lucky?"

"I guess," said Nat, dubiously.

"I'm going to say that you saw . . . hmmm. A seal?"

"Nope," said Nat.

"A mermaid?"

"Come on, mermaids aren't real. Duh. I'm twelve. Not, like, *nine*."

The Bird laughed. "A lot of people think mermaids are real! But you're probably right. There are a lot of stories though, and sometimes when you hear a lot of stories about the same thing, you have to wonder, *Is this real?* Like the Loch Ness Monster. Did I ever tell you that I'm a marine biologist?"

"What? You are? No!" Nat closed her eyes for a second. She could see the pattern of her own blood vessels on the insides of her eyelids. When she was little, she'd thought it was something else. A scary something. She couldn't remember quite what, but she remembered that it frightened her. She wasn't scared now, but she was *something*. "I thought you were a makeup artist," she said, opening her eyes. The *something* feeling was still there.

The Bird laughed again. "Why would you think that? I never even *wear* makeup. Wearing makeup is a lot of work. It takes so much time! Life is too short to worry so much about what you look like."

"My mom is a makeup artist," said Nat.

"Oh, honey. I didn't mean . . . I thought you didn't know who your mom is?"

"I don't want to talk about it now," said Nat. Her voice felt small and velvety, like a cat's footsteps. She wondered if the Bird could even hear her. "I just wanted to tell you about the whales."

"Whales!" the Bird exclaimed. "Well, I am happy to talk about whales all day. Every day. Whales are my favorites. What kind of whales?"

"Orcas," said Nat. She picked up a stone and threw it into the water, where it was swallowed by a wave. She threw another. "Three orcas. They came practically right up onto the beach!"

"Orcas are my second favorite. Did you know they are actually dolphins?" said the Bird. "Humpbacks were my specialty."

"Oh," said Nat. She brightened up. "I like *all* the whales. And dolphins. My middle name is Baleine! That's French for 'whale.'"

"I love that! What a perfectly glorious name! You're very lucky."

"My first name is Nat." She suddenly wanted the Bird to know who she was. "Natalia."

"That's a nice name, too," said the Bird. "Nat. But can I call you Baleine? I like to say it. It has such a nice shape in my mouth."

Nat giggled. "I like it, too. You can call me that." She paused. "No one calls me that, not ever. It's like a secret name."

"Well, then it fits. We are like secret friends. Do you want to know my name?"

Nat shrugged, but obviously the Bird couldn't see her shrug. She didn't want to know the Bird's real name. She wanted her to stay Bird (Mom) forever. Having a Bird (Mom) was better than anything she knew how to explain. But she didn't want to be rude either. "Maybe not yet," she said. "Unless you really really want to tell me."

"I get it," said the Bird. "If you don't know my name, I can be anyone. I think maybe that's just fine. I like the idea of being anyone. I think a lot about being someone else, some-times. I look at people and I think, *Why am I me and why are you you?* Do you ever do that?"

Nat didn't answer. She couldn't think of what to say.

"I like thinking of you as Baleine, more than I like thinking about you as Prank Caller," the Bird went on. She pronounced *Baleine* perfectly, in the French way. Nat felt something like feathers moving softly in her stomach. "Tell me about the whales, little Baleine. Let me just get comfortable. I want to hear everything. I want to hear the whole story."

So Nat told her.

HARRY

Here is a list of everything that is wrong with you, Harry typed.

He reached up and scratched his ear. His ear was always itchy lately. He thought there might be something wrong with it, like scabies or mites, or something even worse. He Googled "scabies." Again. He was pretty convinced that was it: tiny little bugs burrowing through his skin. He scratched his ear harder. Maybe he picked them up at the library when he leaned his head down on the sofa. Or maybe on the bus to the stupid day camp he had to go to while his parents were at work.

The day camp was terrible in more ways than that. It was particularly terrible because it was a camp for *girls*.

Thinking about it gave him the elevator-stomach feeling he hated, where it felt like your body separated from your head somehow when an elevator went too fast. The elevator in the building at his dad's old job in Victoria, where they used to live, did that.

Harry scratched his ear again, so hard it was probably bleeding. It was just a coincidence that it was the same ear that got hurt the year before when a group of boys in his class decided it would be funny to beat him up.

They beat him up because they hated him for knowing who he was.

That is, they beat him up because even though some dumb doctor said he was a girl when he was born, he was really a boy.

The boys who beat him up were not the kind of kids who understood things like that.

No one in that town was.

Maybe no one *anywhere* was.

Only on the Internet did people get it.

So moving was a good idea, for sure. The trouble was that his dad moved with them. Obviously.

And so did Harry's "issue." That's what his dad called it.

Harry deleted everything that he'd typed and started a new list. He wrote the day at the top of it, which was Tuesday. A list of all the things that were wrong with him would take too long. He'd stick to all the things that were wrong with Tuesday. It was easier.

Harry scratched his ear.

Tuesday:
1. *Everything*
2. *Itchy ear*
3. *Day camp*

4. *School starts back next week*
5. *GENDER—having to explain*
6. *Shut up shut up shut up shut up shutup*
   shutupshutupshutuppppppp

Harry stopped typing. The day-of-the-week list was a dumb idea. Everything was wrong, every day, and mostly the same things were wrong, and the same things were itchy.

Harry was suddenly too bored of the topic of himself to try writing another list.

He wanted to scream.

Lists put things in order and made him feel like he had a handle on things, but he didn't actually have a handle on anything at all except for pretty much every Mario game ever. Maybe he'd have a handle on everything else the next day.

Maybe nothing would be itchy.

Probably not, though.

A *good* list always made him feel better. But a bad list, not so much.

He deleted the whole list and shut off the laptop and turned on the PlayStation instead.

This is better, he thought. Video games never hurt your feelings. Video games never looked at you funny when your dad called you Harriet, loudly, at pickup time or when you were the only boy at a girls' day camp. Video games never had so darn much to explain.

The game beeped and played a song. Harry leaned forward to see it better. "Yes!" he said.

His character ran across a tightrope and swung down a tunnel. "Gotcha!"

COD IS TERRIBLE

Dear Solly, Nat wrote.

She was lying on her bed.

"Now *you're* tired," said her dad from the doorway, which he more than filled with his enormous self. He had to stand sideways. "We have to time our naps better, yep yep."

"I'm not napping! I'm writing to Solly. I don't nap. Napping is for losers! And babies."

"Nah! Napping is the best. Man, you have to try it. One day, I'll talk you into it and you'll be like, 'Dad, how come you never told me how great naps are?'"

"I promise I will never say that."

"Yeah, you will!"

"Whatever. I won't though."

"Will so."

"Will not!"

"Will so."

"DAD. I'm trying to do something here!"

"Oh! I'm trying to do something, too." He made a face. "How was the beach?"

"It was beachy. There were . . ." For some reason, the whole story about the whales didn't want to come out of her mouth. *That's weird*, she thought. "I saw . . ." She shrugged. "It was kind of cold," she said. "Lots of seagulls. And rocks. I slipped." She showed her dad her knee. The blood was all dried now. It didn't look like a big deal.

"Ouch. Are you OK, Natters?" Her dad came into the room. Her room, like all the rooms in the trailer, was tiny. It just had her bed, which was basically a shelf, and that was it. There was no room for anything else. All her clothes were in a tiny closet and in the drawer under the bed. Her dad filled up so much of the non-bed space, she felt like she needed to scrunch her body into a corner of the bed in order to breathe. At least sitting down he wasn't so gigantic.

He sat.

"I'm good," she said. "I'm fine. My knee is fine. It's no big deal. Did you have a nice nap? Did you have happy dreams?" That was another one of their jokes. At bedtime, he always said, "Night night, happy dreams, fun tomorrow." No matter what. And in the morning, he said, "Did you have happy dreams?" And if she hadn't, he'd mock-punch her and say, "I told you to have happy dreams!"

"Did I ever!" he said. "The Canadian air makes me sleep like a baby!"

"I hear babies are terrible sleepers. That's why they have to nap during the day, too," said Nat. "Did you cry a lot and poop yourself?"

Her dad threw back his head and laughed, nearly

smashing his head on the shelf that ran along the wall where she kept all her books.

"That's true about babies," he said. "*You* were a good baby though. You slept like a log. I had to keep checking to see if you were dead!"

"Spoiler alert: not dead."

"Not dead," he repeated. "Thank goodness. Anyhoo, I'm going to take the scooter into town for groceries. We need cod!"

"Dad, I hate cod. Please, no. *You* hate cod."

"I was joking about the cod!" He laughed again. There had been an article on the Internet the year before called, "XAN GALLAGHER EATS MORE IN A DAY THAN YOU DO IN A WEEK." The Internet went nuts for it. People tried to eat like him. One guy got really sick and gained five pounds in a week. "He didn't work out!" Nat's dad had said. "What a dummy!" The article said that XAN GALLAGHER ate two pounds of cod every day, which he *had* been doing, when the reporter had asked him. It was his Cod Phase. "I can't ever face cod again." He paused. "Their faces are really tiny."

He laughed at his own joke, bending double in the middle. Everything he did, he did BIG. The books shook on the shelf.

"DAD!"

He stopped laughing. "Nat, I solemnly swear . . ." He put his hand on the book she was sort of reading. His hand was bigger than the book. "I swear on this book that my Cod Phase is over."

"Cod is gross," Nat agreed. "No more Cod Phases allowed. Like, ever."

"I think I'll get salmon, yep yep," he said. "They have great salmon here. Maybe this will be my Salmon Phase. Drumroll, please!" He drummed on her leg with his hands.

"Ouch! Stop. Sure, Dad, whatevs."

"'Whatevs' is not a word."

"Is too."

"Is not."

"DAD, don't you have fish to cook?"

Nat's dad spent two hours every day preparing massive amounts of food and then even more time eating it. He ate about ten times what a normal person ate; fifteen times as much as she, a kid, ate. They had a special fridge installed in the trailer that took up most of the kitchen wall.

Cooking, eating, and working out was his full-time job, when he wasn't doing a movie. And this year, he hadn't even done one.

He was taking a break.

But he never took a break from cooking, eating, and working out.

After he cooked all that food and ate it, he worked out in the Other Trailer.

The Other Trailer was also an Airstream, but it was full of gym equipment. There was even gym equipment attached to the outside of it for the massive, weird elastic-band exercises that he couldn't do inside a small space. In San Francisco, he had used the famous director's home gym, but here they did not have access to a famous director's house and gym equipment. The second trailer they called "Mini-Me" even though it was pretty much the same size as their main trailer.

XAN GALLAGHER was serious about his body. *Too serious*, Nat thought privately. She wondered if he wouldn't probably still be *just* as famous if he ate a normal amount of food and went for a jog once a week or something like normal dads.

"I'm trying to write to Solly!" she said. "Go away!"

"I love you," he said.

"Yeah, you do," she said.

She waited until she heard his scooter start up, putt-putting up the long gravel driveway, before she started writing again. She looked down at what she had so far. "Dear Solly" seemed too formal. She put that one at the bottom of the pile of identical postcards and got out a new one.

Hey, she wrote. *Canada is cool! It's basically like America but the money is more colorful. Ha ha. I saw whales on the beach today. They were really close. School starts in six days. There are about 10 people in this town, so it should be weird.*

She stopped writing and lay back on her bed. Sweat trickled into her hair. Her dad had the fan blowing, but it was still hot—way hotter than down at the beach. He didn't believe in air-conditioning. Something about the refrigerant gases destroying the atmosphere. Sometimes the inside of the trailer was exactly like the inside of a solar oven. She got up. She took the pen and the postcard outside to where her dad had set up the hammocks in the shade of some gigantic trees. His was huge and hers was little. It looked silly next to his, like a toy, like when girls put outfits on their dolls that matched their own.

She climbed into his hammock.

It was covered with needles from the trees and some sticky sap.

She stuck her fingers in the sap and stuck them together, and then wished she hadn't. Sap was hard to get off.

Then she sap-glued the pen between her fingers so she'd be forced to finish writing.

Lying in her dad's hammock was like lying in the sail of a boat. She held on to the pen and swung back and forth for a few minutes, and then she reread what she'd written so far. There were actually about thirteen thousand people in this town, but Solly would know she was Exaggerating For Dramatic Effect. That was something that they did. She stopped swinging. (*EFDE*), she added in parentheses, in case Solly had forgotten. Sometimes she felt like Solly had mentally deleted all their inside jokes the very second Nat left San Francisco. Purposely. Like she needed to empty out her brain space to make room for a new friend's inside jokes.

I hope you have a good first day at school! (Wear white socks for gym.) You probably will already have had it by the time you get this.

Her writing was messy because it was hard to write lying down. Besides, she had run out of room and had to write the end of the last sentence in tiny letters around the address part. She filled in Solly's information, which she knew from memory. She made the *o* in Solly's name into a heart and then colored it in.

Then in even tinier letters, upside down, across the top, she wrote her new address, which was a post office box, not an actual house number. Then she put a star beside it.

She turned the postcard over. Luckily, there was lots of white space on the Canada flag. **This is TOP SECRET. Do not share this with anyone, especially p_zzi, I'm not kidding, I will NEVER talk to you again.*

That filled up the whole area around the maple leaf. She drew a frowny face on the leaf itself, and then she felt bad.

She hoped she hadn't desecrated the flag or something. She hoped Canada wouldn't be mad.

Solly would probably laugh at it and show her new best friend, whoever that was going to be, and they would laugh together about what a nerd Nat was and wonder how such a dorky kid could have such a cool dad.

("Overrated," Nat heard Solly say, in her mind.)

Suddenly, Nat felt so tired. She closed her eyes. She would think about mailing the postcard the next day, or maybe never, or more likely she'd just leave it on the table and her dad would mail it for her.

Or he wouldn't.

She didn't care, either way.

She was still mad at Solly.

Maybe she always would be.

She hadn't decided yet.

A BEAR ON A BIKE

For lunch on Nat's first day of school, XAN GALLAGHER packed four glass (never plastic) containers with fresh food. One was Caesar salad, one was fruit salad, one was just salmon, and one was hard-boiled eggs.

"Dad," she said. "That's way too much food. I'm not going to a weight lifting competition. I'm going to a tiny school in the middle of nowhere. They'll probably all eat wheatgrass or something."

"Wheatgrass! Man, I love that stuff. I can put it in a smoothie!"

"Dad! I was kidding. I don't want a *grass smoothie.*"

"OK. I do though. Man, I have a craving. Is that what you're wearing?"

Nat looked down at what she was wearing, which was jeans—she hadn't worn shorts since the Knee Incident—and a plain orange T-shirt. She was also wearing the hearts-with-eyes sneakers.

"Um, yeah? Why? What's wrong with it?"

"Nothing!" he said. "You look great! You look like *you*!"

"Thanks, I guess. Why are you being weird?"

"I'm just excited for you! Excited to see the new school! See the new people! Meet some parents! Yep yep. What should I wear? What do you think?"

"You aren't coming! Dad, no. No. I mean, 'nope nope.'"

"Of course I'm coming! Too far to walk. We have to take the scooter."

"Dad, you can't!" Nat leaned against the counter. She took a sip of orange juice and a bite from the mammoth bowl of scrambled eggs that her dad had put out. "Is this *six* eggs?"

"No! That would be crazy. It's five eggs. Only five! Protein is good for growing bodies! And brains!"

"I'm not eating *five* eggs for breakfast. You are so weird."

"This isn't weird, I always make you five eggs. It's just sometimes I eat some of them. I get hungry just making them."

Nat stirred the eggs. They looked like congealed yellow milk. She made a face.

"You're just nervous about school! I get it. I do. The first day on a new set is like that. It's like, 'Who will my friends be? How will I meet people?'"

Nat stared at him. "Dad," she said. "You're XAN GALLAGHER. It's not like you have to walk around introducing yourself to craft services and hoping they remember you next time you have a craving for a pound of mackerel."

"I do though! They might know who I am, but they don't *know* me. I don't *know* them. I have to put myself out there! I have to learn who they are! It's the same!"

"Sure, fine, the same." Nat rolled her eyes. "Either way,

can you please drop me off at the end of the road and I'll walk the last part?"

Nat's dad's face fell. "Oh!" he said. "Yeah, OK. Fine! I can do that! Yep yep."

"How are you so famous for being an actor when you're such a terrible actor? Now I can *tell* that your feelings are hurt! Now I *have* to let you come!"

"I can come? Oh man, thanks, Nat-a-Tat. I hope I meet some people who can be our friends. You know, *normal* people. We're gonna have a normal life here, I just know it."

Nat grinned in spite of herself. "Sure, Dad. Normal. I'm sure there will be a lot of normal people at Justin Trudeau Middle School who we can befriend."

"Great, I'm going to change my T-shirt. Would it be weird if I wore orange, too?"

"DAD! We can't be twins! We aren't Kate and Cait!"

He laughed hugely, slapping his hand on the counter. "Gotcha!" he said. "I was joking!"

"You are a laugh riot, Dad," said Nat. "I can't think why you don't go into comedy instead of all this acting stuff. You'd have to work out less! Stand-up comics are usually not in good shape. I'm going to brush my teeth."

In the tiny bathroom, she inspected her face carefully. Her dad was right—she looked like herself. She made a face and stuck out her tongue.

When she was little, the press was always grilling her dad about whether Nat was trying to be a boy or was maybe even transgender. They were *beyond* excited about this possibility. There was even a headline that she saw in the checkout line one day that said something dumb like, "TOMBOY? NO, SAYS XAN THE MAN, SHE'S A

NATGIRL." She had to read it three times to understand what it meant.

That was the day she decided to grow out her hair.

It was the exact *moment* when she realized that people were judging her.

And not just judging her, but wanting something from her. Wanting her to be something *special*.

Up until then, it had been about her dad and only about her dad.

But now it was about *her*.

And she hated it.

So even though she'd liked having short hair that she didn't have to fuss with, she decided on the spot to grow it out, so that she looked like just a normal girl.

Not a boy.

Not even a tomboy.

She didn't want to give them *anything* to talk about.

But hair, as it turned out, took a long time to grow. It was only just past the tops of her shoulders now. She brushed it hard. One website that she read said that if you brushed your hair a lot, it would grow faster, because it stimulated circulation to your scalp. She brushed until her scalp hurt, then she pulled her hair into a ponytail and inspected the result.

"Too much face," she said, and then took it out again.

She let it fall forward. Maybe she should cut bangs; then she'd have even less visible face skin. Suddenly, *face skin* seemed too personal to show the world, even the world of Justin Trudeau Middle School.

She picked up the nail scissors and started with one snip. Her dad thumped on the door. "We'll be late!" he bellowed, nearly giving her a heart attack.

"I'm *coming*," Nat said. She put the scissors back. She could finish it later. Maybe. But probably not. She already regretted the snip. She rinsed her mouth with mouthwash. *Good breath is more important than what you look like anyway*, she thought. You could look like a million bucks, but if you had bad breath, no one would care. You'd be friendless and alone, probably forever.

"Nat!"

"Dad!"

"Let's go!"

"Coming," she singsonged. She made a face in the mirror and then opened the door. "Good luck, me," she whispered.

Nat peeked outside. Her dad was already sitting on the scooter, like he could barely contain his excitement to leave for even one more second. It was a special scooter, custom-sized for him, but he still looked silly, like a bear on a bicycle. It was a hot day. She opened the windows and the skylights to let some air in. The heat from the sun was amplifying the foresty smells. She had to take a big, deep breath to inhale the cool saltiness of the farther-away sea air.

Her dad revved the engine and hit the horn. *Toot toot.*

Nat let the breath out, picked up her lunch, and put it in her backpack. Then she put her backpack on her back. Everything she was doing felt magnified and slow.

"Ready," Nat said, not that he could hear her.

She slipped the phone into her jeans pocket, just in case.

NAT HAD KNOWN THAT letting her dad bring her to school might be a mistake, and she was right. They had barely pulled into the parking lot when people started going bananas. XAN GALLAGHER was recognizable from one hundred feet away. Probably farther. Maybe the astronauts on the space station could even recognize him from space. It took about twenty-seven seconds (*exactly* twenty-seven seconds, actually; she counted) for a small crowd to form. Nat slipped off the back of the scooter and ducked into the school without saying goodbye. She didn't make eye contact with anyone. She could hear her dad, behind her, being jovial, and she cringed.

Being jovial was another one of his *things*. Which was fine! He was a jovial guy. But there was always something about seeing him being jovial to strangers that made her feel funny.

He was trying too hard.

It was as if he needed to be liked just a tiny bit too much.

He was even jovial when Nat knew that he wasn't feeling that way, although this morning he really was at peak joviality. She grinned in spite of herself.

This morning, it wasn't an act.

She hoped he would make a normal friend. She just somehow doubted that was possible.

"YEP YEP," she heard a kid yell.

Nat hoped none of the people who were snapping photos with their iPhones would put the pictures on the Internet, but she also knew that was too much to hope for.

Her sneakers were squeaking on the floor. It sounded as though she were being followed by a tiny troupe of noisy mice.

Squeak, squeak, squeak.

The sound made her shiver like nails on a chalkboard.

The hallway was empty and echoey.

The lockers were all painted a pale yellow color. Sunlight streamed in the high, square windows and made diamond-shaped patterns on the floor. She could see dust motes in the illuminated air. When she was little, she had thought they were fairies. For a second, she missed being little. She was obviously growing up.

Now she could see dust for what it was: dust.

She wasn't sure she liked this version of herself.

The whole place smelled like new paint. A teacher poked her head out of the classroom. "Are you new?" she said. "I'm sorry, but students have to wait outside for the bell."

Canadians were always sorry; Nat had already noticed this.

"I just have to go to the bathroom," Nat lied. "I'll go back out after."

"Oh! OK. Sorry!"

Nat smiled, because she couldn't help it.

"It's down there, on the right." The teacher pointed.

"Thanks," said Nat. Then, just to see what it would be like, "Sorry!"

"Welcome to Justin Trudeau Middle!" said the teacher. She left off the word "School."

"OK thank," said Nat. She left off the "you" on purpose, for a joke, but it made it sound just like she didn't know how to say "thank you," not like she was making a joke at all. "Ha ha," she added.

The teacher smiled.

Nat squeaked down the rest of the hallway and went into the bathroom. It looked like every school bathroom ever, but everything in there was pale yellow, too, except the toilets and sinks. Those were white. But the floor, the tile, the hand dryer, and the soap dispenser were all the same yellow. *Lemony*, she observed.

It did not *smell* lemony.

It smelled like a bathroom.

Nat tried to breathe not-too-deeply. She went into the stall, but she didn't really need to go, so she came out again. There was no graffiti in there. The walls were all too clean. She'd never seen a school bathroom without something scratched into the paint, even if it was just a smiley or a dumb swear.

She found a place to sit, under the shelf that ran along the wall below the mirror. The shelf must be for putting on your makeup or fixing your hair. Did people here do that? At her last school, makeup wasn't allowed, but Solly always wore mascara and lip gloss, like she was daring the teachers to say something.

They never did.

Even the teachers were a little bit scared of Solly.

Nat sat there, half hidden, waiting for her dad to leave in a cloud of joviality, waiting for the bell to sound, waiting for *something*.

She didn't even know what.

She missed Solly and San Francisco so much that her stomach hurt.

The door opened and then shut again. Someone else walked into the bathroom.

From her viewpoint, she could only see jeans and Converse sneakers. The jeans and Converse sneakers did not look like *girl* jeans and *girl* Converse sneakers. Had she come into the wrong bathroom? Nat shrank herself deeper into the corner. The person would only see her if they looked. The shelf was hiding her.

Sort of.

Nat held her breath.

Then her phone rang. The person jumped, literally. "Holy crap!" the voice said. "You scared me to death. I'm dead now. I'm a ghost. Thanks a lot."

"I'm sorry!" said Nat. She was trying to get her phone out of her back pocket and she hit her head on the shelf. By the time she wedged the phone free, it had stopped ringing. Her phone hardly ever rang. The only person who had ever called her was Solly, and Solly wouldn't be calling her this early in the morning.

Would she? Maybe she would.

Nat looked at the missed call. *Solly.*

Weird, she thought.

"I'm so sorry," she said out loud. She crawled out from her spot and stood up. The person was a boy. "This is awkward."

"Yeah," he said. "It is."

She stared at him.

A boy.

In the girls' bathroom.

Why wasn't he explaining himself? Why wasn't *he* apologizing?

His hair was pulled back into a ponytail. It was as long as a girl's hair, but he was *definitely* not a girl. Nat didn't know exactly how she knew that, but she could just tell.

It was obvious.

He had a widish nose and greenish eyes and a nice face. She almost said that out loud, "Nice face," but she caught herself just in time.

"You're a boy," she went with instead, as a way of prompting him to explain. She looked at the door. "Am *I* in the wrong bathroom?"

"You're good," he said. "You're not. It's complicated." He held out his hand. "Hi, I'm Harry."

"Nat," said Nat. She stared at his hand. On his wrist, there was an orca. It was either a tattoo or it was drawn on with a marker, but it was really good. *That* was definitely a sign.

But was he showing it to her? Or was she supposed to shake his hand? Was this a Canadian thing?

"Nice tattoo," she said at the same time as she said, "Nice orca," so what came out was "Nice tattorca."

"Thanks, I just drew it. This morning. In the car. It's not permanent or anything." His hand was still out, so she shook it. It was wet. She had never really touched a boy on purpose before. She wiped her hand off on her jeans and blushed.

"Sorry," he said. "That's water, not, like, sweat."

"OK," she said. She stuffed her hand and her phone into her pocket, which was really uncomfortable.

"Hey, did you know XAN GALLAGHER is here?" Harry was fixing his hair in the mirror by wetting his hand and smoothing it against his scalp. His hair looked like it might be wildly, fantastically curly if it escaped from the ponytail, like it was just waiting for an opportunity to break free.

"Um, yeah. I guess. I saw him. Why are you doing that to your hair?"

"I hate it. I wish I could be bald, like XAN. XAN THE MAN. He's great," the boy said, fervently. "He's the best actor in the world. Plus, he's nice. Everyone says that he's nice. Do you think he lives here now? That's weird. *No one* lives here. Do you think he lives here?"

"He's OK." Nat was smiling now. "Yeah, he lives here."

"I nearly hyperventilated. That is so amazing that he's here."

Nat was acutely aware of the fact that her blush wasn't fading. It was just getting bigger and brighter and louder the longer they stood there, like her face was a stereo and the volume was being turned up. She *should* tell him that XAN GALLAGHER was her dad. She knew she should. But she couldn't figure out how to say it. It was already too late.

Her eyes started to water. Harry stared at her, like he was either waiting for her to say something or like he just couldn't believe how red her face could actually get.

"You—" he started.

"You're in the wrong bathroom," she interrupted.

"Oh! Yeah, that. I can explain . . ." But his voice was drowned out by the school bell. It was the loudest bell Nat had ever heard. And it went on.

And on.

And on.

Nat's ears were ringing when it finally stopped.

"We should go," said Harry.

Which was fine by Nat. "Yeah," she said.

She wasn't sure she wanted to hear what he was going to say before he was cut off by the bell.

It seemed like maybe, pretty obviously, it was going to be *complicated*.

THE THING ABOUT HARRY

Nat knew that Harry was once called Harriet because of Mr. Hajeezi.

Mr. Hajeezi was her new teacher. He had long hair, which he wore in dreadlocks. Hanging on the wall behind his desk, there was a guitar, a ukulele, and something else that Nat couldn't identify. A stringed something. There was also a large porcelain peacock on a shelf and a very tiny model of a toilet on his desk.

Weird, but promising, Nat thought.

The first thing Mr. Hajeezi did was to arrange the classroom alphabetically. He called everyone out by name, one by one. When he got to Nat's name—"Natalia?"—she raised her hand and quickly said, "Actually, it's Nat." Then he pointed to the desk he wanted her to sit in. She crossed her fingers that the person who was going to sit next to her would be her new BFF. That would make everything so much easier.

"Harriet," said Mr. Hajeezi.

No one answered.

"Harriet Brasch?" he said again.

He looked around the room. "Harriet must be absent today," he said out loud. "But I have the right number of students in the room." He counted. "Sixteen? Sixteen. Strange."

He kept going down the list, and when he was done, Harry was still sitting on the floor. By himself.

"And you are?" said Mr. Hajeezi.

"Harry," said Harry, his voice cracking but firm. He looked down at the floor. He looked so uncomfortable that Nat suddenly, without knowing how she knew, just *knew*.

Harry was *Harriet*.

Why hadn't he just done what she had done, just said, "Actually, it's Harry"?

"Huh," said Mr. Hajeezi. "Must be a mistake on the form. I'm just going to go down to the office and correct the record."

Harry turned pale, then red, then pale again.

His face finally settled on white: the color of a piece of paper. A piece of paper that wanted to be folded into the shape of a crane so it could fly directly out the window and disappear into the foggy sky.

"*I'm* Harriet," he mumbled. "Forget it. I mean, don't worry about it."

"Sorry?" said Mr. Hajeezi, which Nat understood now was a Canadian way of saying, "Pardon me?"

"I'm Harriet Brasch, OK?" Harry was shouting. "I'm *Harriet*. GO AHEAD AND STARE, EVERYONE."

Then he ran out of the room, his Converse squeaking just like Nat's had squeaked until the sound was gone.

They must have just waxed the floor, she thought, goose bumps rising on her arms.

"Oh," said Mr. Hajeezi. "Oh man. Shoot."

The two girls who Nat had had her eye on as potential BFFs giggled. The giggles turned into full-on laughter. A wave of *myötähäpea*, which is a Finnish word for sympathetic embarrassment and also the very first untranslatable foreign word that Nat had learned, crashed over her.

She liked to roll *myötähäpea* around in her head. It was a perfect marble of a word, red and swirly in the middle and definitely made of glass.

"Stop that," said Mr. Hajeezi. "This isn't funny. I need to . . ." His voice trailed off. Nat wondered what he needed to do. It seemed to her that what he needed to do was to go get Harry and to apologize. She raised her hand, but then she quickly put it back down again. She couldn't tell a teacher what to do.

The class became quiet.

Then someone mumbled, "Harriet," in a terrible, sing-songy way.

And then everyone in the room was laughing, except for Mr. Hajeezi and Nat.

Nat found that she was standing up. She didn't really decide to do it; it just happened. She felt funny; her ears were ringing. She ran down the hall after Harry, so fast that her shoes didn't even squeak. She wasn't running, she was flying. She flung the door open and then ran out into the fog, which had rolled in sometime between her dad dropping her off—which seemed like a million years ago—and now.

The whole playground seemed wrapped in the hush of it, the whiteness making everything a shadow.

She stepped onto the field and yelled his name. "HARRY!"

At first, he didn't answer. Then she heard a quiet, "What do you want." It didn't really sound like a question.

Harry was on the playground structure, sitting inside a tunnel on top of a climbing wall. The playground wasn't separated into boys' and girls' here. It was just one playground, small and ramshackle. It looked magical in the fog, like it was a ship and the field itself was a calm, foggy sea.

My last school would have been unbearable for Harry, Nat thought. *Which playground would he have run to?*

Nat walked over to the structure so she was standing directly under him. She could see his outline through the holes in the tunnel. She cleared her throat. "Um," she said. She wanted to say just the right thing, but she didn't know what it was.

"I don't want to talk about it," Harry said.

"OK," she said. "I don't really either. Like, I don't know what to say, even if I did want to talk about it."

"Maybe I will later," he said. "Just not right now."

"Doesn't matter." Nat shrugged but she knew he couldn't see her. "Hang on, I'm climbing up." She scaled the wall easily—it was made for really little kids—and scooted into the tunnel.

He looked at her.

"Hi," she said.

He almost smiled. "Hi."

"So, I should tell you that XAN GALLAGHER is my dad."

"He *is*?"

"Yes. I'm sorry, I should have said. Before. In the bathroom."

He laughed in a way that didn't sound like a "ha ha" kind of laugh. "No big deal," he said. "But, yeah, you should have said. I was going on and on! What are you doing here?"

"Here in this tunnel or here in Sooke?"

"Sooke."

"Getting away from the paparazzi," she said. "Plus, we like beaches."

"Oh," he said.

"I saw whales," she told him. She didn't look right at him; instead she looked out the end of the tunnel, away from him. A huge bird flew by. There was no traffic nearby, so she could actually hear the *thwap thwap* of the bird's wings pushing against the air. "On our first day here, that's when I saw them. They were scratching their bellies on the beach."

"That's *cool*," he said. "I really really like whales."

"Me too." Nat thought about all the whales she had seen, all over the world, but she couldn't tell him, because it would feel like showing off. She kept her mouth closed.

Nat could hear all of her own breaths and Harry's. She wished she could think of something good to say. The sprinklers came on and sprayed the field with huge swaths of water, ticking and tocking like giant clocks.

Then the principal appeared out of the mist, like an apparition.

She was an older lady who had the hunched-over back of someone who has been carrying too much, too far, and for too long. Her hair was silvery gray, and Nat could see the comb marks in it. It was as thin as a baby's.

The principal walked all the way over to where they were sitting and looked up at them and sighed. Then she shook her head. "I *knew* this would happen. I told him, but he . . . Never mind."

"But how did you know?" Nat wanted to ask. "What is 'this'? Who is 'him'?" But she didn't.

It wasn't her business.

At least, she didn't think it was.

Nat and Harry looked at each other. He nodded.

He climbed out one end of the tunnel. She climbed out the other.

He jumped to the ground. She carefully found footholds and climbed down, one step at a time.

Walking back into the classroom, Nat's legs felt heavy, like they were made of stone. She couldn't even imagine how Harry felt.

"There," said the principal, at the classroom door.

They could hear that everyone inside was talking and laughing, but when they opened the door, the whole room fell silent.

Mr. Hajeezi stared at them. He looked embarrassed.

"Well," he said, finally. He was almost-not-quite smiling and almost-not-quite frowning. It was a hard facial expression to read. "Well," he repeated.

Harry took a deep breath. Nat could tell he was going to say something. Nat was surprised. If it were her, she would have ducked into the back row and kept her head down. Instead, she stayed next to him, in case he needed her. Harry was clearly a person who did things differently than she did. She liked that about him already. He was brave. She put her hand on her phone in her pocket in case she might have to call 911. Harry looked like he might faint.

He steadied himself by holding on to the corner of Mr. Hajeezi's desk and cleared his throat.

"Go ahead, Harriet," said Mr. Hajeezi, stepping back.

The class stared. Nat took one step to the side and put half her body behind the coat rack. She felt too visible. She didn't like it. She didn't know what to do with her hand that wasn't in her phone pocket. She touched her face and then her hair. She wished she'd cut those bangs, after all. She found the one short part with her fingers and tugged on it. Then she stuffed her fingers into her belt loops.

Harry was staring at the collection of clocks on the back of the classroom wall that showed the time where they were, and in New York City, and in Paris, and in Hong Kong. Nat had been to all of those places. Nat could tell that Harry's knees were shaking. He looked like he was going to fall over. He looked like he *wanted* to fall over, preferably into the huge sinkhole that he was hoping would open up right in front of him, before he could talk.

At least, that's how she would have felt.

His lips were very white. "I was born a girl," he blurted, so quickly that there were no spaces between his words and Nat had to replay them in her head more slowly just to understand what he said. "I mean, I wasn't, but that's what they thought. That's what the doctor said. My parents named me Harriet. But then it turns out that I'm not a girl. I'm a boy. I'm sure you don't get it. I didn't get it either, when I first figured it out. I'm not sure I even get it now, so don't ask me a bunch of stuff that I can't answer. I just know it's true." The more he talked, the more his voice sounded calm. "Not everyone gets it. My dad doesn't get it." He made a face.

A couple of kids laughed.

"My dad left when I was three!" a kid yelled from the back row.

"I like my dad," said the girl with very long, blond hair. She blinked, prettily.

"Hey, did anyone else see XAN GALLAGHER this morning?" a boy in the front row asked. "He's *someone's* dad!"

"His daughter's name is Natalia Rose!" someone else called. Nat drew back farther behind the coats. It wouldn't take them long to realize that she was *Natalia Rose*, would it? Why didn't they already know? Did she just not look glamorous enough to be XAN GALLAGHER's kid? She frowned.

Harry did not turn to look at her.

He did not tell the kids that Nat was "Natalia Rose."

She loved him so much for that, she felt like her heart actually flapped, its wings *thwapping* like the bird's they had seen outside.

Everyone in the room started talking all at once. Harry/Harriet was forgotten. He shifted uneasily from foot to foot. Mr. Hajeezi clapped his hands, once, twice, three times, in a pattern.

The class quieted.

"Are you finished?" Mr. Hajeezi said to Harry. His face was kind, but he also looked relieved. Everything was out in the open and no one was crying, which Nat supposed was a win from a teacher's point of view.

Harry's face was, by then, normal colors again, but his eyes looked like they were going to overflow. Nat took her hand out from her belt loop and was surprised that it was shaking.

"I'd just rather be called Harry. That's all," finished Harry, looking both relieved and miserable.

"Great job, Har . . . ," said Mr. Hajeezi. He let the name trail off like that, like he didn't know what to do.

It sounded like he said, "Great job, Hair."

"Great job, Hair," Nat whispered to Harry.

He laughed.

The girl with the long, beautiful hair leaned over to the girl next to her and whispered something, too. Then *they* both laughed in a way that was definitely mean. Nat found her fists curling at her sides.

"Thank you, Harriet," the girl called out. "Thank you for telling us your sad story." Her voice was like a silk ribbon.

Nat knew two things right away: That girl was the most popular girl in the class. And that girl was terrible.

Harry collapsed back into the desk that was beside Nat's desk. It was the only desk that wasn't taken. Nat followed him and sat back down at her own desk. Her heart was beating too hard. Harry's foot tapped the floor in an uneven rhythm.

It's fine, Nat tried to say, telepathically. She believed wholeheartedly that telepathy was a real thing that worked. It definitely worked with animals, she'd noticed. And sometimes it worked with people. People tended to block it, though. She could almost feel it when that happened, like she was trying to send a message to someone through a curtain or even a brick wall. Harry had a curtain. "It's fine," she mouthed at him when she finally caught his eye. (Mouthing sometimes worked when telepathy didn't.) He stared at her and then slowly looked away.

"Yep yep," a boy's voice called out, and someone else said, "XAN THE MAN!"

"Back to work now," said Mr. H. "If anyone has any questions for Harry, please write them down and we will discuss them after lunch."

IT TURNED OUT THAT even at a school that professed to be open and accepting, kids could be the worst. Mr. Hajeezi crumpled most of the questions up and put them in the big blue recycling bucket at the front of the room.

He sighed.

"The most commonly asked question is one that I can answer." He smiled at Harry. (*I am smiling gently at Harry!* he was thinking so loudly that Nat could almost hear it. That was a kind of telepathy, too.) "The question is, 'Why does Mr. H call Harry Harriet when he said to call him Harry? That's rude.'"

That was Nat's question.

She held her breath.

Mr. H paused and scratched at his arm. He had a skin condition. Tiny flakes of his skin showered down on his desk in a little flurry. He sighed. "Sometimes," he said, "we do what parents request because our job as facilitators is not to make choices for our students, but to help them navigate the lives in which they exist."

Nat raised her eyebrows at Harry.

"The lives in which they exist," she mouthed. Then she rolled her eyes.

She watched Harry watching her mouth. She couldn't tell if he understood or thought she was rude or what.

And then Harry laughed.

Making Harry laugh was a great feeling. It felt like the time when she and her dad were up in the mountains somewhere. It was very cold, with deep snow. One night, they sat on the front porch of the house they had rented and blew bubbles, which froze instantly into fragile ice balloons. They lined them up in a row and then tapped each one with a tiny silver hammer and they exploded in tinkling shards of light. It was magical. Nat did not know how or why her dad had a tiny silver hammer. He was just the kind of person who sometimes had a tiny silver hammer exactly when you needed one.

Harry's laugh made her think of that tinkling.

Harry's laugh made her heart *tinkle*.

SOLLY/SOLEIL

The letter was waiting on Nat's bed when she got home from school.

Her dad must have picked up the mail while she was gone. She didn't notice it at first, because she was still thinking about Harry.

Or rather, about his former life, when people called him Harriet.

When people thought he was someone who he wasn't.

Hair, she thought, and giggled.

"How was your day?" Nat's dad had asked when he'd picked her up at three o'clock. He was on the scooter. The crowd was even bigger than before. They were shouting and waving, although Nat's dad appeared not to even notice. Sometimes he was impenetrable, like he was encased in a soundproof bubble. "Tell me everything! Was it great?"

"Dad," she said, "just go. Go! I'll tell you at home. I'll tell you later." She looked at the crowd. "From now on, I want to walk home," she added. "This is ridiculous."

Everyone had seen Nat climb onto the back of XAN GALLAGHER's scooter.

And just like that, everyone *knew*.

She also felt that they were somehow disappointed, and she hated that she felt badly that she wasn't someone more exciting, even if only for a second.

Well, she thought, *too bad for them*. At least she'd had one whole day when she could just be Nat, and not NATALIA ROSE, DAUGHTER OF XAN GALLAGHER.

Nat's insides felt like a piece of twine that had been tied into such a complicated knot that it was hard to tell if it was a knot-tied-on-purpose or just an unfixable mess. And seeing the letter lying there on her bed, with Solly's familiar handwriting on the front, didn't make it better.

If anything, it pulled the twine tighter.

Nat's dad was in the kitchen, cooking chicken. Specifically, cooking four chickens at the same time. They smelled delicious. He was singing a song from the last movie he had done, which was an animated film about a mouse who thought he was a rat. "I'm not who you think I am," he sang, "I'm not who you want me to be, but the glorious part of all of this heart, is that under my fur, I'm just meeeeeee."

"DAD," she yelled. "I can't even think."

"Sorry!" he called back.

"You're turning Canadian already," she said. "Sorry yourself."

"Sorry for being sorry! Yep yep."

She could tell even from her room that he was smiling.

"Sorry for YOU," she said. "You great big nut. I never said you should mail that postcard to Solly!"

"Sorry!" he yelled. "SOOOOOOORRRY!"

"Stop!" she yelled back.

Nat picked up the letter and inspected the handwriting. It was written in purple pen. Solly always used purple. The swoops and swooshes were as dramatic as she was. Nat sniffed it and then felt weird about that. It probably smelled like the mailman's hands! What was she thinking?

It actually smelled like grapes.

She held the letter up to the light. Solly had already broken the rules. For one thing, the whole point of the Great Postcard Project was *postcards*. The letter was heavy, and when she squished it around with her fingers, she could feel something in the envelope that wasn't paper. She wanted to see what it was, and she also didn't want to see.

"I'm going outside," she told her dad. "Go ahead and serenade the chickens if you need to."

Nat's head spun a little as she stepped out the door. She had no idea why she felt so strange. The letter was as heavy as lead.

She walked over to the edge of the clearing and sat on a big rock that had a view through the trees to the ocean. The rock was warm from the sun. It was a little bit windy, enough that the envelope flapped in her hands, like it wanted to blow away.

She looked for whales' fins in the waves.

Every single day, since the day the whales had come, she'd gone down to the beach to sit and wait for them to come again. But they hadn't.

Not yet.

Today she didn't even feel like going down there. Too much had happened.

School had happened.

XAN GALLAGHER, outed as her dad, had happened.

And Harry was once called Harriet.

Harry, Harriet.

He was Harry. He was 100 percent Harry.

Harriet was a mistake, that's all.

A mistake that clung on to school records and in the minds of people who didn't get it. But Harry wasn't Harriet.

"Harry, not Harriet."

She said that part out loud, partly to try it on for size, and partly because it was almost a tongue twister. "Red leather, yellow leather," she said.

She tore open the envelope. The thing inside along with the folded paper was a bracelet. It was made from string that was the color of a brown paper bag. It was tied into knots. There were three beads on it. One said B. The next said F. The third was another F.

BFF.

But were they? Still?

After what Solly did?

"I don't think so," said Nat. She threw the bracelet into the bushes. It got hung up on a branch briefly, and then it fell out of sight. She felt bad about that for a split second, and then she didn't.

Nat unfolded the letter and began to read, even though the wind kept flapping the paper in her hand and her hair into her eyes, like it was trying to demand her attention.

Sooooooo Natters,

Guess what?

Some BIG things have happened since you left. Why did it take you so long to send your address? I was going CRAZY.

The things are Super Huge Things (SHTs).

The hugest.

The MOST HUGE things to ever happen to a person, short of being murdered in the woods. LOL! Not that being murdered in the woods would be funny, but you know what I mean.

Anyway, the first SHT is that I kissed Evan Walker at the pier. We were just hanging out, you know? (His mom is my mom's new BFF. They met at hot yoga.) (His mom has had her entire face filled with fat from her own butt. She looks like a wax museum person who was too close to the heater and who has started to melt. Not kidding.) Sooooo, we were like walking and talking and then he was standing right next to me, pointing at some boat or something, and then BAM his lips were on my lips! It was weird but so good and good and weird. I don't even like-like Evan Walker. But I like-liked kissing him. It is ever complicated, like you'd say.

The second even bigger thing is that I got my period. The very next morning. AFTER THE KISS. I went to the bathroom and THERE IT WAS. Did the kiss make me a WOMAN? I can't wait to see how big my boobs are going to be. If they are bigger than Mom's, she's going to freak.

I feel TOTALLY different. Like GROWN UP.
You know?
>*Do you have your period yet? You'd tell me, right?*

There was a big scribbled-out sentence here. Solly had crossed it out every which way so it was impossible to read. There was only one letter that Nat could make out, which was a capital *L*.

The scribbled-out bit was the worst part of the letter.

>*Mom is having surgery on her face to make her lips bigger now. She is going to look so stupid. In related news, Mom is still terrrrrrrible. The worst. She says hi!*
>*I have to go. The whole class is going to the market today. We have to buy four different kinds of vegetables and then make it into soup for homeless people. I'm going to buy beets so my soup will be gloriously pink.*
>*I LOVE YOU!!!!!!!!!!!!*
>*Love,*
>*Me*
>*PS—Now that I'm a woman, I've decided that from now on, I'm going to use my full name, Soleil. Pronounced "Sol-yay."* ☺
>*SMOOCHES, BABY!*
>*Soleil (SolYay!)*
>*PPS—Write back and tell me all the SHTs that have happened to you.*

Nat carefully refolded the letter, making each crease doubly sharp with her fingernails. She wanted to call Solly and shout at her. She wanted to say, "What is with this dumb bracelet? We aren't even friends now!"

She took the phone out of her pocket and looked at it.

She had had the phone for exactly one year.

A lot can happen in a year, she thought. *Sometimes, too much.*

Instead of dialing Solly though, she pressed the contact button for Bird (Mom). She wanted to tell Bird (Mom) about Harry. Bird would know the right things to say. She would probably understand.

She wanted to tell Bird (Mom) everything.

And she didn't want to tell Solly anything at all.

HARRY

Observations on the First Day of School, Harry typed on his laptop. *It would have been fine, but Dad told the teacher that he had to call me Harriet and then it got stupid fast, and I'm stupid so I panicked.*

Note to self: Panicking is stupid.

Dad is stupid.

Everything is stupid.

Harry read what he had typed. It wasn't bad in that it was true, but still, it wasn't good either. If his dad saw it, he would kill Harry. Harry started hitting the backspace key and watched the word "stupid" disappear, one letter at a time.

One day, he was going to write a whole entire book about what it was like to be a boy who had been identified as a girl—"transgender" was the word for it, according to Google, not like he had an expert around to ask or anything—and then everyone would understand.

Maybe even *he* would understand.

But he didn't quite understand the *why* of it. Particularly the *why me* part. It's just who he was.

He just wanted to be a kid. To play video games. To learn new tricks on his skateboard. To have a group of boys to hang out with and to just *do* stuff.

The thing was that sometimes a thing could happen to you, and sometimes it could be really personal, but you couldn't explain *why*. You didn't know what it was, what misfired when, or if it even was a misfire or if it just *was*, like having brown eyes or curly hair. Personally, he didn't think it was a bad thing. If he could change anything about himself, it actually would be his hair.

But he would, eventually, be able to do that.

Sooner or later, he'd be able to just go ahead and cut his hair short, without his parents having to approve it.

That's what he'd say in his book, *The Book with All the Answers*, in a non-annoying way. What he wrote would make other kids feel OK in their own skin.

If he were to write a book, it would 100 percent not be annoying.

It would answer *everything* to everyone's satisfaction.

No kid would be in trouble ever again for being who they were! They definitely wouldn't get bullied about it.

It would make it OK, not just for kids like Harry, but for dads like Harry's dad.

Basically, it would be a magic, miracle book.

"Duh," Harry said out loud. "As if." Then he mentally crumpled up his own idea and threw it away. Why would *he* be able to do this thing?

Writing a book was hard.

Impossible, even.

Writing lists was easier.

He highlighted everything that he'd typed and erased it. Then he started a new list.

Goals For This School Year:
1. *Don't freak out.*
2. *Make friends with boys (Best friends) (OK to be friends with girls but just acquaintances, sort of).*
3. *Always use the bathroom before leaving home so you NEVER have to use the GIRL'S bathroom at school. DUH.*

He underlined the "<u>DUH</u>."

That about summed it up, he thought.

Harry closed his laptop and turned the Xbox on. His short-term goal was to play through all the new levels of this video game in record time. That was an easier goal than, say, writing a book to explain inexplicable things.

"Kapow," he said.

THE THINGS YOU FIND
WHEN YOU AREN'T LOOKING

The first time Nat went to Harry's house after school, she found a collection of magazines in the downstairs bathroom cupboard when she was looking for a roll of toilet paper. The magazines were wrinkly, and some of them were really old. They were pretty much all celebrity magazines. Her dad never bought these magazines or let her buy them, not that she wanted to. She'd seen the covers on the newsstands; she'd read the headlines. If she reached for one, he'd give her that look, let out a belly laugh and make a face and say something like, "If you want an interview, Nat-a-Tat, I'd be happy to give you one. Yep yep. Or even my ortograph."

When she was little, she didn't know how to pronounce "autograph" and now it was one of their inside jokes.

She liked having inside jokes with her dad more than she wanted to read the magazines.

Nat picked up the whole pile of magazines, took them out of the cupboard, and fanned them out on the counter. Some had pretty actresses on the front. Some of them were people she knew. Some of them were friends with her dad.

There were even some that featured XAN GALLAGHER.

Nat's heart was beating funny in her chest. It felt like her blood was suddenly too watery, like it had turned into a whole ocean and was whooshing through her veins too quickly.

As though someone else was controlling her hands, Nat separated the XAN GALLAGHER magazines from the others and made a smaller pile of just those. Then she looked at the covers, one by one. There he was with his eyebrow up on one, two, three of them.

"XAN THE MAN."

"THE RETURN OF XAN."

"XAN COMES BACK."

Nat wondered what they thought he was coming back from. XAN GALLAGHER never went away. He was always there.

She pulled one more magazine from the pile.

XAN GALLAGHER was on the cover, wearing a tuxedo.

The tuxedo had a wide, turquoise sash.

That was weird. Nat looked more closely.

It wasn't a sash.

It was a baby carrier.

And there, with just a tuft of hair sticking out the very top, was her very own head.

Suddenly, Nat knew that if she opened up this magazine, she was going to know who her mom really was. Realizing that made her feel dizzy. She sat down on the floor, which was flecked with a gold pattern that sparkled in the light.

She lay all the way down on it. The walls spun and then held still. She pressed her cheek against the sparkles and held her breath for three whole minutes, watching the numbers on her phone flip from 3:31 to 3:32 to 3:33. Then she let the breath out: 3:33 seemed like it should be lucky. Next to the time, the little weather icon showed a sun, which wasn't even true. It was foggy.

It was almost always foggy here, just like in San Francisco.

Nat sat up again and put the magazine on her lap.

She needed to talk to someone. She wanted to call Bird (Mom) but she didn't want Harry to hear her talking on the phone in the bathroom. He would think that was weird. Besides, she didn't know what she would say.

"Are you going to be in there forever?" Harry yelled.

"Probably not," she yelled back. "Maybe another minute though."

"Weirdo," he said. He tapped a tune out on the door. She could hear him breathing.

And then, finally, she heard his footsteps walking away.

The magazine smelled musty, like it had been read in the bathtub and put away damp. The date on the magazine was February 28, 2005. That was the day after her dad won his Oscar. The headline said, "XAN THE MAN IS XAN THE DAD: XAN'S NEW BABY MAKES HER DEBUT AT THE OSCARS."

The idea of someone reading this very magazine in the bathtub, looking at photos of her dad and of her as a baby, made Nat feel terrible, like someone was rubbing Styrofoam against her teeth.

Superimposed over her dad's smiling face, there was a smaller photo of him on a surfboard, wearing a very long, striped, knitted hat. He looked silly, which made her smile, but also made her feel embarrassed on his behalf. There is a word for that in German, which is *fremdschämen*.

"*Fremdschämen*," Nat whispered.

Feeling *fremdschämen* for her dad was not a new feeling. It happened a lot.

She opened the magazine to the article. Her hands made the decision before her brain did, but as soon as her brain caught up, it made her slam the magazine shut again. She hadn't read any words, but she *had* seen some photos. One of the photos was of her dad with a woman. The woman was beautiful and also familiar. Nat blinked. She had black hair that was blowing around her face, and she was smiling. Her eyes were behind sunglasses. Even just glancing at her chin and cheeks and the way her head was tossed back, Nat could tell she was famous. Famous people took up a different type of space in photos than people who weren't famous. Also, they glowed.

This woman glowed.

She was definitely *not* a makeup artist.

She was someone who makeup artists made up. *Is that the right term?* she wondered. *"Made up"?* It *was* a little bit like they made a new version of the person they were working on. Her dad sometimes looked like a total stranger after makeup: an old man or a monster, or worse, a *stranger*.

Nat's hands went cold and clammy.

"You are made up," she said to the face in the magazine, then she looked away. She didn't read any of the small print beside the photo. She closed her eyes, but she could still almost see the face, as though it had been burned into her retinas.

Her heart kept sloshing in a watery way, like it was murmuring a secret that it wanted her to hear.

"Are you my mother?" she mouthed to the magazine, and then she felt dizzy again and lay down on the floor. She was panting like a dog in the sun. She wondered if she was dying.

This was why her dad didn't want her to read the magazines.

This was why she had to carefully separate her dad in her mind from XAN GALLAGHER.

Nat closed her eyes again and pictured herself underwater, bubbles rising to the surface, no sounds coming from anywhere except her own heartbeat. When she thought about hearts, she thought about blue whales. Blue whales were the biggest whales in the whole species. Their hearts were big enough that another, smaller whale—like a baby humpback or an adult orca—could easily swim through their gigantic veins.

She had been in the bathroom for a long time. Harry probably thought she was dead. She wasn't sure that she wasn't, but probably not. She could hear the TV was on now in the other room. Maybe he had even forgotten she was there.

Nat put the magazine down on the floor. She took the rest of the magazines and put them on the floor, too, separately from the *one*.

She nudged the rest of the XAN magazines with her foot and the pile spilled over messily, cover after cover showing itself to her.

"XAN GALLAGHER: SEXIEST MAN ALIVE THREE YEARS RUNNING"

"XAN THE MAN: HE'S WRITING A BOOK!"

"XAN LEADS PIPELINE PROTEST—BUT WHO IS THAT GIRL?"

She stacked the XAN magazines at the bottom of the bigger pile and put them carefully back in the closet. She put the one from February 28, 2005, right there on top of the pile, closed the door, and gave it a kick. The kick was so loud that the TV went quiet. Harry must have muted it.

He probably thought she was nuts.

Probably he wouldn't want to be her friend anymore, and she needed a friend, she really did. She wanted to press a big "RESTART" button on this whole playdate. Even the word "playdate" was all wrong.

They were *twelve*.

They were hanging out, that's all.

Or they would be, if she hadn't spent the whole time in the bathroom.

She turned on the faucet so Harry wouldn't think she was dead.

Harry knocked on the door. "Mom says I have to ask if you're OK in there."

"I'm fine," she said, louder than she needed to. She laughed so that he would know nothing was wrong.

Harry knocked again, harder. "What?" he said. "Are you *crying*?"

"*Coming!*" Nat shouted, still running the faucet. "Just washing my hands!"

Then, without thinking about it, she opened the cupboard door again and took *the* magazine. She rolled it up and stuffed it down the leg of her jeans.

"What are you *doing* in there?" said Harry.

"I'm *coming*, I said." She looked at herself in the mirror and there she was, the same as before.

She put her hand on the door handle and made herself turn it. She put a smile on her face. "Hi," she said to Harry.

"Why are you making a face?" he said.

"I don't know," she said. "Sometimes I do that."

"OK."

"Don't be scared," she said.

"I'm not!" he said. "Why would I be scared?"

Nat followed Harry back down the tiny hallway into the room that his mom had called the playroom.

Playroom/playdate, Nat thought.

Both were terrible words.

"Go down to the playroom!" Harry's mom had said after she'd fed them a snack.

Harry's mom seemed perfectly, *quintessentially* normal. The snack was some kind of orange cheese goo spread onto celery sticks, salty crackers, and chocolate chip cookies. It was the best snack Nat had ever eaten.

Harry was *so* lucky.

The "playroom" had a sectional couch that was bigger than Nat's whole living room and kitchen combined. There was a TV that was connected to an Xbox, a PlayStation, *and* a Wii U. Nat felt *flattened* by envy. From the side, she probably looked like a piece of paper, that's how flat she felt. Her dad didn't believe in video games. He believed in being outside. He believed in fresh air and trees.

Nat liked those things, too. If she didn't go to the beach every single day, she might not see the whales again. And the whales were a billion times better than any old Xbox. Even thinking about them made her heart feel lighter, floaty, like when you run down a hill really fast and your feet don't even really touch the ground.

So why did seeing all this *stuff* make her feel so flat? She flopped backward onto the couch and folded her legs, origami-style, into her body.

"What are you doing?" said Harry. "Is that yoga?"

"Yes," she said, because it was easier than trying to explain. "Ohmmm," she said. "That's meditation."

"Okaaaaaaay," he said. "You're being super weird."

"I'm not," said Nat, and she crossed her eyes. "I'm just jealous of all your stuff. I don't have any stuff. My dad is a minimalist."

Something dark passed over Harry's face. "My dad is a jerk," he said.

Nat stopped smiling. She didn't know what to say.

After all, Harry might have a lot of *stuff*, but he also had a dad problem.

She didn't have a dad problem.

Not really.

Unless having a famous dad is a problem, which it was, in a lot of ways that probably Harry wouldn't understand because to him having XAN GALLAGHER as a dad probably looked pretty great.

It was Harry's dad who told the school that Harry was Harriet.

It was Harry's dad who told them that Harry was a girl and must be referred to as "she," even though Harry said he was a "he" and, as far as Nat was concerned, this should be up to Harry.

"Forget it," said Harry. "I shouldn't have said that."

He smelled like Doritos and laundry soap, which was weird because they hadn't eaten Doritos.

"Did you know that all dogs' feet smell like Doritos?" she said.

"I didn't know you had a dog!"

"I don't. But my best friend . . . I mean, my old best friend. My friend, Solly. She had a dog. Has a dog. She still has it."

"Huh," said Harry. "Doritos are good."

"They smell like dogs' feet," said Nat. "How can you eat them?"

Harry rubbed his stomach. "I'd like some right now," he said. "Mmmmmm, dog-foot chips! My favorite."

They giggled.

The leather on the couch was cool and smooth under Nat's hand. She rubbed her hand on it. "This is a *really* nice couch," she said, which she knew was the wrong thing.

"I don't know who my mom is," she mouthed, but didn't say out loud.

"I saw something in that magazine and I'm freaking out," she added.

My mom is a makeup artist. She tried to believe that one, but now she wasn't sure. She closed her eyes. *She is,* Nat told herself. *She's French. She's a makeup artist. She loves whales. My mom is made up. Made up with makeup.* She didn't want to cry. She wanted to tell him though. She wanted to say something. She just didn't know what, exactly, to say.

"Why are you moving your mouth like that?" Harry said. "You're not making any sound. I can't hear you."

Nat shrugged.

"Do you believe in telepathy?" she said.

"What's that? You mean like mind reading?" He snorted. "Duh. No."

Nat flinched.

She decided right then and there that she wouldn't tell Harry anything about her mom until he asked.

She knew he would never ask.

She picked up all four game controllers and laid them out beside her on the couch. "What should we play?" she said.

"Duh," he said, like it was obvious.

She wasn't sure she liked how he said "duh" all the time, but she knew you could like a person without liking everything about them. She tried to erase her bad thought about how he said "duh." It wasn't up to her to judge. That was another one of her dad's things, the thing about never judging people. "People are weirdos!" he'd say. "Freaks and weirdos! All of us! It's what makes us so great!"

Harry went to one of the game consoles and fiddled with it, then came back.

Being with Harry outside of school felt different; the atmosphere shifted around them. It was, she thought, like looking at the pavement in a heat wave. Everything felt shimmery and surreal, not like real life.

"What are you girls up to?" Harry's mom materialized out of nowhere. She was carrying a hamper full of dirty laundry with the cat balanced on the top. "This cat," she said, and laughed, putting the hamper down.

When Harry's mom said "girls," Nat felt something in her mouth that burned. She wondered if she might throw up. She swished the spit around in her mouth and swallowed. It tasted bad.

"Mom." Harry frowned. "We're playing video games, OK? Can you leave us alone?"

"Is that rude?" his mom said. "Harriet?"

"Don't call me Harriet!" he shouted.

Nat couldn't believe how fast he got mad. She'd never seen anyone get mad as quickly as Harry did, except for her dad, and that was just that one time.

"Your dad says . . ." Harry's mom said.

Nat looked around; she wanted to crawl under the sofa and hide but there was only about an inch of space. There was no way that she would fit. She considered just running away. She could keep running until she was back at the Airstream trailer, where her dad was probably right now steaming twenty-seven pounds of shrimp. The shrimp here was really good. She wished she were there with him now, sneaking some shrimp from the basket.

Nat hadn't known that it was possible to feel homesick for your own house when you were just hanging out with a friend after school.

"Don't talk about it!" yelled Harry. "Can't we just not talk about it for ten seconds?"

"I'm just trying to do the right thing here," said Harry's mom.

Nat glanced at the window, which was one of the half windows that people have in basements. She was eye level with the ground. She pictured herself climbing up and out and then crawling away, but she knew she wouldn't. She wasn't the kind of person to abandon a friend. "I—" she started.

"It's your name!" his mom interrupted. She had a steely determination in her voice. Her words glinted like roofing nails. "Your father and I named you Harriet."

"I don't want to fight about this right now!" Harry yelled.

Nat cleared her throat. Both Harry and his mom stared at Nat like they'd forgotten that she was there. She was definitely there. She took a deep breath; it smelled like cat (which was nothing like Doritos) and leather. She thought about what she should say.

"Oh my goodness," said Harry's mom. "That was *so* rude of us. I'm sorry, Nat. We didn't mean to make you uncomfortable!"

"Why do you call her Nat? That's a boy's name! If you call her Nat, you have to call me Harry," said Harry. "She's a girl! She doesn't even look like a boy!" He looked at her. "Well, she does a little."

"I'm a girl," said Nat quickly. "I used to have short hair and people said I was a tomboy, but I was just . . ." She let the sentence trail away. It was too complicated in the moment to explain about her Tomboy Years. It had to do with her dad wanting her to hide her true self from the media, just like he did.

Except he didn't. XAN GALLAGHER was XAN GALLAGHER, period. He wasn't different when he was just her dad, he was just sometimes less jovial.

Nat tapped her fingers against her cheek, and then she looked at the cat, which—like her—didn't seem to know where to go but looked like he wanted to run. The cat meowed.

You can just jump down, Nat told the cat telepathically, and he did. Cats were very in tune like that. Nat smiled.

The cat's departure unbalanced the laundry, which spilled out all over the floor. Then it was like all the air rushed out of Harry's mom at once, and she sagged against the door frame. "You're right," she said quietly. "I'm so sorry." Then she walked away, leaving the mess behind.

Harry still hadn't said anything.

He seemed paralyzed. His mouth was open a little bit. Nat was tempted to stick her finger in his mouth. That's what she would have done to Solly if Solly made that face. But Harry wasn't Solly, so she didn't.

Nat picked up one of the game controllers, the gold one.

Harry was still not talking.

Nat got up and pressed the reset button on the game, which had gone to sleep. "Ready?" she said.

Harry nodded.

He had freckles in a perfect arch that went over his nose. It looked like an upside-down smile, or a sad face, if you thought of it that way. Nat was starting to understand why Harry looked so sad all the time.

It was because of *Harriet.*

It was because his mom was trying to do the right thing, and by trying to do the right thing, she was doing the wrong thing.

It was because his dad wasn't even trying to do the right thing at all.

Having a dad who did not understand about his Harry-ness must have felt insurmountable. "Insurmountable" was one of Nat's favorite English words. There were some good ones, after all. It was a word that made her think of mountains too high to climb, glistening with snow and ice, sharply carving lines into the sky. Also, it contained the word "mount," which made her think of the creepy bear head she had noticed hanging on the living room wall in the upstairs of Harry's house, which they had to pass on their way to the stairs that led to the playroom.

The more she thought about it, the more *insurmountable* became reshaped as a headless bear in her mind.

She shivered.

Nat hadn't explained to Harry about the words she collected—all kinds of words, from regular ones to foreign ones to made-up ones—and how they made shapes in her head, the foreign ones more roughly hewn than the English ones, which were so sanded down and polished by being spoken out loud so much around her that they were all uniformly smooth and sometimes not meaningful enough.

She tried to concentrate on the game.

She didn't know how to play it, and her character kept dying. Harry's didn't.

Just then, he shouted "HEY" at the screen. She watched as his character fell down a tunnel.

"Watch out!" she said, way too late. "I don't really know how to play this," she added. "It's harder than it looks."

"It's not hard!"

"Did I just die? How am I supposed to do this?"

"Argh!" he yelled. He stood up and started jumping up and down. "It helps when I jump!" he explained, even though she hadn't asked. "It totally helps!"

Nat stood up and started jumping, too, her sock feet landing with gentle thuds on the thick carpet while her character re-spawned for the tenth time. The game played a jaunty, enthusiastic song.

Nat and Harry jumped and jumped in Harry's basement. Nat was a little worried that the magazine in her jeans was

a) showing or b) about to slide down and out the bottom of her pants.

How would she explain that?

She stopped jumping.

"Why aren't you jumping?" Harry said.

"I got tired," she said, sitting down.

"OK." He sat down, too.

"When I was little, I saved all my fingernail clippings in a jar, because I didn't want any part of me to get thrown in the garbage," Harry said, for what seemed like no reason.

"What about your toenail clippings?" Nat's character ran into a bad guy and evaporated. The game bleeped. Even the music sounded disappointed in her.

"Toenails are gross! I threw those out."

"I'm glad you have such super-high standards," she said. "Now I know we'll be friends."

"Duh," said Harry, but he looked at her funny and then he shook his head. She wasn't sure if that meant they were friends or that they weren't.

"*Unguim*," said Nat. *Unguim* was the Latin word for fingernail.

"Whatever," said Harry. His character grabbed the giant diamond from the top of the turret and raised his hands in a victory dance. The video game played a jaunty tune.

"I won," he said, but he didn't sound as happy about it as Nat would have expected.

HARRY

Nat was the first person Harry met.

Nat was the person he sat next to.

Nat was the nicest one.

But Harry did not want to be best friends with Nat. Nat was a girl, and his whole plan was to start the school year with a posse of boys, doing only boy things.

It was because Nat was so easy to hang out with that this was happening. That the coolest boy in his class, Seth, and those guys didn't want him in their squad and wouldn't let him sit with them at lunch.

He was so frustrated. He didn't know what to do about it or how to deal with it. And the stupidest part of it was that NAT WAS THE ONLY PERSON HE COULD TALK TO ABOUT IT.

Harry picked up the phone and dialed her number, which she'd written on the inside of his math textbook.

"Hello?"

"It's me," he said. "What are you doing?"

"I'm at the beach," Nat said. Harry could hear the wind blowing through the receiver. "I'm waiting for whales."

"Stay there," he said. "I'm coming."

He yelled to his mom, "I'm going to practice on the board!"

"Be back by dinner!" she answered. She was on Facebook on her computer. She was always on Facebook on her computer. Harry hoped she was maybe finding a group of parents of trans kids or something, the good kind of parents, the nice supportive ones. He knew they were out there. He looked over her shoulder. It was a group of people who collected vintage dresses. He rolled his eyes. "Mom," he said.

"What?" she said. "I love these."

"Those dresses look like cartoons," he said. "When would you wear those?"

She shrugged. "I don't know. Maybe one day your father and I will go somewhere that I need to dress up. Are you going to the skateboard park?"

"Nah," he said. "Just around."

"Wear a helmet!" she called after him. He waved in response.

He went to the garage and got his longboard. It was painted with a skull and crossbones, all black and silver and BOYISH. He loved his board. He dropped it on the pavement and hopped on. It was all downhill to Nat's place; he'd barely even have to break a sweat. He could just coast, almost the entire way.

POSTCARD NUMBER 2

Hi Soleil, Nat wrote at the top of the next postcard on the pile.

It felt like she was writing to someone she didn't know, so she didn't know what to say. What did you write on a postcard to a stranger?

Writing to a stranger might actually be easier than writing to someone who used to be a friend, but was maybe not a friend now and actually maybe never was.

Nat glowered at what she'd written so far.

"Soleil" looked all wrong.

It wasn't Solly's name. Not the Solly Nat knew. She guessed maybe it was the name of this new version of Solly who kissed boys and had her period and wanted to grow bigger boobs.

Nat did not want those things.

Not yet.

"I'm just not ready," she told Stick Monkey. She had taken

Stick Monkey out of the box and put him on the shelf next to her head. "I will be eventually. Maybe."

She looked back at the postcard. She wanted desperately to talk to Solly about the magazine, which she'd put in the box where Stick Monkey used to be. She wanted to ask Solly if she should look.

But that was dumb.

Solly already knew who Nat's mother was.

Solly had already Googled it.

Nat knew this because one day, when they were in a fight, Solly had said, "Who are you really talking to when you say you're talking to your mom on the phone?"

Nat's blood had run cold. She had started to shiver, hard. "My mom, duh. Why?" She tried to make her voice sound natural.

"Uh, because your mom is—"

"Shut up," Nat had said, before Solly could finish her sentence. She put her hands over her ears, like she was three years old or something. She closed her eyes. She could still hear Solly, but she couldn't make out the words. Then she'd grabbed her backpack and put it on so fast that she didn't realize it was upside down. She'd run the whole way home, dropping her homework all over the street.

Sometimes, people just aren't who you think they are. It takes a long time to really know a person, like maybe a year.

Maybe longer.

Maybe it took a whole lifetime.

Having a great time, wish you were here, Nat wrote in huge block letters. She went over and over them again until they were thick and heavy and showed through the other side because she pressed so hard.

Then she wrote her name in cursive: *Natalia Rose Baleine Gallagher.*

If Solly was going to be Soleil, she could not be plain old Nat. That's how it worked. It was math. But x does not equal y. Nat did not equal Solly. Not anymore. Maybe she never had.

Anyway, she did not very much feel like a Natalia Rose.

Natalia Rose felt like a name she was eventually, *maybe*, going to grow into.

Natalia Rose felt like someone she wasn't ready for yet.

Underneath her name, in very tiny letters, she wrote, *Congratulations.* It was so small, she wondered if Solly would even see it. She probably wouldn't bother to look. She'd be too busy kissing Evan and looking in the mirror to see if her boobs had arrived yet, like they might come by FedEx in the night and just appear by magic in the morning.

Nat, for one, was sincerely hoping that it didn't work like that. Well, she knew it wouldn't *literally* work like that, but she still hoped it wouldn't work in *any way* like that. She looked down at her chest: still flat.

Nat felt nothing but relief.

SCIENCE FAIR

The silky-haired, ribbon-voiced mean girl was called Heaven.

Sometimes people are just grossly misnamed, Nat thought.

Like Solly, whose name meant "sun" in French. Solly wasn't always very sunshiney—although she was at first, when they were new friends.

Back when they were both on the same page.

Before everything changed.

Sometimes Nat worried that there was something wrong with her, that she was good only at beginnings, but not middles and definitely not endings.

It was hard to explain, even to herself, but even when she was angriest at Solly, she didn't hate her. She loved her. She just didn't *like* her very much.

It was complicated.

But with Heaven, it wasn't that way at all. It was simple.

She didn't like her at all. Nat was worried she actually *hated* Heaven, and she didn't want to be someone who hated anyone. Heaven was acting as though Nat were auditioning to be her friend, which couldn't be more wrong. Nat didn't want anything to do with Heaven. If she had to pick a friend who wasn't Harry, she'd pick one of the nicer, quieter girls, like Maggie or Amelia, who sat in the back and secretly read e-readers on their laps instead of listening to Mr. Hajeezi. But they were already a tight pair, like the pair that Nat and Solly had been. Heaven's group was bigger and looser, and she could probably "get in" if she wanted to, but she really, truly didn't.

She didn't want to be friends with anyone else except Harry.

But Harry didn't feel the same way, as it turned out.

He had sat next to her on the log at the bottom of the path.

He had stared out at the sea, instead of looking right at her.

And he had explained that she was "wrecking" things for him.

Nat almost couldn't stand it. She felt like she was on fire. She'd wanted to throw herself into the waves or scream or both. She blinked hard to stop herself from crying right then and there, sitting in the science lab with stupid Heaven doing this stupid project.

"Why are you *staring* at me?" said Heaven. She touched her hair. She did that a lot. It bugged Nat. But what about Heaven didn't bug her?

Nat looked away. "I wasn't staring. I was thinking."

"You were. I saw you. When you're caught, you have to admit it. You could just say 'sorry,'" said Heaven.

"Fine, sorry, whatever." Nat put her head down on the cool, shiny black counter of the science lab, where she and Heaven were meant to be making oobleck. She felt funny. Feverish or something. Her body was hurting. Either she was sick, or it was because of what happened the day before with Harry. Or because of what happened after that, when Harry left, walking up the path without Nat and rolling away down the road.

The after thing was that she and her dad had seen the Lion.

It was a lot different being famous in Canada than it was being famous in America. The locals treated XAN GALLAGHER very politely in Canada, Nat had noticed, like he had a brain injury or a mental disorder.

"Sorry, Mr. Gallagher?" they said, turning their apology into a question at the end. "A bit of a crowd has gathered by the entrance; would you like to use the back door?"

In San Francisco, people were always screaming when they saw XAN GALLAGHER in public. No one offered them the back door when they lived in America. They all *wanted* things from him, like he owed them: a photo or an autograph or a handful of his famous shirt. And if someone made a grab at him, everyone else followed suit, until sometimes there was a mini-riot of people all grabbing for her dad's clothing.

They took pictures in Canada, too. Sometimes. But it was a lot quieter.

It was a lot better.

"It's no problem," her dad had said, back in SF and NY and all the other places. "Photos are free. This guy's just makin' his living. We all gotta work! It's the price of

fame." But Nat knew that he hated being followed and photographed. He especially hated when *she* was followed and
photographed.

But he never let on how much it bugged him.

Sometimes he even hugged the photographers, lifting
them right off their feet. "Give 'em a story!" he said. "I'm
givin' you a story!"

But while Nat's dad might have *said* it was "no problem,"
if it weren't a problem, they wouldn't keep moving and keep
moving and keep moving.

The night before, Nat and her dad found out—again—
that you can't outrun fame. It just packs its bags and comes
padding along right behind you, camera raised.

If by "it," Nat meant "the Lion."

They'd gone up to the Food Mart to get ice cream. Nat's
dad always bought her ice cream when she was sad, and he
knew she was sad. He'd tried to jolly her out of it, or to get
her to explain it, but she'd refused. So he'd decided that ice
cream was the only thing for it.

Nat was just reaching into the freezer to get the last all-
fruit, no-sugar sherbet for her dad—she'd already gotten the
mint chocolate chip real stuff for herself—when her dad froze
in his tracks and made a ribbiting sound, almost like a frog.

Nat looked, and there was the Lion, camera aimed,
crouching behind a display of corn on the cob.

"No," she said. Her heart lurched.

Nat's dad didn't pick up the Lion that time and give him
a hug, but he raised his hand in a half wave and did his signature one-eyebrow raise. Nat could tell he was trying.

The Lion yelled, "GOT IT, MAN!" and scurried away
with his photo.

Just like in SF.

Nat put the sherbet in the basket her dad was carrying.

But then she noticed that her dad's hands were shaking the tiniest bit. *That's very un-Dad-like*, she'd thought. Now Nat still had that thought in her head, but she didn't know what to do with it.

It's hard to imagine someone as big and jovial and famous and safe and giant as her dad actually being anxious, but why else would his hands shake?

After the Lion left, her dad had walked two aisles over and selected a box of sugary cereal. His body was a temple, he said often, but sometimes his temple worshipped on its knees at the altar of Fruity Pebbles.

It was his one weakness.

He said it was because it tasted like his childhood. It reminded him of being a kid, of the time before he was XAN GALLAGHER.

"We all contain *multitudes*," he'd told Nat. "Everyone isn't ever all one thing."

Nat hated sugar not because of the taste, but because it made her teeth feel squeaky and strange. She liked crisp fruit and crunchy almost-but-not-quite-burned toast, food that was sharp and convincing in her mouth.

BUT she also liked mint chocolate chip ice cream, so she got it.

It made perfect sense to her.

"Yep yep," she said.

By the time they got to the checkout, he wasn't shaking anymore, but she could tell that he was upset. She could tell that Canada had been ruined now, for her dad.

Nat knew at that moment they for sure wouldn't be

staying past June. She tried not to think about it though. Thinking about it hurt more than she would have thought. Thinking about it made her want to cry, and she was already close to crying because of Harry.

She was miserable for the rest of the day. Her dad seemed miserable, too. At least, he left her alone, which he almost never did. He didn't even work out.

Everything had gone bad, all at the same time, like milk you accidentally left out on the counter, and when you poured it, all you had was curdled lumps.

OOBLECK WAS WATER AND cornstarch mixed together. There was nothing complicated about it; it was just those two things. Heaven and Nat sat next to each other, using the school's iPad, and watched a bunch of YouTube videos of people making it. That was the "research" part of their science fair project.

It was, according to the Internet, a popular thing to make in preschools. It obviously should have been very easy.

But *their* oobleck was a mess. It refused to come together. It was impossible to stir. It turned as hard as a rock under the tines of the fork, but turned to water as soon as they stopped trying.

"You do it this time," said Heaven. "It feels gross. I have to wash my hands."

It was their tenth attempt. They had almost no cornstarch left.

"Fine," said Nat. "No problem."

Heaven swished away, flipping her hair over her shoulder as she walked. She was all about the hair. Nat flipped her own hair, but then felt dumb, so she pretended she was just trying to stretch her neck. She did not want to be a hair flipper. She did not want to be anything like Heaven.

Heaven was awful.

Since the day before, everything had felt awful.

Maybe she *was* sick, she decided. She had eaten two spoonfuls of Fruity Pebbles to try to cheer her dad up. Every time he bought them, he was sure that she'd love them. And every time, she didn't.

Even thinking about them made something in her stomach churn and threaten.

Nat stuck a fork into the cornstarch and water and tried once more to stir it into something that resembled what was in the videos, but she couldn't.

The stuff was still like concrete. Then she tilted the bowl from side to side and it turned into watery soup. It was supposed to be *oozy*. Not *soupy*. Goo. Not water.

Nothing was as it was supposed to be.

Certainly not Nat.

Definitely not Harry, who was supposed to be her BFF.

Not even Canada, which was supposed to be paparazzi-free.

And especially not XAN GALLAGHER, who was supposed to be superhuman and not ever anxious. Definitely never *shaky*.

"Everything is wrong," she said out loud. "Nothing is working." She slammed the fork down on the worktop.

"It's not my fault," said Heaven. "I was following the instructions. You must have messed it up."

They both stared at the oozy mess.

The magic of oobleck was in its impenetrable surface tension. (Nat wondered if *people* could have impenetrable surface tension. She felt like she could definitely use some.) They had watched one video where someone filled a whole pool with oobleck and people rode bikes on it. As long as they were moving, it was fine, but if they stopped pedaling, they sank.

There was no chance anyone could ride a bike on the surface of their oobleck.

Nat dumped in some more cornstarch.

"It might be OK," she said. Heaven delicately wiped her hands on a paper towel. "Maybe it's supposed to start out like this."

"I hate this lame project," said Heaven. "I wanted to make a volcano."

"Oh," said Nat. "Well, I hate it, too." She wondered privately if Heaven meant that she hated working with Nat and that she would rather work with her real friend, Shay. Shay was very pretty but, like Heaven, was pretty mean. *They deserved each other*, Nat thought. She didn't want anything to do with either of them. But the rest of the girls in the class—Amber, Ashley, and Catrina—were all in Heaven's "squad," too.

Shay was working with a boy named Kevin. Kevin was cute and tall and smart and pretty nice, a combo that should make him crush-worthy, but Nat didn't have a crush. She didn't want one.

Maybe she never would.

Besides, Kevin was best friends with Seth, and Seth was the reason why Harry didn't want to hang out with Nat.

All Nat wanted was the kind of friend you could call and say, "Something happened!" and that person would say, "What? What happened? Are you OK?" That kind of friend.

She'd thought she had one, in Harry.

Duh, she thought.

She *got* it—why he'd want to be in with Kevin and Seth—but it sucked. She knew that it wasn't personal.

But it also was.

Nat blinked some more. She didn't want to start crying right there in the classroom while her fork bounced off the surface of the mess she was making. "My eyes hurt," she told Heaven, just in case she'd noticed all the blinking Nat had been doing. "Something has fumes maybe."

Heaven sniffed the air. "I don't smell anything," she said. "Your face is all blotchy."

"Allergies," lied Nat. "Maybe I'm allergic to cornstarch."

"You should take a pill or something," said Heaven. It sounded almost like she cared. "You could go to the sick room and lie down."

"Thanks," said Nat. "But I'm OK." She smiled at Heaven. "Thanks," she repeated.

Maybe if she got to know Heaven and Shay, she *would* like them. No one was *all* bad. Maybe they were just jerks about Harry because their parents were terrible. You couldn't blame someone for having rotten parents. Take Solly, for example. *Her* mother was truly terrible.

And Solly was at least *half* bad, in that she had done some mean, dumb things. But Nat couldn't really fault her for being excited about boobs and boys and her period when her mom was sort of famous for having huge boobs and lots of boyfriends. (Nothing period-related though.) Lots of people were like that. Boys-and-boobs people. Maybe even most people. It was just her, Nat, who didn't want to think about it.

"Why do you keep saying 'thanks'?" said Heaven. "I didn't even do anything. You don't have to be *grateful*."

"Rude," muttered Nat.

"Sorry?" said Heaven.

"I'm not grateful," said Nat. She closed her eyes.

Solly, she thought, as loudly as she could. *SOLLY.*

"I guess you think you're too good to be grateful because your dad is famous." Heaven rolled her eyes, Solly-style.

"I—" Nat started. Then she stopped. "Whatever." She was suddenly having trouble breathing. It was like Heaven and Solly had merged into one person. But they couldn't do that, because she hated Heaven.

She didn't hate Solly.

Did she?

Solly had done that one huge terrible thing, but Nat didn't want to think about *that*. Sometimes she wished she could just erase her brain and not have to think about anything that had already happened. A break from thinking would be nice.

Nat would call Solly when she got home, she decided. She may not have a BFF here but she still sort of had Solly, and Solly, at least, would *get* it. She would scorn Heaven and her posse of hair-flipping morons. She would understand how cool Harry was and how much it sucked that he didn't really want to be friends.

Solly would approve of Harry. She liked people who were who they were meant to be, even if it meant they were purple-haired people in a sea of blondes and brunettes.

"Let's just put the food coloring in and get it over with." Heaven sighed. "It's good enough. It's fine. I'm bored of this already."

"Sure," said Nat, trying to sound like she cared. "Great idea!"

"You do it," said Heaven. "Food coloring takes forever to wash off your hands, and I don't want to have green and blue blotches."

"I don't either!"

"But you don't care what you look like," said Heaven. "People like you just don't have to worry about it."

"I do so!"

"You do?" Heaven sounded so dubious that Nat questioned it herself.

"Not always," admitted Nat. "I just don't think what I look like is very interesting."

"You're *lucky*," said Heaven.

"What?" said Nat. She heard what Heaven said, she just wasn't sure she understood it. People like her? Lucky? She wanted to know what Heaven meant. "Sorry?" she added.

"Nothing," said Heaven. "Nothing for you to be *grateful* for, anyway. It wasn't a compliment. Let's dump this stuff onto the speaker and see what it does."

The point of the project was to make the oobleck dance. With the food coloring mixed in, it would gyrate mysteriously to music. Or at least, it was supposed to.

It did in all the videos.

Nat glopped the oobleck into the cup that was balanced on the speaker, and Heaven turned the music up. Loud. And then louder. The song was so loud that the windows in the lab were shaking and the other kids were groaning and covering their ears.

"Gracie sucks!" shouted Seth from the back row.

Seth was working with Harry on a project about genes.

It was Harry's idea. When Harry had told Nat about it, she thought he meant to work on it *with* her. Nat knew that he was doing it because he was looking for something to explain why he's a boy but was born with parts that didn't match. Nat hoped that he figured it out. They had only gotten as far as how to tell if a pea plant was going to be green or yellow. But that scientist guy, Mendel, didn't really get into the complications of being transgender, she didn't think.

Nat also didn't think Seth knew that's why Harry chose the project in the first place.

She didn't think *he'd* get it.

She knew a person like Seth would never really get Harry. Not like she did.

But Harry wanted to work on the project with Seth and not Nat. Nat's feelings were so hurt that even looking up at Seth brought tears to her eyes. Again. She had no idea why Heaven picked her as a partner. She'd only said yes because she'd been so caught off guard. Heaven definitely seemed like the type to try to befriend her for being XAN GALLAGHER's daughter, but she hadn't exactly been friendly so far, so the whole thing was pretty confusing.

"This is *Gracie*?" she said.

"What?" shouted Heaven.

"GRACIE?" Nat tried again.

"Isn't it AWESOME? She's making a total comeback. She's ancient. From the eighties."

"I know her!" said Nat, but she didn't explain. It seemed too hard and the music was too loud and the oobleck still wasn't moving, it was just lying there in the cup, like it was too exhausted or sad to even consider a small shimmy.

Mr. Hajeezi clapped his hands. "ENOUGH!" he yelled.

"Turn it off and try again tomorrow, girls! This music will make us all crazy!" He pulled the plug on the stereo.

"That's a terrible song," said Harry from the back row. "I agree with you, Seth." He sounded like he was trying too hard. He sounded so formal. *He could stand to take a page from XAN GALLAGHER's book*, Nat thought. *He could use some* joviality, *at least*.

"Dude," said Seth. That was how Seth talked, in one-word bursts.

"Yeah," said Harry, mimicking his tone.

Nat cringed. She coughed loudly, to cover up both Harry's voice and the feeling she was having.

The terrible, awful feeling that came from knowing that she *got* Harry, and that she might be the only one; that Harry was her best friend, but that he didn't want to be.

Part Two

MEXICO

BEBIDA/BOOBIDA

Harry and Nat were riding the bikes into town.

The town was on the Baja Peninsula.

Everything about the fact that they were there, in Mexico, together, was so strange to Nat that she could hardly get her head around it. But there they were, pedaling up a steep hill, sweating like crazy and squinting in the dazzling sunlight.

The bikes came with the house that Nat's dad had rented on Airbnb. It was wrong to call it a house. It was a glass palace. The house was the kind of house that famous people stay in when they are on vacation and want to be hidden away from everyone else in the world. It was *not* the kind of house that the Brasches were used to, or had ever seen before, except on TV. It was four whole stories of glittering glass and polished floors and swimming pools and a rooftop deck where you could see for miles and miles.

The Brasches—especially Harry—were trying very hard to pretend the whole thing was *completely* normal, but Nat kept catching them whispering in one room or another, picking up a weird brass sculpture and inspecting it carefully, like robbers, assessing it for value. Once, she caught Mrs. Brasch taking a photo of the toilet. To be fair, it was an interesting toilet. It had a lot of different push buttons on the back. In the tank, there was a clear window where there seemed to be a tiny aquarium with actual fish.

"Gross," Harry had said, and Nat privately agreed. Why *were* there fish in the toilet? It seemed super cruel to the fish, like keeping a whale in a tank at SeaWorld or something, except worse, because it was a *toilet*.

But also not as bad. Because fish were fish, not whales.

Nat thought those things, all in a jumble, but she didn't answer. She was still feeling prickly toward Harry for mostly ignoring her all fall and winter while he got closer and closer to Seth and his "squad" and farther and farther from Nat.

Nat had remained mostly alone. She was sort of, she guessed, friends with Maggie and Amelia, but maybe they just didn't mind her being around because she sat with them and read a book. Or pretended to read a book.

It could be worse, Nat thought. Maggie and Amelia were sometimes funny, with the dry kind of sense of humor that Nat had seen only in British films. They were *quietly* funny. Nat liked that. She didn't like it enough to want to invite the girls over or to hang out with them on weekends though, so mostly she was pretty lonely until her dad decided to make it his own personal mission to be BFFs with the entire Brasch family. He even went hunting, once, with Mr. Brasch. "It wasn't my thing!" he exclaimed joyfully when he got home afterward. "But I think I know what to do! I think I've got this! You and Harry! I'm going to fix everything! You'll never have to hang out with Hell again!"

Nat had giggled. "Heaven, Dad. Not Hell."

"Oh, right!" he'd said, and slapped the table so hard that a bowl of apples had toppled over. He'd picked them up off the floor and juggled them while raising his eyebrow.

"DAD," she'd said. "Do you even like Mr. Brasch?"

"Des? Oh, sure! Sure, I like Des! He's a different kind of guy. You know, very straitlaced. Old-school. Pretty religious, too. He's a good person! He just doesn't know how to be one all the time. But we'll get him there! I'm gonna help him!"

"Dad," she'd said. "Not everyone wants your help, you know."

But he had been busy catching one of the apples in his gigantic mouth.

"DAD."

Whatever he'd said and done had worked, though. Nat's dad claimed that Mr. Brasch was really "trying hard" to understand Harry, thanks to him. He also somehow magicked this trip into happening.

That was the best part.

Nat pedaled up to Harry. "I was thinking that the toilet fish are probably actually pretty happy. Think of all the people they get to see! Always something going on."

He slowed down a little so she could keep up. "Uh, OK. All those fish get to see are people's backsides. Which are private. Anyway, even with the weird fish, this place is amazing. I wouldn't have thought your dad would pick a place like *this*. Like if any house is an insult to the Earth or whatever, it's a house like this one."

"He's trying to impress your parents," Nat told him. "He does stuff like this when he wants people to like him."

"Why does he want my parents to like him? He's this huge movie star! He can have John Cena over for dinner! Or whoever! My dad is a jerk and my mom is just a normal person. They don't know *anyone*. They don't know how to act in front of your dad. It sort of feels like he's adopted them or something. My dad's talking about all kinds of weird stuff he's never mentioned before. And he joined a gym. Like he's going to start lifting weights now? And my mom blushes whenever she says your dad's name. It's gross. They are sort of creeping me out."

"Oh, I don't know," said Nat, but she did know. "I guess he just likes them. He likes normal people."

"Uh, they are *not* normal."

The truth was that her dad wanted to impress the Brasches so that Harry would be her real friend again.

But she could hardly say *that*. So instead she shrugged. "They seem pretty normal to him, I guess."

"What does he know?" said Harry. He started pedaling faster. "He's so far from normal, he has NO idea."

Nat wondered if that was true. Maybe it was.

Maybe it was true of her, too.

I love you, she said to her dad, telepathically, as she watched Harry distance himself from her, pedaling faster and faster, like he was desperate to get away.

Her dad didn't answer, because *duh*, but she could pretty much perfectly imagine that he would've said, "Yeah, you do."

And then he'd have laughed.

THE BIKES, IN CONTRAST to the house, were rickety and old, spotted with rust and mysterious algae. They looked as though someone found them one day at the bottom of the ocean and hauled them back to the house, relics from the deep.

The bike Nat was riding was green and much too small for her, which was quite something, as she was a very small person for her age. Especially for her age as it would be on Monday, which was thirteen.

The trip was a present for Nat's birthday. All she wanted, she'd told her dad, was to go somewhere to see whales. She was desperate to see them. She felt like seeing whales would fix everything. Somehow.

She didn't say "see whales with Harry." He had thought of that on his own.

Maybe he knew.

Maybe he could tell because of that day when Harry met her at the beach and Nat had cried because no whales came. At least, that's what she'd told him.

She'd wanted whales to be their friendship *thing* that had started on the day she had said "Nice tattorca!" and he had laughed. Not *at* her; *with* her.

Whales were important to Nat. But they were also important to Harry. They must have been, or why the tattorca in the first place? Somehow, she just knew that if she could show Harry how connected she was to whales, he would like her back as much as she liked him.

Whales would make them best friends again.

All through October and November and December and January, Harry had worked hard to get in with Seth and Kevin and those guys, and it had worked, to a certain extent. After school, he hung out with them at the skate park, leaning on his board and scuffing his shoes on the ground. He shouted things like "Dude!" and "Yeah!" She'd seen him. She wasn't following him or anything—it's just that sometimes she got her dad to pick her up there instead of at school. Sometimes she felt like walking.

Seeing him there, she could tell that he was happy. That he was feeling more comfortable in his own skin. And she was truly happy for him. Sometimes she *totally* understood, and that understanding felt like something inside her was cracking open, but in a good way.

She *got* it.

She *got* him.

And wasn't that really what love was all about? Getting someone? Being gotten?

Nat hadn't really gotten Solly. She'd thought she did, but she had been proven wrong after all.

Her best friend from the year before, Mika, now seemed like someone she just barely knew. They had only been ten! Babies.

In fact, other than Harry and the Bird, her dad was pretty much the only person she just got, 100 percent. She was at about 75 percent with the Bird. (You can't really know someone you've never even met, after all.) And *maybe* 86 percent with Harry.

Eighty-six percent was an A.

Nat grinned. Now she was in Mexico, with Harry, and they would see whales, and he would finally *get* her back. Then it would be perfect.

Or close enough.

At least until June. In June, Nat and her dad were going to

move to France. Her dad was filming a movie about a Maori warrior who inherited a French vineyard. Nat was going to have an on-set tutor. She wouldn't even have a chance to make a normal school best friend next year.

Nat wasn't that keen on France. Not just because of the tutor. But because there weren't any whales there—at least, not where they would be living.

On the other hand, France might mean that she would get to meet her (French) mother. *Ma mère*, she thought, and smiled.

"What?" Harry yelled. "Did you say something?"

"No, nothing," she yelled back.

Harry's bike was blue. It was too big for him. It had a bent front wheel, like someone had run it over with a car.

When Nat pedaled sitting down, her knees hit the handlebars over and over again and she felt like a toddler, so she gave up and stood, bending forward awkwardly to reach the handlebars. Her dad refused to rent a car because of carbon emissions. They had used up more than their share by flying there in the first place. He was donating money to charity like crazy to make up for it. She hoped he wouldn't give it *all* away. Carbon emission reduction was another one of his things.

Sometimes it seemed like her dad was making himself bigger and bigger and bigger so that he could lift up the whole world on his shoulders and take care of it. He would feed it a lot of lean protein and kale smoothies. He would clean it up from the inside out. Somehow.

"You gotta walk the walk," he said all the time. "Talk the talk."

He said (and tweeted) that one quite a lot, often enough

that it, too, had become a *thing*. Nat had even seen it on bumper stickers.

"Wait up!" Nat called to Harry. She pedaled harder to try to catch up. He was way more athletic than she was. Faster. Stronger. Taller.

All-around better, she thought, privately. Harry was someone who really knew who he was.

She wasn't. *Who was she?*

Maybe that was the problem.

Her dad knew who *he* was.

Harry knew who *he* was.

The Bird knew who *she* was.

Even Solly knew who *she* was.

But did Nat?

She didn't like thinking about it. It made her feel funny. Light-headed, like she'd just seen blood.

"Harry!" She was panting hard already.

"Hurry up!" Harry yelled back. He coasted back toward her and then turned and pedaled up the hill again like it was nothing. Nat's legs burned. The town was still two more miles away. Maybe she wouldn't make it. Maybe she'd just die, right there, by the side of the road.

"Wait," she gasped. "Up." *Gasp.* "For." *Gasp.* "Me."

"Town" was not the right word for where they were going anyway. The word "town" made Nat think of crowds of people, of neatly parked cars, of buildings with clean edges, lined up in an even row, with colored awnings and lit-up signs. Here, the scattered handful of spread-out buildings all seemed to tilt either one way or another, like they were caught in the act of sighing. When Nat and Harry finally crested the top of the hill, they could see it laid out before them, like a third-grade diorama project that had been knocked sideways on the school bus and maybe had been stepped on by more than one someone.

"That's *it?*" said Harry, dubiously. He wasn't even slightly winded.

"It's probably better than it looks from here." Nat tried to sound normal and not like she was about to die. "Things are usually better up close." But even as she said it, she wasn't sure. This was her first time in this part of Mexico. She really had no idea.

"Dude," Harry said.

Nat didn't say anything. "Dude" wasn't a thing you had to answer. Besides, she wasn't a dude at all.

It was so quiet. They could hear the wind pushing through the low-flung shrubs on the brown hills and the sound of their own breathing. They kept pedaling. They passed a house with a trailer parked in front that had a clothesline covered with T-shirts emblazoned with the words *BAJA—BEEN THERE, SURFED THAT.* Beside the trailer, there was a restaurant that looked permanently closed. There were boards on the windows. But it still had a folding billboard out front that said *Una copa de vino: buena bebida, buena comida.* Glued over that, there was a loose piece of tattered paper. On it, someone had written *15 PESOS BEER* in marker.

"This place looks like where the zombie apocalypse is gonna start," said Harry, skidding to a stop.

Nat stopped, too, dragging her sneaker through the dust.

"*Buena bebida, buena comida,*" she read. Her voice sounded weird, all wooden and splintery. Of all the languages in the world, Spanish was the hardest for her to speak. The words didn't have sharp enough corners. It made them harder to hold on to. German was very prickly, almost like Velcro. She had no problem saying *weltschmerz*, for example. It was one of her favorites. It was a word that described a feeling of a weary sadness about everything in the world, something that she was feeling quite a bit too much of lately.

"*Weltschmerz*," she murmured.

"What?" said Harry.

"*No entiendo*," said Nat, instead of answering.

When Nat and her dad lived in San Francisco, people often assumed Nat was Mexican. She learned to say "*No entiendo*," which meant, "I don't understand." And "*Lo siento, no hablo español*," which meant, "Sorry, I don't speak Spanish."

Harry wandered over to the trailer. "Helllloooooo," he called. "There's no one here." He held a T-shirt up to himself and posed. The T-shirt was huge. It hung down to his knees, like a dress. "Should I buy this?"

"*No entiendo*," she repeated.

"What?" he said. "Why do you keep saying that?"

"It looks like a dress," Nat told him, and he hung it back up again, quick. Harry was dress-phobic, for obvious reasons. She felt mean for saying it, but also too *weltschmerz*-y to say "sorry."

"You could get one," he said.

"Me and my dad are No-Stuff People. You know that. I already told you."

"Oh yeah. I guess I forgot. But what does that even mean?"

"It just means we don't have stuff. Stuff takes too much time and space. I mean, it's like having stuff means you are responsible for the stuff."

"I don't think it takes a lot to look after a T-shirt," Harry said. "It's not like a puppy or something."

Nat shrugged. Sometimes her dad's things were hard to explain, even if they made perfect sense to her. Everything that mattered to her, she stored in her head, like words and whales. Well, memories of whales; not the whales themselves.

"You don't own stuff!" her dad liked to say. "Stuff owns *you*!"

But Nat did like how the T-shirts billowed on the line, like giant pillowcases, dusty from the road and wind. She held up her hands and took a pretend photo: Harry and the T-shirts against the gray of the sky and the brown dusty everything.

"Insta-perfect," she said.

"Upload that, stat," said Harry, wiping his forehead on one of the shirts. "Put it on the Twitter."

Saying "the Twitter" was one of their inside jokes. Harry's dad didn't know anything about social media. "Is that the Facebook?" he said sometimes when Harry and Nat were talking about something he didn't understand. "Will you put that on the Twitter?"

"Someone might buy that! And now it's all sweaty! Don't be gross," Nat said.

"It's a bonus. I've, like, imbued it with magic," he said. "The Magic of Harry." He grabbed an imaginary mic like a rock star, shaking his sweat into the audience.

Nat laughed. This was her favorite version of Harry. Not the slumpy, skateboarding *dude* version. This was more like the sitting-on-the-beach-waiting-for-whales version, but not the part where he was rejecting her. Her heart surged. She *really* liked him.

Maybe she even like-liked him.

The thought made her blush.

"I'm hot," she said quickly.

"Yeah," he said. "You're all red."

"I know, duh. Let's get out of the sun." She was starting to *duh* more and more often now. Her dad said that you ended up mimicking people you liked. So now she was an eye roller (Solly) who *duh*'d (Harry). She hoped her next BFF wouldn't do anything too weird. One of those things was fine, but doing too many of them was probably not so good.

It made her even less herself.

Too much of herself was taken up by being other people.

The sun was dead center in the sky, and even behind the veil of clouds, it was blinding, big, and mean. Harry got on his bike. "Go time?" he said.

Nat nodded. *"Buena bebida,"* she said. *"Bebida bebida bebida."*

As soon as she stopped saying it, it tried to escape from her memory, like a fish slipping through holes in a net. "Bediba. Bebida, babida, boobida," she chanted.

Then she blushed even harder.

"Boob" was not a word she said out loud, ever, especially not in front of Harry. Maybe in a *whisper* to Solly, but even that was mostly just Solly talking and Nat listening. There was just something about thinking about all of that growing-up stuff that made Nat's heart race. When they had Life Class in school, she had nearly passed out. Everyone thought it was because she was squeamish about blood, but it wasn't that. It was more like there was a voice in her head that was shouting and then echoing, like her brain was a canyon.

The voice was saying, *You're not ready for this yet. Not yet! Not yet! Not yet!*

Maybe one day Nat would be ready, and then she would be BFFs with Solly again. She would *get* her. Like magic. And Solly would get her back, because obviously, Nat would have caught up. Then it would be like when they were first becoming friends and Nat felt like Solly could read her mind. And Nat felt like she knew what Solly was thinking without having to ask.

"Solly, Solly, Sol," she said out loud while she pedaled. She reminded herself to buy a postcard. Solly was still doing letters, not postcards. She didn't seem to notice that Nat's replies were sporadic and didn't say anything, sometimes literally. Right before she got on the plane, in the airport, she mailed Solly a postcard with a picture of a frog in a sunhat and sunglasses. On the back, Nat wrote, *Why are frogs always happy?* It was a riddle but the kind with no answer. A hypothetical riddle, or something like that.

She was going to make up an answer and write it upside down at the bottom, but Harry wanted to get doughnuts before they got on the plane, so she didn't. The answer, she decided, would be something about how they can just eat what bugs them. Eating bugs! But was that funny? She had no idea anymore. She was just sending the postcards so that Solly would write back. She didn't want to read about boobs and kissing, but she didn't want Solly to stop telling her those things, either.

Solly had perfect handwriting, which was nice to read. Her *A*'s and *O*'s and *E*'s were all almost perfectly rounded, like a real font.

In her last letter, Solly didn't mention that her mom had a new hit song. She didn't mention her mom at all. She talked mostly about her new haircut (something about ombre balayage highlights), and there was also a long story about who said what to who at a party that Nat couldn't even imagine. It sounded like a teenager's party, which was normal, obviously. They were almost teenagers. But reading about it made Nat anxious. Would she know what to do at a party like that? Would she know what to say to a boy she was alone with on a porch?

Nat couldn't figure out why the fact that Gracie had a hit again didn't make it into the letter, above the part where someone she didn't know threw up in the swimming pool. Did Solly think they didn't have music in Canada? Maybe she just didn't want to remind Nat that her mom was famous, in case Nat tried to exact her revenge, a type of revenge that would *only* be possible if Solly were as famous as Nat.

Famous for being the kid of someone famous, that is.

Nat squinted up the road. Harry was way ahead now. She had to pedal about a hundred times for every one time Harry did on his too-big bike.

"What?" Harry yelled then, for no reason.

"I didn't say anything!" Nat yelled back. "I'm coming! Wait up!"

WATER IS UNIVERSAL

Between the low hills, which seemed to be inhabited by nobody, the wind was moaning like a hurt animal.

"The wind sounds like an animal that's been hit by a car," said Nat, when she finally caught up.

"Dude," said Harry. He made a sad face. "That's sad. It sounds worse now."

"Sorry! Maybe it was a really terrible animal that deserved to die." Nat licked her dry lips and she tasted sweat and dirt and salt.

"What kind of animal deserves to die?" said Harry. "All animals are better than people."

"Truth," agreed Nat. She grinned. Harry was so much more himself—his great self—without Seth.

Like he was reading her mind, he said, "Seth has horses. They are so awesome. He's going to teach me how to ride."

"Oh," said Nat. "Cool."

Maybe Seth wasn't so bad.

Maybe he was.

Probably.

She'd never actually talked to him. In her mind, he was the Enemy, and that was that.

"I know you don't like him," Harry said.

"I do so," lied Nat. "He's fine. He's just a boy." She shrugged.

Harry gave her a look.

"I just don't get him. Because he's a boy, I guess."

"*I'm* a boy," said Harry. His voice was sharp. It made her think of a blade, thin as paper.

"I know!" She winced. "I didn't mean . . ."

"Forget it," he said.

They both stared down the road. It looked endless, in the same way the trip itself suddenly seemed endless. The road was paved, but the wind was working hard to smother it with sand and dust. The heat shimmered over everything.

Nat and Harry weaved crookedly around in the middle of the road, zigzagging tire tracks into the sand that the wind quickly erased. Every once in a while a bird flew over, casting a shadow on the ground that made Nat think of pterodactyls.

"It's like we're time traveling," she said, panting. "Dinosaurs!" She was trying to find common ground. She felt like they'd just had a fight. She wasn't really sure though. Maybe she was overthinking it.

Maybe she was overthinking Harry in general.

He was just a boy. A regular person who didn't overthink everything like she did.

"What?" yelled Harry.

Nat wondered if maybe Harry needed his hearing checked.

Harry said "What?" about a hundred times per day. Not just to her; to everyone.

"*Nothing!*" Her bike wobbled, churning up extra dirt, which blew directly into her eyes. Nat wasn't wearing sunglasses. She hated the way they tinted everything yellow. Harry, on the other hand, was wearing aviators that were so big his cheeks were almost completely hidden.

Harry let go of the handlebars. "No hands!" He raised his palms flat up into the air.

Nat couldn't do no-hands, but she took one of her hands off and put it on her leg for a second. Her hand left a sweaty handprint on her dusty skin. Then she put it quickly back on the handlebar. They hadn't brought Band-Aids, and she didn't want to fall and bleed and faint, right there in the middle of the road. Harry wasn't watching anyway—he was way ahead, the wind pushing his hair away from him, back over his shoulders, the bike going straight as an arrow, his hands whipping through the air like wings.

On the last long steep part, they coasted with no brakes, going so fast that the bumps all blurred together to make one vibration. When they finally slammed on their brakes and skidded to a halt, they had to spit dirt out of their mouths and wipe bugs off their faces. "They eat what bugs them!" Nat said to herself. She laughed. It was funny, after all. She wished she'd written that on the postcard.

Maybe she'd send it on a separate one. She imagined Solly reading it. She pictured her rolling her eyes.

Maybe not, then, she decided.

"What?" said Harry.

"Nothing," said Nat. It was too hard to explain.

Harry gave her a look. "Weirdo."

The place where they had stopped seemed to be a bus station, but it didn't look like any buses had been there for a hundred years. The sign said *Central de Autobúses*.

"The zombies have already been here." Harry made a gesture with his finger across his throat.

"Stop it," said Nat. Her dad was in a zombie movie once. She saw it when she was about six and woke up screaming every night for almost a whole year, imagining her dad with his eyeball hanging out. It didn't matter how many times he told her it was just makeup. She *knew* that. It was still scary.

The wind was desperately trying to pull off all the flyers advertising surf lessons and *cerveza*, and they were flapping like thousands of moths half burned to a light bulb. "Mothy," said Nat, but Harry didn't even say, "What?"

Instead, he sat down on the metal bench. "Ouch." He pressed his whole hand flat against it. "This is *burning*. I bet you could cook a grilled cheese on this. Maybe my leg meat is cooking. Zombies probably like cooked meat better anyway." He crossed his eyes and made a zombie groaning noise. "I bet my hair is crazy, huh."

Nat's eyes were full of grit. "Your hair's fine," she lied. "Me and Dad once fried an egg on a sidewalk. In Australia," she added. "There was a heat wave."

"Oh." Harry twisted his hair up with both hands. "Did you eat it?"

"What? The egg?" Nat shook her head. "Too dirty."

Harry's dad wouldn't let Harry cut his hair, even though he wanted to more than anything. "Not under my roof," he said every time Harry asked. Harry's hair was down past his shoulders in big loose curls that tightened up in the heat and sprang upward and outward with reckless abandon when he sweated.

"You're lying. It's all *poufy*." Harry let it go, and it escaped like so many snakes hissing and uncoiling all at once. "I give up." Harry dropped his head down, scuffing his shoe in the dirt.

"No one's looking. Who cares? The zombies?"

Harry shrugged. He swung his foot in a half circle. In the reflection on his aviators, Nat could see that her own hair was sticking out all over. It looked like she hadn't brushed it in a week.

"We're *both* in wild disarray," she said. "Can you stop doing that?" She coughed. "Wild disarray" made her think of wildflowers in a meadow, a hurly-burly of colors and smells. "Wild disarray," she mouthed again.

"Sorry," he said, darkly, stopping.

"Your hair looks totally *fine*! Windblown, maybe. So does mine. It doesn't matter! Check this out." She tiptoed across the dusty sand in front of the bench, back and forth. "*Hanyauku*," she explained. "It means 'to tiptoe in warm sand.' It's from Namibia."

Harry stared at her. Then he grinned, and it was like someone reached into his face and flicked on a light switch. "Oh, *there* you are," she wanted to say. The Harry she loved was in there, she could see it. He was maybe just taking a while to go from being Seth's friend Harry to being Nat's friend Harry. That was fine by her.

"It probably means more like when the sand is too hot to touch with your bare feet, like when you can't *stand* to touch it because it's going to burn your skin right off? Or else it wouldn't really need its own word."

Right away, as soon as he said it, Nat knew he was right, that she got it *slightly* wrong. It changed the shape of the word in her head from a word that was as oval as an egg to something more like the end of a hot poker. "*Hanyauku*," she repeated, sharply, feeling how the word was now hot enough to leave a scar. "Yep."

Nat sat down next to him. The bench burned the back of her legs, too. "This is too hot to sit on! Why are you sitting here?"

"Don't sit on it!" he said.

"I'm already sitting!"

He pushed her and she almost fell off, and she pushed him back and he landed with a *thump* on the ground. "Ha," she said.

"Ha yourself." Harry wasn't looking at Nat. He was staring toward the rolling hills. No matter what direction you looked, everything looked the same except the ocean, but that was hidden behind the buildings. Nat worried Harry was disappointed, that this wasn't the postcard-pretty place he was expecting.

Nat still couldn't believe it had happened, that her dad had somehow made this happen.

It was a *miracle* that Harry was here, when you considered that Mr. Brasch still thought Nat's dad was a hippie. Nat knew this because her dad told her about his outings with Mr. Brasch. "Hippie!" he'd say, laughing. "Man, that guy is a blast. I just don't think that word means what he thinks it means!"

"Hippie" was Mr. Brasch's worst insult though. If he had a bad experience at the grocery store or at work, he always muttered about hippies under his breath.

Nat's dad didn't seem to get that. Or maybe he did.

Harry had had to get a passport. It was his first time out

of Canada. Nat had been traveling for her whole life. She couldn't really imagine what it would be like to never have gone anywhere else in the world, to never have seen anything. Canada was plenty nice, but it was not *enough*.

"This place isn't what I thought it would be," said Harry. "Why aren't there any people?"

"Every place is weird." Nat tried not to sound like someone who had already been everywhere and knew everything. "In different ways. This town is just really small. Dad likes to get away from people-packed places. It gets weird, even for him, when people grab at his shirt and scream."

Harry gave her a funny look, the one she couldn't read. "I guess I wouldn't know."

"OK," said Nat. It was awkward being famous. People didn't really understand it. She had thought Harry was different. He'd never made too big a deal about her dad after he found out that XAN GALLAGHER and her dad were the same person. But maybe she just super badly wanted him to be that way, to be a person who wasn't seduced by the XAN GALLAGHER part of her life

They got back on their bikes. The road flattened out and they passed a building that might have been a bank, three decrepit gas stations in a row, a post office that looked haunted, and finally a 7-Eleven with a half-full parking lot. A few people were standing around, leaning on the hoods of cars, wearing board shorts or bikinis, drinking Big Gulps.

Surfers.

There was a VW camper van with a couple of people sitting on the roof. They all looked American. "Look!" said Harry. "Dudes."

A dog came rushing up to Harry and Nat, barking.

"Hey now." Harry stopped pedaling and leaned forward. "Hey you." The dog was yellow and tufty-looking.

Hey Tufty, Nat said to it, using telepathy. *Sit,* she tried, with her mind. Tufty sat. "Can dogs smile?" she asked Harry. "He looks like he's smiling."

"Maybe his lips are just stuck like that. Want a Slurpee? I'm thirsty." Harry reached into his pocket for money.

"No! I don't want anything I can get in America. The point of not being at home is to not be at home." Nat's dad said that all the time when they were in, say, Croatia, and she wanted a cheeseburger from McDonald's.

Harry pulled his glasses down and looked at her over the top of them. "We don't live in America," he said.

"Well, true. But you can get Slurpees in Canada, too. Anyway, let's find a place that sells something Mexican."

"What's Mexican?" he said.

"Water?"

"How is water Mexican? Every place has water. Anyway, I'm sure you can get water at 7-Eleven. And I think you're not supposed to drink the water in Mexico." He scratched his ear, which was another one of his habits that she had started to notice. "Mom said."

"That just means water from the *tap.* Bottled water is fine. Anyway, they have lots of soda drinks that are Mexican. I bet they have Coke. And Jarritos. Let's get some Jarritos." She tried to pronounce it right, with the *J* sounding like a *Y* and the *R*'s rolling like rocks down a hill. It felt like a stick, stuck between her teeth.

"Jarritos," repeated Harry. He pronounced it perfectly. "Sure."

The year before, Nat and her dad were in Mexico, too,

but in a place called Coba. They climbed up a million stairs on Ixmoja, which is a huge pyramid. Nat was so thirsty at the top, she broke her no-sugar rule and drank a Jarritos, because that was all that her dad had brought in his backpack. It was cold and bubbly.

She was about to tell her dad that maybe she even liked it, sugar and all, when a tourist recognized her dad and screamed, "OH MY GOD, IT'S XAN GALLAGHER!" and dove in for a photo, pushing Nat out of the way. Nat dropped the bottle, which broke, and also nearly fell to her death down those steep, scary steps, skinning both her knees badly, the blood ruining her shoes.

Now when she thought about Jarritos, she felt panicky and light-headed.

Nat opened her mouth to tell Harry the story, then decided not to, in case saying it out loud made her faint or made her seem like a show-off. She sighed.

"You'd drink Jarritos?" he said. "Is it like Coke? What about the sugar?"

Nat shook her head. "It's fruity. You'll like it. I don't want any, actually. But they'll have water, too. But we have to find a real Mexican store, OK?"

"Mom says—"

"*Bottled* water, I promise. It'll be fine! It's fine anyway!"

"Water is water." Harry scowled. "You wanted something Mexican."

"Water is universal," she said, but then she realized she was just making his point. She wasn't sure why she was being so stubborn. She wanted to feel unprickly, but she couldn't. She wanted to be normal and have fun, but it was like she was in her own way and couldn't get out of it. "Tell your mom," she muttered. Her irritation maybe had something to do with Harry always mentioning his mom.

Harry had never even *asked* about her mom, so she had never lied.

Harry had never asked about the Bird, either, but why would he?

She hadn't told Harry about her.

She hadn't told anyone.

Nat felt for the phone in her back pocket. It was there. She liked the idea that no matter where she was in the world, the Bird was with her, even though she was actually in LA. She always answered, no matter what time it was. She always wanted to talk to Nat. Basically, she was Nat's number two person, right after her dad.

Even though she was a stranger.

Harry was her number three. She wondered what number she was on his list. She probably didn't even crack the top ten.

She frowned.

They weren't friends.

Maybe they weren't anything.

Maybe he was just here for the free trip to Mexico.

Her heart did something funny in her chest that made her think of a skipping rope churning through dust. She coughed.

"*Fine,*" Harry repeated. "Water is universal. Whatever." Nat couldn't see his eyes behind the glasses, but he seemed mad.

She stared straight into the sun for a second. She imagined it burning a hole right through her shirt, and then her skin, right into her heart. "I'll have a Jarritos," she conceded. "If it's really important to you."

"I don't care what you drink!"

Nat's holey heart made a *thlurp*ing sound. Her legs hurt from stand-pedaling. If Harry weren't there with her, she'd be lying in the hammock with her dad, reading a book. Or letting him teach her how to surf. Again. (She never seemed to quite get it, even though he'd started taking her out on his board when she was just a baby.) They'd maybe be singing something silly in the kitchen while they made frozen drinks from organic bananas and some rare fruit that her dad had discovered in a local's yard and learned about after talking to the owner—his new BFF—for forty-five minutes. She suddenly had a yearning for her dad and their regular-together life, a life without extras like Harry or the Brasches.

Without *complications*, like needing to have a BFF.

She just *wanted* one.

One BFF who would get her and who she could talk to about stuff and hang out with without wondering if she was doing it right.

"Ugh," she said out loud, by mistake.

Harry didn't even say "What?" for a change, because he was busy ignoring her.

"We should go back to—" Nat started to say, but then they turned a corner and they were in an empty parking lot at a SUPERMARKET. That's what the sign said in huge, bright white letters. In smaller letters underneath, it said MERCADO. "Why is that sign in English?" said Nat. "Weird."

"Is it open?" Harry sounded doubtful. "It looks like one of those stores in Japan that was abandoned after the tidal wave. We should have brought a camera and filmed this stuff. I bet it would go viral on the Internet."

"Huh." Nat hoped it was not abandoned and that it sold water. Her mouth was as dry as the road, the sand, the sky, all of Mexico. On the other hand, Harry sounded really happy about the possibility that it was empty. "Maybe."

On Harry's bedroom wall at home, he had a bunch of photos of abandoned theme parks. Nat thought they looked spooky, but he seemed to really like them. She wondered how it made him feel to look at those falling-over roller coasters, the bumper cars rusted into place. It made her feel sad and hollow. But he must have felt something better than that, or he wouldn't have tacked the pictures to his wall.

Harry was *deep*.

Nat liked that about Harry.

She liked kind of knowing what he was thinking, but she also liked that he had dark, secret corners that she couldn't see into.

She *wanted* to know. That was the difference between Harry and, say, Heaven. She had a feeling that Heaven's dark, secret corners were full of scary clowns and probably spiders, not that she cared. It was just that Heaven was the opposite of Harry in every way. She was like a photo negative of him.

Yet she was the most popular girl in the class. One day, maybe after she graduated from high school, Nat hoped she would understand what made a person popular and what made them not popular. It almost never had anything to do with being kind, that's what she'd observed so far. Sometimes the kindest kid was the most popular. But sometimes it was a mean girl. And anyway, who decided these things? Was it the person themselves? *Maybe I should decide to be popular*, she thought. *Then I'd have tons of friends and I wouldn't have to think about it so much.*

On the other hand, being popular also seemed like a lot of work. Almost like being famous, but on a different scale.

Popular kids had to always be "on."

Nat didn't think she had the energy to be always "on."

Maybe she preferred to be "off."

THE SUPERMARKET MERCADO

The door was the push-open kind, not automatic like grocery stores at home, and inside it was the exact same temperature as it was outside, only not at all dusty. It smelled like pine-scented cleaner. "The air-conditioner is broken," the girl behind the counter said, without looking up from the book she was reading. She was sitting on a high stool and her feet were on the counter.

"Thank you," said Nat.

Harry nudged her. "Should we whisper?" he whispered. "She's reading."

"Don't be dumb," said Nat. She rolled her eyes.

Nat and Harry started walking up and down the aisles. In aisle three, there was one other person. She was an old lady, wearing a bright pink, off-the-shoulder blouse. The blouse, and the pinkness of it, gave Nat the impression that the old lady was a dancer. Nat smiled at her. The lady was slowly putting things into her cart and taking them out again, inspecting each item carefully. When she noticed Nat, she gave her the stink-eye. Then, in slow motion, she put a tin of something back on the shelf and slapped it so hard it fell off and rolled a few feet, landing at Nat's feet.

"Oh!" said Nat. "Sorry."

The old lady looked like the next thing that she wanted to slap was Nat.

"Harry." Nat touched his arm. "Let's go."

"No *way*! We can't go now! This place is awesome!" Harry whisper-shouted. "This stuff is *seriously* cool. Check it out."

He pointed. There were all the regular kinds of cereal, but the packaging looked different. It looked old-fashioned.

"This cereal box looks like it's from 1977," said Harry. "Vintage. Do you think it's stale?"

"That cereal is made from sugar and sugar and more sugar and some sugar," Nat told him. "Sugar doesn't really go bad."

"I'm going to buy this. This is *amazing*. I could probably sell it on eBay for a hundred dollars. How much is it?"

Nat shrugged. She could clearly see the price marked on the shelf that said 52 pesos, but if she could see it, so could he. Harry's mom had given him Mexican money when they left, as well as some American dollars, "Just in case!"

Nat's dad always forgot that people have to pay for things. He was above money. He existed on another plane.

"I'm sure I have enough," said Harry. "How expensive could cereal be, anyway?"

"Look!" Nat pointed to a small fridge that was stocked with Coke. She picked out a Diet Coke for herself and a regular Coke for Harry. "Mexican Coke is different from

American Coke. And Canadian Coke, for that matter," she explained. "In Mexico they use cane sugar." She traded her Diet Coke for a bottle of water. Fake sugar gave her just as bad a feeling as real sugar, cane or otherwise.

"Water bottles are bad for the environment," said Harry.

"So are Coke bottles," she said.

"Are they?"

"I don't know," she admitted. "Maybe. Probably."

"They're glass," he said. "It's better. Different, anyway." But he put the bottle back and picked up a can instead. "Cans are the best. I think. Maybe. I don't know. Do you?"

Nat kept bumping into moments like this, moments where she felt like she didn't know anything at all. The world made her feel stupid. "*Pâro*," she whispered. *Pâro* was a word from her favorite website, *The Dictionary of Obscure Sorrows*, which was a bunch of made-up words for things that there weren't words for already. It was almost, but not quite, as good as foreign words. It was a place where you could find words that *should* exist, but don't.

Pâro means that no matter how hard you try to do the right thing, you're usually messing it up.

"How much is it?" Harry asked the cashier, using the loud, slow, clipped voice that people used to communicate with non-English speakers. Nat shuddered. "How man-y pe-sos?" Harry enunciated loudly.

The cashier stared at him and blinked slowly, once, twice, three times. She was very pretty. She had waist-length hair and was wearing a T-shirt that said *Imagine Unicorns*. She had the best fingernails that Nat had ever seen. Her nails had tiny jewels embedded in them. She put her book down.

She picked up the cereal box and swiped it over the scanner. *52 pesos*, the screen showed.

Nat was so embarrassed. Money was money! It looked different everywhere, but it all had *numbers* written on it. You didn't have to speak Spanish to understand that a peso was a peso!

Nat wanted to explain to the cashier that Harry wasn't the dumb jerk he looked like, but she kept her mouth shut. The cashier's smile went nowhere near her eyes; it stayed firmly down around her teeth in a grimace. "Give it to me," she said to Harry, using the same slow voice that he had used. She took the whole stack of cash from his hand.

"Hey," he said.

Nat felt so *greng-jai*, she wanted to cry. (*Greng-jai* was a Thai word for the feeling you got when you were putting someone out.) "Count your own money!" she mouthed at Harry.

The cashier counted Harry's money out slowly in Spanish.

"Gracias, señorita," he said. His accent was fine, but there was something about the way he hit each syllable too loudly that made Nat want to walk away. She didn't understand why he was speaking Spanish when the cashier clearly spoke English.

It was condescending.

Nat nudged him.

"What?" he said.

"Nothing," she mouthed. "Never mind."

"I can't hear you," he said.

Nat made a face.

"*What?*" he said, again.

The cashier put the cereal into a bag, the kind of plastic bag that sea turtles often mistake for jellyfish and die eating. Nat took it out again. "We don't want a plastic bag," she explained. "Sorry. But they kill turtles."

"How can I carry it without a bag?" said Harry.

He put it back in the bag.

"There is a turtle's blood on your hands now," Nat told him.

He shrugged. "There's no basket on the bike!" But he gave the bag back to the cashier. She didn't say anything, but she sort of looked like she wanted to punch them both, or maybe that's just what Nat would have wanted if it were her. The cashier shrugged instead, the universal body language of "Go away, you are bothering me."

Backpfeifengesicht—*a face badly in need of a fist*, Nat thought. It was a German word. The Germans had a lot of great words for things; words that just nailed very particular feelings. She had to stop herself from saying it out loud. It was her own face that was *backpfeifengesicht* in this scenario. "Sorry," she said, making it worse. She tugged on Harry's arm. "Let's go!"

The old lady in the pink blouse started slamming her cans and bottles onto the counter. One. At. A. Time. She was wearing sunglasses on her head that were exactly like Harry's.

"Well, bye!" Nat said to the cashier in her friendliest voice. "Thank you!" She wanted the old lady to know that she was a good person. A friendly person! Practically Canadian! Not a monster who deserved to be slapped like a can of beans and left for dead in aisle three.

"Wait!" the cashier blurted. "I have something for you!"

She reached under the counter and she passed the brochure around Nat and put it into Harry's hand.

"Gracias," he said again, too crisply.

"Terrible," Nat mumbled. The cashier gave her a look that may or may not have meant, "Your friend is terrible."

"Yes," Nat said to her, which she realized didn't make sense as soon as it left her mouth, but there it was, her "yes" floating out of her mouth and over the counter to the cashier, who turned her back on it, leaving it hanging there like an unanswered phone call.

The worst.

The old lady immediately started talking rapid-fire in Spanish, probably about how Nat and Harry were terrible, which Nat agreed with 100 percent, without fully knowing why.

Nat unscrewed the cap from the water and drank it in three huge gulps while sending the old lady a telepathic message, which was, *Sorry, sorry, sorry.*

"Are you *coming*, Nat?" said Harry. He stuffed the brochure into his pocket and tapped her on the head with the cereal box.

"Let's go. I mean, yes. I'm coming. YES." She said the last "YES" loudly to reclaim the "yes" that went unanswered. She put the empty bottle of water in the garbage can and rushed out the door, just as the old lady yelled something. Do they not throw away empty bottles here? Pâro! Pâro! Nat thought.

"Hey!" Harry followed her through the door, shoving it open with his elbows. "Hold the door! You could have broken my nose!"

"Never lead with your face." She held up her arms. "Use these."

He rolled his eyes. Did he pick up that habit from her? She got it from Solly. Maybe that's how these things spread, one person to the next. Contagious, like the flu. "Thanks a lot."

"Sorry!"

"What's your problem, anyway?"

"Nothing," said Nat. "I don't know."

"Are we fighting? This feels like we're fighting. I don't like fighting." Harry shifted from one foot to another. "Like, I really don't."

"*Pickleflitz,*" Nat said. It was a word that she just made up on the spot. It meant "Nothing sorry something I don't know" all at once. She sat down, right there on the ground. It was hot.

"What?" Harry plopped himself down next to her in the dust. He opened his Coke and bubbles fizzled out. He took a long sip. "Aaaaaah," he said. "Actually, it kind of tastes the same." He burped. The yellow dog wandered up to them and lifted his leg.

That's private, Tufty, Nat told him, telepathically. *You could have done that around the corner.*

Tufty hung his head.

"What did you say?" Harry repeated.

"I didn't say anything," she lied. "If I did, I forget."

"Yeah, you said *pickleflitz* or something," he said. "Did you make up that word? Or is that a real thing in Polish or whatever?"

"You must have heard me wrong." Nat eyed his Coke. "Is that empty yet?"

Harry tipped the can out, and a couple of drops hit the ground and instantly evaporated. "Look, it says *refresco* on it. I'm keeping the can. It was very *refresco.*"

He got on his bike, the can in one hand, the cereal box under his arm. The bike wobbled. "I am *refresco*ed!" he shouted. Tufty ran in a circle around him. "Do you think this dog belongs to anyone?"

"I think it's a stray."

"Yeah, it looks like it." He pedaled a few times in a circle around where Nat was standing, holding her bike. She slung her leg over the seat. The bike seemed to have shrunk even more while they were in the store.

Tufty barked three times and then ran toward the door of the SUPERMARKET MERCADO. He belonged to the cashier, Nat decided. Or, better yet, he was waiting for the old lady so he could walk her home, carrying her groceries in his teeth. Nat liked the idea of that. The old lady probably even had a better name for him than Tufty and even though she was the sort of old lady who slapped cans and insulted children, she was hopefully very kind to dogs. That's how it would happen in a movie, anyway.

Harry was getting ahead of Nat. "Wait for me!" she yelled. She had to ride fast to catch up. They couldn't talk on the way back because it was uphill, the kind of long slow uphill that made you think you might die before you got to the top. The sun had burned through the clouds and everything was blue and silvery bright, awash with heat. They had to pedal so hard that they didn't have enough air left to waste on words. The brochure flapped in Harry's back pocket. Nat could see a photo of a humpback whale, front and center.

Whales were why they had come.

Finally, she thought.

NOPE NOPE

XAN GALLAGHER ran his hand over the front of the shiny Whale Experience Factory brochure that the cashier had given to Harry. Then he squinted at Nat and shook his head slowly from side to side. "Now, Nat-a-Tat," he drawled. "That's no way to see whales."

He was swinging in a hammock on the beach side of the house, one dirty, bare foot hanging over the side. His toenails were the size of pancakes. Tiny pancakes, but still pancakes.

"What?" Nat was distracted by the idea of toenail pancakes. *Unguis pancakeus*, she thought. She didn't know the Latin word for pancake. "You should think about washing your feet. Anyway, the whole point of this trip was to see the baby grays! I promised Harry whales. He's never seen a gray whale up close." She was actually pretty sure he hadn't seen gray whales from far away, either, but she left that part out.

"Naaaaah," he said. "Think about it! We can see them

from here. With the telescope. We don't need to pollute their sea, kiddo, with sound and oil. We don't need to chase them around their own living room, pointing cameras and shouting."

Nat felt her heart sinking all the way to the ground, where she imagined it flopping around like a fist-sized fish out of water. She looked down, but there was nothing but sandy dirt, clumps of grass, and a few tiny wildflowers the size of pencil leads. She kicked a loose stone with her sneaker. Her shoe was brown with dust. You could hardly make out the eyes on the hearts, imploring her.

"Dad," she said. "Please. It's my birthday."

"Whale watching boats are basically whale paparazzi," her dad went on. "Think about it! Whale Experience *Factory*. You don't want anything to do with that. Can't imagine what an outfit like that is doing in a place like this." He smiled his big, easy, famous smile, the one that seemed to slide over his face like an omelet sliding cleanly out of a pan. "Yep yep," he summarized, like that was that.

"Harry bought Fruity Pebbles in town," she told her dad.

"For real? Awesome!" he said. "Oh man, I *love* those things. Yeah!" He fist-bumped her, but because her fist wasn't up, he accidentally punched her in the shoulder.

"Ouch. DAD. That hurt!"

"Oh man, I'm sorry, Natters." He looked at his fist like it had a mind of its own. "Man, this thing."

"Dad, it's *your* fist. Just don't hit me with it."

He raised his eyebrow.

"Come on, Dad. This is really super important to me."

"Oh, is it *reeeeaaaalllllllly* super important? Well, I tell you, Natters, it's just as important to the whales that you don't hunt 'em down and shoot 'em, even if you're just using a camera."

"I don't even have a camera."

"You know what I mean," he said.

"I hate you," Nat mouthed.

He wasn't looking at her anyway. Instead, he was staring off into the distance like he was posing for a shoot. Then slowly, like he was pretending he didn't know she was looking at him, he crossed his eyes. Nat laughed, even though she was mad.

"Everything is terrible," she said.

"What—what now?" The hammock rocked wildly as her dad sat up. He made a sweeping gesture with one of his huge arms and then beamed, as though he personally were responsible for the enormous house, the view, the turquoise blue infinity pool, the flowering shrubs, and the gravelly hill that rolled right down to the aqua sea. "I think you mean, 'Everything is *exquisite*.'"

Nat snorted. "What. Ever." She took the brochure out of his hand. She should have gotten Harry to ask. Her dad liked Harry. Especially if he was wielding Fruity Pebbles.

"Look around!" her dad shouted. "Just look! This place is amazing! This is *paradise*!" He started to play a fake ukulele. One of his tattoos was her name, Natalia Rose G., written in fancy script across his chest. The *G* was crammed in at the end like an afterthought, or as though the tattoo guy didn't plan it and just ran out of room for the whole *Gallagher*.

And there was no room at all for the *Baleine*, which was the best part.

The Mom part.

The part that had been deleted.

She opened her mouth to ask him why he hadn't just asked the guy to write smaller, to include the whale, but then she closed it again.

She didn't want to know.

The "Rose" jumped up and down on his pecs while he fake-played. (Pecs were man boobs, or at least that's what they looked like. If she ever said that out loud, he would have corrected her. "Muscles, not boobs," he'd say. Which was true, but a boob was a boob.) She giggled.

"The world, the world, the world is a sewer," he sang. "Look close and you can see how it stinks."

"What an uplifting song," she said, sarcastically.

"It has over five hundred million views on YouTube!" he said. "America loves this song."

"America has terrible taste." She stuck out her tongue.

Harry was squashing his face against the glass and gesturing with his hands. The gestures meant, "Have you asked him? Has he said yes?"

Yep-yep-yep-yep, Nat said sarcastically in her head, kicking another, bigger rock. It didn't budge. She kicked it harder and then harder again and then so hard that something in her toe snapped like a dry twig. "Ouch! Dad!"

Her dad was really getting into his solo. The hammock was swinging wildly. "The STENCH of LIFE is LOVELY . . ." he wailed. "The STENCH OF IT ALL, the . . ."

"OUCH," Nat repeated, pointedly. "DAD."

Her dad stopped singing and grunted in much the same way he did in *Tumbleweed* when he got his left foot stuck in a leg-hold trap and had to saw it off with his pocket knife, which took an excruciating seventeen minutes on the screen. Grunting was a lot of his performance in *Tumbleweed.*

Grunting and, in one scene, *drooling* in a way that made Nat sick to even think about. The drool didn't bother the Oscar judges apparently. They must have had strong stomachs.

"I've really badly hurt my toe on this dumb rock." She was standing on one foot, like a flamingo.

"Good thing you're wearin' shoes." Her dad winked.

"That's very sympathetic," she said. "Thank you. I think I've broken my toe. There probably isn't even a hospital here!"

"Are you going to die?" He clutched at his chest. "Noooooooooo." He rocked backward on the hammock and flipped out of it and somehow landed on his feet. For a huge guy, he was very graceful. Nat sat down on a rainbow-painted chair. Her toe was pulsing like it had its own heart. "I think it's broken, for real. I'm not joking. Can you stop being so jokey? Seriously."

"Well, kiddo, you know what they say: Some rocks just ain't for kickin'." Her dad had a way of declaring things that made them sound important, like they should be embroidered on a throw pillow.

"*Literally* no one says that, Dad."

"Well, they'll start now. Some rocks just ain't for kickin'," he repeated. "See? I'm a person and I'm saying it, so people *do* say it." He bellowed with laughter and, mid-laugh, he grabbed her foot and yanked her shoe off without untying it first.

"Hey!" she said. "Don't—"

"Shhhh." He stared at her face, then abruptly he pressed down hard on her toe with both his thumbs. It was so shockingly painful that she almost kicked him right in the nose. "Stop it! That *hurts*!"

"I just want to try something. Hush for a sec. You've gotta be open to it."

"I'm open, I'm open," she lied. He pressed some more. The pain felt like a musical note that was being played right through her. Then, just as suddenly, it muted, or at least she couldn't feel it as much. "Oh!" she said, without meaning to. She racked her brain for a foreign or even made-up word that meant the suddenly ecstatic feeling you had when pain stopped, but she couldn't think of one. She hid her smile behind her hand.

"Anyway, about them whales—"

"*Those* whales," Nat corrected him.

"Uh-huh," he said. Even without looking at his face, she knew that he was "squinting thoughtfully." Sometimes he forgot to stop being an actor even when he wasn't working. "Seeing *them* whales from that giant clown-colored inflatable boat, that just isn't an authentic experience. That's not *truth*. It's not real. That's like . . . taking an elevator up a tree instead of climbing it yourself."

Harry was jumping up and down in the window. He seemed to be hurling himself against the glass, but it wasn't making any sound. Nat held up her hand and telepathically told him, *Not yet.*

Harry pressed his whole face against the glass and crossed his eyes and pulled at his hair. He was not as good at listening to her telepathic messages as Tufty, the dog. People never were. She sighed.

"Dad, it's *nothing* like a tree elevator, which don't actually exist, by the way. It's just a thing to do. It's not a lifetime commitment to the whale watching industry. It's just one trip. One boat. You don't have to come! Not everything has to be so . . ." She looked around and then gestured at the sea. "*Organic*," she finished.

As if on cue, a bee buzzed toward them and landed on XAN GALLAGHER's famous wrist. They both watched it climb over his arm hair like it was traversing the surface of an impossible planet. It finally stopped at the tail of the mermaid tattoo that encircled his bicep and then awkwardly took off, wobbling on the breeze.

"Nothing wrong with *not* being the type of person who goes on 'excursions.'" He made "excursion" sound like something that ought to be spit out before poison control needed to get involved. "How's that toe? Better?"

"Not even a little," she lied. "It might even be worse. This trip—and my birthday!—is totally ruined." She looked him straight in the eye. "UNLESS we can go see the whales." She crammed her foot back into her dirty shoe. It was filled with grit and pebbles.

"Well, kiddo, as it happens, today I was down on that beach out front and I met a guy with a boat. Good guy. Great guy. *Really* amazing guy. A true American hero, if you think about it."

"He's probably Mexican, Dad. This is *Mexico*."

"Salt-of-the-earth guy . . ." he went on. "Salt-of-the-sea, too." He laughed. His laugh made her think of giant beach balls being tossed around a crowded pool, ricocheting off people's heads. "Ouch!" she imagined them yelling. "Stop it!"

Nat picked flakes of paint off the rainbow chair that she was sitting in, in the right order: red, then orange, then yellow, green, blue, indigo, violet. She lined up the flakes on her knee. The sun was as warm and thick as honey. Her legs were hot in her jeans. Her head was burning.

"I need sunscreen," she interrupted.

"—thing is with guys like him, they just understand about the vibrations in the water—" Her dad was still talking. "—and the whale *music*. They're in *tune*. It's a *true* symphony, that's what it is. It connects to the soul of the fish and all them scallops and shrimps and lobster, and even cod . . ." He didn't seem to notice whether or not she was listening, which she was not. She was searching the horizon for evidence of whales. *Come to me*, she told them, telepathically. *Come now*. Harry was practically climbing the glass now; he was splayed out against it like a starfish. ". . . and the beach absorbs it and the waves *contain* it. It's a dance, nature in perfect harmony! Think about it!"

"Those. It's *those* scallops. I'm probably getting skin cancer as we speak." Nat pressed her finger hard on her forearm and examined the white fingerprint it made on her skin.

"It isn't anyone's God-given right to pay some outfit to take them to see whales up close, to look into their huge ancient eyes and . . ."

The not-listening was what happened to people after they'd been in movies, after they'd been on magazine covers, after they got used to people taking their photo in the grocery store. It made Nat sad to think about how her dad went from being a normal kid—a boy named Alex who once broke his arm falling off a rope in PE class in the fifth grade—to being an actor to being XAN GALLAGHER, King of the Twitter Hashtag #yepyep, #nonlistener. Nat wondered what his fans would think if they knew he was using Twitter on a laptop from the 1990s and not what they probably imagined was the newest, best phone available. Of course, his fans knew all about his feelings about cellular phones. *They* still used them, but they must know he didn't.

She sighed.

"What do ya say, Natters? The real thing, or some plasticized, packaged junk you could see on the TV?"

A hummingbird hovered in front of them, staring, like he wanted an answer from Nat, too. She was tempted to mention that her dad's movies were frequently also on TV. Were they "plasticized packaged junk"? The hummingbird's wings made a whirring sound. XAN GALLAGHER raised his hands and took a pretend photo. "Insta-perfect," he said, furrowing his brow. The bird, who had no idea that XAN GALLAGHER was a famous person, zoomed away, straight up into the now-blue sky.

"Yeah, OK. Whatever." Nat brushed the rainbow of paint off her knee. It floated down to the ground like very tiny, colorful feathers. "What*ever*," she repeated, hitting the word harder, so that he understood that she didn't care, even though she did. She gave Harry a big thumbs-down with both hands, but she couldn't see him anymore. Maybe he gave up. Maybe he knocked himself unconscious on the glass. Or, more likely, maybe he was just watching them whales on TV.

Those *whales*, she corrected herself.

"Yep yep," her dad said. "*That's* my Nat-a-Tat." The hammock started swaying again, back and forth, back and forth. He closed his eyes.

"I love you," she mouthed. He was a weirdo and had whackadoo ideas about pretty much everything, but she couldn't help loving him anyway. He was *lovable*, not just to her (and she shared his genes), but to the whole world.

There was plenty of proof of that.

His eyes stayed closed but they crinkled at the corners. "I love you, too, kiddo," he said.

He made his hands into the shape of a heart.

"Yeah, you do," she said.

"Yep yep," he said. He opened one eye. "Tell Harry I'd love some of that cereal."

"Yeah," she said. "Whatever."

HARRY

Harry didn't bring his laptop with him to Mexico, and writing lists without a computer was hard. He couldn't remember the last time he had handwritten anything for fun. He didn't write postcards, like Nat told him she did. He never wrote letters. He just wasn't a person who wrote stuff.

He *typed* stuff.

He was a typer.

He had a lot of things he wanted to write down about Mexico. Like, *observations*.

So instead of typing it, he wrote everything he knew about Mexico down, but in his head.

Which was really so much better and easier anyway. You couldn't mess up stuff you wrote in your head. It always worked perfectly. It was when you tried to write it down that it started sounding dumb.

Observations about Mexico, he wrote, smoothly, in his imagination.

1. Hot
2. Dry
3. Nice ocean water
4. Good surfing (looks good from the beach)
5. Nice people
6. Being rich would be good!!!!!!!!!!!!!!!!!!

Harry added a whole row of mental exclamation marks after that one. The house where they were staying was so nice. It probably cost more for a night than their house at home did for a year. He couldn't figure out why Nat and her dad lived in a trailer. They could afford a palace, probably. They could even build this exact same house overlooking French Beach and be the envy of pretty much everyone. Not that they weren't already, but still.

7. Mexican hot salsa is way hotter than Canadian hot salsa.

Harry had requested spicy salsa at lunch and so had Nat, and he had nearly stopped breathing, it was so hot. His throat had slammed closed, and for a second, he had forgotten how to breathe. Nat had eaten all of it, scooping great mouthfuls onto her chips like it was nothing. "Is your tongue deaf?" he had asked, and then they had both laughed so hard, they got the hiccups.

"Is your tongue deaf?" she kept repeating.

He stopped writing his list and whispered it to himself. "Is your tongue deaf?" He snorted and laughed again. *Still funny*, he thought. It was a good thing he wasn't really writing it down, because if he was and someone saw it, they would probably think he was weird, and he wouldn't be able to stand it.

8. *Is your tongue deaf?* ☺
9. *Cool cereal boxes*
10. *Learn to surf?*

Harry sat up.

Maybe he could ask XAN GALLAGHER to teach him how to surf. He lay back down and closed his eyes. He could imagine it happening. XAN GALLAGHER was super friendly, and Harry was positive that if he asked, XAN THE MAN would sweep him up into a huge bear hug and drag him to the beach, and maybe even hurl him into the water like a . . . coconut or something. (There were no coconuts in Mexico—it just looked as though there should be.)

He didn't want to be thrown into the water.

On the other hand, being taught to surf by XAN GALLAGHER would be so rad. Beyond rad. Whatever word was bigger, cooler, and more amazing than "rad."

Seth would die of jealousy.

Maybe Harry's dad would see Harry surfing with XAN GALLAGHER and he'd realize how cool Harry was, too.

"I should have brought my laptop," said Harry, but he was sort of glad he hadn't. It was nice to not have to feel like he needed to be writing a book or making a list or explaining something to someone about who he was.

It was nice to not have to think about an answer and to just *be.*

He got up from his bed and walked around his room. His room at home could fit into the closet of this room.

This room was huge. Just to see if it would echo, he shouted the word "DUDE." It did sort of resonate. Harry shook his head. "This is crazy," he said to himself. He was suddenly so glad to be there, in this weird fancy house, with Nat and her dad.

He unpacked his swimsuit and changed into it. He'd see if Nat wanted to go for a swim in the pool. It was OK to be really good friends with Nat here in Mexico, even if it wasn't so much OK at school. No one would see him. He could still be in with Seth at home, but here, who cared? He grinned.

In the bathroom, he carefully rewrapped his chest with an Ace bandage so it wouldn't show through his swim shirt. He made a face at himself in the mirror. He couldn't wait to be an adult who could make his own decisions about his body.

And his boobs.

And he wouldn't have to ask his dad about it.

He wouldn't have to explain it to anyone.

He looked out the window at the pool. No one was in it, and it looked like something you'd see in a commercial for lottery tickets. It was huge and still and the perfect color blue. It had an infinity edge, which made it look like you could swim off the side and through the air and into the ocean in a single stroke.

This place was seriously amazing.

"Dude," he said out loud, again, which pretty much summed it up.

Then he went out of his room to find Nat. The house felt so vast and empty around him, he suddenly knew what it must be like to be a fish in an aquarium, except this was a house with proper furniture and not just, say, a plastic diver who blew bubbles and a plastic log.

He went into the living room. The largeness of the house was creeping him out. Then he remembered what Nat had told him about how her dad did yoga when he was stressed. He, Harry, was no XAN GALLAGHER, but if it worked for XAN THE MAN, maybe it would work for him, too.

He had literally no idea how people did yoga.

Harry lay down on the floor. He started to tug on his own arms and legs. Maybe if he could jam his leg behind his head, he'd feel better. The room spun a bit. Harry picked up his right leg. He stuffed his head under it. It hurt, but maybe he did feel better, at least a little.

The trouble was that now he was also a little stuck.

THE 34B FROG

The last thing Nat got from Solly before they left for Baja arrived on the Tuesday before they left and it wasn't a letter.

It was a page ripped out of a Victoria's Secret catalogue.

Victoria's Secret was a store that sold bras and underwear. There was one bra circled in the middle of the page with a black Sharpie. Stuck on it, on a yellow Post-it note, she had written, *34B*, then a series of exclamation marks. It took Nat a minute to even figure out what it meant.

Then she understood.

Solly's boobs had finally arrived.

Nat couldn't stop thinking about them, which sounded creepier than it was.

She wanted to stop thinking about them.

Solly's boobs.

Her own future boobs.

Boobs in general.

She just couldn't.

She didn't know why Solly's new bra was suddenly front and center in her brain. Brains were weird like that, always pushing stuff forward that you didn't want to think about.

"Dumb brain," she said out loud.

Nat went into the house through the sliding glass doors. Harry was on the living room floor in his swim trunks. One of his legs was behind his neck. It didn't look like yoga though. It looked really painful.

"What are you *doing*?" Nat asked.

Harry jumped, or he would have, if he weren't stuck. Instead, he sort of twitched.

"I was looking for you. I was going to ask you if you wanted to go for a swim," said Harry, from under his own leg.

Nat laughed. "Um," she said. "Did you think I was on the back of your leg or something?"

"No, why?" Harry sounded like he was trying not to laugh. But maybe he was trying not to cry.

"Harry, are you stuck?"

Harry snorted. Then he was laughing. He tipped over. His leg was still behind his neck.

"Sort of," he admitted. "I mean, I'm doing yoga." He was laughing really hard now. Nat laughed, too.

"I'll save you, Harry!" she said.

She went over and helped him get his leg from behind his head. She hoped it didn't hurt too much. It seemed like it would. Afterward, they lay on the floor next to each other.

"Thanks," said Harry.

"*De nada*," said Nat. That was Spanish for "It's nothing." "That's what friends are for," she added. "Like specifically to help you get your leg unstuck from behind your head."

They both laughed again. "Then I'm glad you're my friend," said Harry. "Don't you *dare* tell anyone."

"Whatever." Nat shrugged. Her heart started beating faster. At first, it took her a second to figure out what she was feeling; then she realized she was just mad.

"I know you won't tell," he said quickly. "I was just saying."

"Whatever, I said," Nat repeated. "Just what*ever*."

They lay there for a minute watching the huge ceiling fans stirring the cool air around the cavernous room. The ceilings were made from white boards. It looked like it could be the ceiling of a barn. It was a really pretty ceiling, Nat thought. But then again, her standard for ceilings was set by the ceiling of the Airstream, which was pretty low and kind of rounded at the edges. It was fine, but it was nothing like this. She could get used to *this*.

"Oh, Dad said whale watching boats disturb the whales' peace or something, so we can't go," Nat said, finally. "We have to go out on a boat with some weird old dude he met on the beach instead so we have an authentic experience." She paused, waiting for a reaction. When Harry didn't say anything, she added, "We'll probably be kidnapped. Dad says it's like basically the difference between running into a celebrity in an airport and taking a phone photo and paying someone to take you on a tour of the stars' homes. I wasn't really listening, but that was the gist of it."

"Oh man," said Harry. "Dude."

"I know," Nat agreed. "Dad is sometimes kind of a . . ." She trailed off.

". . . hippie," they said at the same time. They smiled at each other. Nat was still mad, but she also wasn't.

It was complicated.

"What do you think your parents will say? Like will they let you do it?" said Nat. She had a suspicion that normal parents might not say yes to sending a kid out with a stranger on a boat to have an "authentic" experience.

Harry sat up. He shrugged. He pointed out the window, where they could see the place where Mr. and Mrs. Brasch had set up chairs down at the beach below the house. They had been sitting down there all day, by themselves, ignoring both Harry and XAN GALLAGHER, which probably hurt his feelings. Nat hoped not.

She also hoped they weren't burned to a crisp.

"They don't seem to care," said Harry. "They haven't said anything about anything since we got here. I think their minds have been completely blown by all of this." He gestured around the room.

"Yeah," said Nat. Then, "My dad really wants to be friends with them."

Harry rolled his eyes. "I don't think they get that," he said. "I think they think he feels sorry for them or something."

Nat closed her eyes. Watching Harry's parents sitting on their chairs in the distance made Nat furious. XAN GALLAGHER brought them here so he could befriend them! How dare they!

"Jerks," she said out loud. Then she felt bad. They were still Harry's parents, after all.

"Nah, they're OK," Harry said. "I mean, they aren't anything like your dad. You're lucky. He's rad. Do you think he'd teach me to surf?"

Nat shrugged.

"Rad" was a Seth word. A *"Seth-ism,"* she thought. "Rad," she echoed. Then, "Yeah, he probably would."

Thinking about her dad teaching Harry how to surf made her feel weird inside though. She wasn't sure what the feeling was. *Maybe it's jealousy,* she thought.

Her dad did *really* like Harry.

Harry is like the son he's always wanted, she thought, and something hot and bitter rose in her throat.

She burped.

"Gross," said Harry. "That was the loudest burp that anyone has ever burped."

"*Sorry* to be so *loud* with my almost-throwing-up," she snapped.

"Huh?" said Harry. "I was just impressed, that's all."

Nat got up. "Whatever!" she shouted.

She stomped up the stairs.

She was feeling something like rage simmering just under her skin. The French had a word for that kind of irritation, an *itching* irritation. That word was *dépit.* Nat was *dépit* about everything and nothing in particular.

"I am *dépit* about *everything,*" she said to no one, shaking her fist at the heavens, or—in this case—the skylight. "This is *de pits!*"

Nat went into her room and flopped down on her perfectly made bed. The air-conditioned air was as shiny and solid as platinum. Nat took a big breath and then blew it out, half expecting a metallic bubble to appear.

She slid her phone out of her pocket.

She didn't even know, for sure, if it worked here.

She opened it up. It said 1:33 p.m. Then there was a picture of the sun.

"Duh," she said.

Nat got off the bed, went to the closet, and opened the door. She hadn't unpacked—what was the point?—but her suitcase was open on the rack. She lifted out the handful of T-shirts and jeans, as well as her yellow swimsuit. She unzipped the pocket on the inside of the suitcase and pulled out Solly's bra picture, which she had folded into the shape of a frog.

Nat went back to the bed and sat down. She made the frog jump a few times. She was pretty good at origami.

Through the huge, floor-to-ceiling window, she could see her dad sitting at one of the many outdoor tables with the Brasches, who had finally come up from the beach. They looked very pink.

Karma, she thought.

She could see by the way her dad was gesturing that he was telling a story. They sat back like an audience and watched. That's how it was for him. Mostly people didn't talk *with* him, they waited for him to perform, like they were at a show. Her heart squeezed with a bunch of feelings for her dad that happened all at once, a collision of them in her veins. *I love you*, she sent to him, telepathically, and made a heart with her hands.

He couldn't see her because there was one-way glass in all the bedrooms and bathrooms.

From outside, the windows looked like mirrors. She could watch for as long as she wanted without them noticing. That made her feel weird, like a spy. Still, she didn't look away.

But suddenly he looked up at her window. He held his hands up in a heart shape.

Nat laughed.

Her dad and the Brasches were now drinking from tall glasses with tiny umbrellas sticking out of them. Nat used to love those umbrellas. There was a time, not so long ago, when she would have collected them from the adults' glasses to play with for the afternoon. She would have built sand-castles around them, tiny little cities with umbrella roofs. She and her dad used to call them monkey umbrellas. "For very tiny monkeys," her dad would add.

That was when she was a kid though.

And now, she sort of wasn't a kid anymore.

She would be a *teenager* in one more day.

"*Natsukashii*," she told the frog. She assumed the frog would understand, because the word was Japanese, and so was origami. *Natsukashii* was a sad, nostalgic feeling for something that would never come again. She felt *natsukashii* about Solly and the tiny umbrellas. Maybe she felt *natsukashii* about everything.

Nat started to cry. She cried until she was all cried out. Then she felt better. She sat up. She couldn't explain why she'd felt so jarringly and suddenly sad. It had passed like a squall.

She picked up the phone again. She badly wanted to talk to Bird (Mom) about something. Not specifically about Mexico or her dad or even about Harry, but just to hear her voice.

Nat had just pressed the Bird (Mom) contact on her phone when there was a banging at the door. She pressed "disconnect."

"YOU ALMOST GAVE ME A HEART ATTACK!" she shouted.

"It's just me," said Harry. "Are you getting changed? Are we going swimming?"

"I forgot," said Nat. She put her hand on her heart, which was racing like she'd been running her hardest. She was a good, fast runner. She looked at her face in the huge mirror that was on the wall. Her skin was red and blotchy, and her eyes looked swollen. *Pickleflitz*, she thought.

"What?" said Harry.

"I JUST NEED A FEW MINUTES," she yelled.

"Don't freak out," he said, in his normal voice. She could tell that his face was pressed to the crack in the door by the way it was muffled. "I wasn't going to come in or anything."

"I'll be down in a minute. Don't wait."

"What?" said Harry.

"I'LL BE DOWN IN A MINUTE," Nat repeated, but she stopped because she could hear him laughing.

"I was kidding!" he said. "I could totally hear you."

"You have a mysterious sense of humor," she told the closed door.

"That's why you like me," he said. She could hear his footsteps disappearing down the hall, and then the door to his room opening and closing again.

Nat put the phone down and picked up her yellow bathing suit. She bought it the summer before in Greece. She loved Greece. The white buildings against the blue of the sky! The silky sand beaches! The food! She hoped the bathing suit still fit. She hadn't worn it for a while.

Looking out the window, it was impossible to remember the gray dustiness of the morning. The water in the pool was calm and glittery. She watched as Harry walked over to the stairs and into the water. She could tell he was on his tiptoes.

Harry was wearing a swimming shirt and long surf shorts that came down to his knees. Nat closed the blinds.

Sometimes she thought it would be so much easier to be a boy than to be a girl, but then she remembered how complicated it was to be Harry and she took it back. Maybe it was impossible to know how easy or hard anything was for anyone. Everyone had so much going on that you couldn't see.

"Never mind," she said out loud.

Nat took the yellow bathing suit into the bathroom.

Without looking at herself in the mirror, she hurriedly stuffed herself into it. The straps felt too short. The bathing suit was *definitely* tight. She straightened up and looked at herself in the mirror.

She did a double take.

Somehow—overnight?—*something* had happened.

It's like a horror movie, she thought.

It was happening.

Nat stood sideways and then straight ahead. No matter which angle she looked at herself from, *they* were definitely starting.

She was getting boobs.

"Boobida," she whispered, but it wasn't even slightly funny. She squashed them down flat with her hands, but that hurt, so she stopped. She sat down on the toilet again, with the seat closed, and thought about crying. This *is exactly what mothers are for!* She needed her mom. She needed *a* mom.

It was completely unfair that she had no mom.

"Who is my mother?" she wanted to shout to her dad, where he was still sitting and laughing with the Brasches. He held his hands above his head. He made a victory gesture and then doubled over, laughing. "It's not funny!" she wanted to shout. "Tell me right now! Tell me everything! I need her!"

Would he answer?

Would he actually *tell* her?

Nat went back to the bedroom, picked up the phone and pressed Bird (Mom) before she could be interrupted again.

The phone rang.

Then it rang again.

Nat listened to the phone ringing somewhere in a little house in LA that had a view of the ocean from up high on the hills when the smog wasn't too thick. She pictured the Bird, who she imagined had long black hair and probably wore long, floaty tunics. Maybe even bright pink ones, like the old lady in the grocery store. Except the Bird wasn't that old. She definitely wasn't mean.

Nat counted the rings: thirteen.

Then she hung up.

This was the first time ever that the Bird hadn't answered her call.

Weird, Nat thought. Maybe she was in the shower.

Or maybe her phone was broken.

Or maybe . . .

She didn't want to think about it, but she couldn't help it: Maybe the Bird just didn't feel like talking to Nat. Who was Nat to her? Just a prank caller who kept calling back.

Nat grabbed a towel off the pile of perfectly folded striped towels—the striped ones were for the pool, the white for inside—and headed out. The air was heavy and humid and smelled like flowers.

"Hey," called Harry from his inflatable mattress. "There you are. Finally. I thought you were dead or something."

"Ha ha," she said. "Funny."

"I've always thought it's weird when someone says something is funny but then they don't laugh," he said.

"Ha ha," said Nat again.

"Saying 'ha ha' isn't laughing," he said. "Weirdo."

Nat rolled her eyes. She walked on tiptoes across the pool deck, which was horribly hot to walk on. *Hanyauku*, she thought. But it wasn't sand, so it didn't count.

"You look different," blurted Harry. "Like . . . you know." He blinked. He looked really embarrassed, like he had meant to think that and not actually say it out loud.

Nat chewed on her lip for a second without answering. "It's OK," she said, softly. "Just don't." She tried to think what she would have said if Solly had said the same thing. She maybe would have laughed, even though she felt uncomfortable. She was being different around Harry because he was a boy.

Or maybe she was being *extra* different because he was a boy who was complicated.

So maybe she was being a jerk, sort of in the same way Harry was being a jerk when he assumed the cashier at the SUPERMARKET MERCADO didn't speak English.

And she was similarly *assuming* a lot of things, like that Harry wouldn't want to talk about girl stuff.

Maybe he *did* want to talk about girl stuff.

Maybe it was her problem, not his. She didn't want to talk about girl stuff with *him*.

Because she liked him.

Duh.

"Let's talk about something else," she said. "Like *anything* else."

"Fine by me." Harry started kicking his feet off the side of the float, and the spray splashed over her in a wave. "It's not exactly my favorite topic."

"So why did you bring it up?"

"I didn't! I didn't mean to. I don't know. Maybe I did." Harry frowned. "Do you ever just say things without thinking first?"

Nat thought about it. "No," she said, finally.

Harry splashed her, a huge wave of water that went into her eyes and up her nose.

"Hey!" She spluttered. She clenched her fists.

"Sorry!" He looked at her hands. "Don't hit me! Jeez!"

"*Backpfeifengesicht*," she mouthed at him.

"I can't hear you when you mouth things," he said. "Dude." He was floating on his back now. He turned his head to get a mouthful of water and then blew it up into the air.

The water was cold and chemical-scented. Nat dove deep and kept her eyes open to watch the bubbles rising away from her. She sat cross-legged on the tile floor and ran her fingers along the paths made by the grout. She counted to two hundred, but then she lost count. Sunbeams broke through the surface of the water, and she let her hands fan out in the beams of light. She couldn't hear anything except her own heartbeat, and everything looked blue and peaceful and perfect.

Nat watched Harry's feet kicking, churning up water as he motored from one side of the pool to the other. Her lungs started to hurt and burn but she counted to ten one more time before she surfaced, dolphin kicking to the far end of the pool, away from Harry. She dangled her arms over the infinity edge and looked out to sea.

Harry swam up next to her, breathing hard, and spit over the side.

"Gross," she told him.

Harry burped.

The water had slicked his hair away from his face. His eyelashes were as long as spider legs. He blinked, and water droplets fell from them in a tiny rain shower. It was pretty in a way that he would hate, if he knew she was thinking it.

Pickleflitz, she thought. Her eyes drifted down to his chest. It was perfectly flat. Not even the smallest bump showed under his swim shirt.

"How do you do that?" she wanted to ask. But she knew she couldn't. That was more private than private. It was bigger than any secret.

Harry leaned closer to her.

Nat panicked.

She let go of the edge of the pool and let herself sink down to the bottom again. She swam low along the tiles, blowing out bubbles. When she surfaced, Harry's back was to her still.

"I'm getting out," she called.

"Already?" he called back. "Don't you want to have races?"

"I said I was getting out!"

"You can change your mind!"

"One race," she relented.

"OK," he said. He dog paddled over to the end of the pool where she was standing. "ONYOURMARKS, GETSETGO!" he said, all blurred together like that, and then he was swimming before she'd even taken a breath.

"No fair!" she yelled, but he couldn't hear her, he was already at the other end of the pool.

"Loser!" he called.

"Takes one to know one."

She dove back under the water and swam along the

bottom. The sunlight was making sparkles on the tiles that reminded her of Harry's downstairs bathroom floor, which made her think of the magazine.

She kept her eyes open wide and corkscrewed around and around under the water. When she looked up at the surface, she could see Harry's face, all distorted and wobbly. Finally, when she felt like she might pass out, she let herself float to the top with her eyes open, limply.

"Are you dead?"

She shook her head no.

Then she sprayed the water she'd been holding in her mouth right into his face. "Hey!" he said, but he was laughing.

"Now I'm getting out," she said.

ON THE ROOF

That night, Harry and Nat decided to sleep outside on the rooftop deck. They took the bedspreads from their beds to use as blankets. It was plenty warm enough on the lounge chairs up there. Nat's dad lit the fire pit for them and gave them a bag of marshmallows.

"I'm going to go downstairs and watch some movies now," he said. "I trust you guys. No funny business, OK?"

"DAD!" said Nat.

"And don't eat ALL them marshmallows," he said. "Some is good, more is better, but all of them? Well, that's the best." He winked.

"Dad," she pleaded.

"I'm going to watch *Star Blazers 6*," he said. "Seems like maybe we should make 7 now, don't you think?"

Nat rolled her eyes. Her dad had been talking about making *Star Blazers 7* for her whole life. *Star Blazers 6* was a cult classic. That meant that nerdy people watched it religiously, memorized the lines, and lined up for hours for XAN GALLAGHER's signature at comic cons every year.

"Can I watch it with you?" said Harry, hopefully.

Nat's dad looked at Harry. "Nope," he said. "Some things a man just has to do alone, you know what I mean?"

Harry nodded, even though Nat could tell that he didn't have a clue.

I'm on a roof in Mexico with a cute boy and a fire and marshmallows, she thought. *I have boobs. Everything is different.*

She was *so* nervous. But Harry wasn't her boyfriend. She didn't know if Harry like-liked girls. Maybe he hadn't decided yet. They were only twelve.

Well, thirteen in two days, for her. But his birthday wasn't until April.

"Well," said her dad. "Night night, happy dreams, fun tomorrow."

Nat blushed. "DAD," she said. "Good night, OK?"

"What?" he said.

"Go!" she yelled.

Harry made that strange snort-laughing sound that he did when he was trying not to laugh. Nat's dad gave them a big, cheery wave and headed back down the stairs, whistling.

"Have a marshmallow," Nat told Harry, tossing him the bag.

"Thanks."

Nat stared into the fire. It was blue, not orange, at the bottom of the flame. Right above the blue, it was see-through, like it wasn't there at all. But that was an illusion. She stuck a marshmallow onto her stick and poked it into the invisible part. It ignited right away. The part you couldn't see was the hottest part of the flame.

She knocked the marshmallow off her stick and let it disappear into the coals.

"The burnt ones are the best ones," said Harry. "What a waste!" He lit his on purpose. In the flare of the flame, she could see his face.

Do not think about how cute he is! she thought.

"No way," she said. "Golden brown is the only way to go." She took her time making the next one perfect, but then she threw it on the coals anyway. She didn't really like marshmallows, but she did like roasting them.

After they had cooked the whole bag, they leaned back in their chairs and looked up at the sky. There was something about how quiet the night was and how many stars were up there and the fire and the marshmallows that made her want to tell Harry everything. But she didn't know what to say. They were quiet for a long time.

"Harry?" she whispered, finally. "Are you awake?"

"Yeah," he said, in his normal voice. "I was looking at the stars and thinking about how everyone says they feel so tiny compared to the stars. You know what's dumb? Not only are those stars tiny, but most of them are already burnt out. It just takes forever for us to see that."

"Yeah," she said.

"You sound funny. Are you OK?"

"I guess I feel sick from the sugar," she said. "I don't like sugar." She had only eaten one marshmallow, but still, that was a lot for her.

"Oh, I forgot," he said.

They were quiet again for a few minutes. Nat cleared her

throat. "Harry?" she said. "You know we move pretty much every year, right?"

"I know," he said. "Where are you going next year?"

"France, Dad says. He's doing a movie there."

"Cool."

"I guess. I think my mom is French."

"But." Harry sat up. "I don't get it." He frowned.

"I don't know who she is," Nat admitted. "My dad has never talked about it and I've never looked it up or anything."

"You've never looked?" He sounded incredulous. "How can you never look?"

Nat felt funny. Mad, again. Definitely defensive. "I just didn't, OK? I never wanted to."

"That's super weird!"

"Forget I brought it up."

"I can't! It's too big a thing to forget."

The night wrapped itself over them, slipping coolly against their skin. Nat shivered. She willed herself not to cry.

"Are you tired?" he said.

"Not really," she said. "The thing is that I do want to know, but I don't want to know. She didn't want to know me. Why would *I* want to know *her*?"

"Yeah," said Harry. "Makes sense."

"Do you get it?" she said.

"Dude." Harry reached over to her. "Where are you?" he said. "I can't see you."

"I'm right here," she said. She reached her hand out toward him, and then her hand was in his hand. He squeezed it.

Then he dropped it like a hot potato.

Her heart made a sound like an orca, a whistling song.

She put her hand on her forehead. It felt warm.

"My dad wants to send me to boarding school next year," he said. Harry's voice sounded small and prickly.

"Oh. Wow. Really? That sounds . . ." She let her voice trail off. She didn't know how to finish it. "Lonely" was the word she wanted to use.

"In Vancouver," he said.

"I love Vancouver!"

"It's a girls' boarding school." Harry's voice crinkled like tinfoil. Nat wondered if he was crying, but she didn't want to look. "They think they can *fix* me."

"Fix you?" Nat repeated. She blinked. The stars blurred and then reformed again. "Harry?" she said. "What?"

"Are you saying 'what' because you didn't hear me or because you think it doesn't make sense?"

"The second one," she said. "It doesn't make sense! It doesn't. It really doesn't. It's just . . . It's crazy. I'm sorry, Harry."

"Yeah," he said. "Me, too."

From far away, Nat heard something that might have been a dog howling, or maybe a coyote.

"Harry?" she said. His breathing was loud and even, like sleep-breathing.

"Yeah," he said.

"I wish that everything wasn't so complicated."

"Yeah," he said. "Me, too, dude."

She really wished he would stop saying *dude*.

They lay there for a really long time without talking. The surf crashed against the beach. They heard doors opening and closing. Music drifted up from downstairs.

"I wonder if my dad watched *Star Blazers 6* with your dad," Harry said.

Nat laughed. "'Hippies!'" she mimicked. There were a lot of people in *Star Blazers 6* who Harry's dad wouldn't like, she knew that.

People who were different.

People who made choices he would hate.

But maybe she just mouthed it or maybe Harry was asleep, because he didn't answer. Nat looked up at the sky. A star shot across the horizon.

She closed her eyes.

She made a wish.

Not that she believed in that kind of thing, but she also didn't *not*.

Just in case, she thought. *You never know.*

THIRTEEN

In the morning, Nat's thirteenth birthday morning, she tried to call the Bird again. The phone rang and rang and rang.

"Something is wrong," she said out loud. "Something has happened."

But she didn't know who to tell.

She didn't know who would be able to help.

She didn't even know the Bird's real name. Or where she lived.

She didn't know anything.

Today was supposed to be a good day. She had a bad feeling that it wasn't going to be.

The bad feeling prickled on the back of her neck, like a spider crawling up into her hair.

DOWNSTAIRS, SHE HEARD THE doorbell ring. She got up from her bed to see who it was, but her dad was already opening the door. She watched from the landing. A boy from a car rental agency wearing a red golf shirt and khakis was standing at the front door. "Dropping off a car for Mr. Brasch," he said. He sounded bored. He actually sounded like someone who was trying to sound bored to audition for the part of someone who sounded bored. It was as if even being bored was an effort for him.

"OK," boomed Nat's dad. "That's GREAT!"

Only my dad, Nat thought, *could get that excited about a car rental drop-off.*

"Whoa, are you . . . like, um, XAN GALLAGHER?" the kid asked, suddenly standing up straighter. His eyes widened. People always did that to her dad's name, half shouted it so it sounded like they were speaking in ALL CAPS.

Nat's dad slowly raised one eyebrow.

"Holy cow. Oh my gosh. Can I take a picture of you?" Now he was tripping over his own words, each one overlapping the other one just enough that it sounded like the whole sentence was one word.

"Are you American?" Nat's dad asked him.

"Yeah," said the kid. "Totally. I mean, I grew up in Ohio?"

"Then no, I'm not XAN GALLAGHER. Are you kidding? I wish! I'm his stunt double. I heard that XAN THE MAN is in Thailand filming *Star Blazers 7*."

"They're making another *Star Blazers*? No WAY! I love those movies."

"Me too! I watched 6 again last night."

"Can I take a picture with you? I gotta. You gotta let me. Man. Please."

"Why?" said XAN GALLAGHER. "I'm not XAN GALLAGHER. Between you and me, I'm pretty mad they didn't ask me to do *SB7*. I did all the other *Star Blazers*! I'm the man! Just not XAN THE MAN. I'm the Other Man." He flexed his bicep. He'd obviously just worked out. His veins were bulging like yarn all over his arm.

"Cooooool." The kid's eyes looked like they were going to pop right out of his head. He scratched his head. He had long, dirty-looking blond hair.

"You a surfer?" said XAN GALLAGHER.

"Oh yeah. Totally. The surfing here is rad."

"OK, then you can take a picture. I surf, too. Put it on Twitter and tag me."

"What's your Twitter handle?"

"@XANGALLAGHER. Want me to spell it?"

"Nah, that's cool. Wait, what? I mean, you use his name? Isn't that, like, illegal or whatever?"

"Yep, totally illegal. Don't tell anyone."

The kid blinked in slow motion. "Yeah, no," he said. "No, yeah."

"Yep yep," said XAN GALLAGHER. "That's what I'm talking about!"

XAN GALLAGHER posed with the kid for the photo, raised eyebrow and all, then he laughed his huge, unmistakable laugh and closed the door and winked up at Nat.

"Let's see how long it takes him to remember why he came," he whispered. Nat laughed. She couldn't stop laughing.

"Ten," said her dad. He started to count backward. "Nine, eight, seven, six, five . . ."

On "one," the door buzzed again.

"Yes?" said Nat's dad. "Can I help you?"

"Um, yeah, I forgot to drop off the car. It's for the Brasches?"

"Let me get them for you," said Nat's dad.

"You *totally* look like XAN GALLAGHER. Look. I mean, I'm not . . . Are you XAN GALLAGHER? Are you, like, messing with me?"

"Yeah, I do look like him! I smell like him, too. Wanna sniff?" He raised his arm up.

The kid sniffed.

Nat thought she might actually fall over laughing. Tears streamed down her face.

"Yeah, like, you sort of stink, no offense?"

"Sorry, man. That's just what XAN GALLAGHER would've done. He's always getting people to sniff his armpits! Don't tell anyone that. I probably shouldn't have said that!"

"He is? He does? That's, like, super weird!"

"Yeah, he's a weirdo."

"Dude. Man. I can't believe this. Are you guys good friends?"

"*Best* friends."

"That's *so* extreme," said the kid.

"It sure is. I have to pinch myself sometimes. To make sure it's not all a dream." XAN GALLAGHER reached over and took the keys from the kid's hand. "I'll give these keys to the Brasches."

"But you got to sign for them. I, like, need a credit card and driver's license."

"No problem. Hang on."

XAN GALLAGHER disappeared in the direction of the

kitchen. Nat made eye contact with the kid, who looked at her sort of funny. "Are you Natalia Rose?" he said.

"No," Nat lied. "I just look like her." She couldn't do it as well as her dad did. The kid looked kind of mad, not amused or confused. She definitely did not want him to sniff her armpit. She held her arms tight against her sides.

"I feel like this is one of those prank shows or something. Is it? Tell me," he said.

Nat shrugged just as her dad reappeared with his gold card. Nat knew that it was his, that across the bottom it said *XAN GALLAGHER*. The kid swiped the card and gave it back. Then he got XAN to sign the form. While he copied out the driver's license information, which also would say *XAN GALLAGHER*.

This is the punch line, Nat told the car rental guy telepathically. *This is where you get it and when you laugh and then he hugs you and he's your new best friend!*

"Thanks," the kid said. "Wow, this has been super trippy. It's cool that you've, like, met XAN GALLAGHER. I'm, like, starstruck. Great to meet you, man. Other Man, I mean. Other XAN THE MAN." He laughed at his own joke.

"You, too." XAN GALLAGHER gave the kid a huge bear hug. "Stay in school!" He stood on the doorstep and waved until the kid was out of sight.

"Great kid," he said, coming back inside and seeing Nat. "What? You know how it is! Everyone loves XAN GALLAGHER!" He came up the stairs and sat next to her.

"Yep yep," she said. "Me, too."

"Yeah, you do," he said.

She leaned against his arm. He really did not smell good.

"You need a shower, Dad," she said. She fanned her hand in front of her face.

"I heard it's your birthday," he stage-whispered. "I've got something great planned. But first, a private talk. You and me."

"A *talk*?"

"We'll be back in time to go see them whales, don't worry."

"I'm not worried," she lied, but she was.

Just a little.

There were a lot of things that "little talks" could be about, and she wasn't sure she was ready for any of them.

In fact, she was pretty sure she wasn't.

"Get your sneakers on," he said. "Meet you out back in ten."

"Got it," she said. "Shower, Dad. I mean it. I'll give you fifteen. You need to do a lot of washing."

"Well, there's a lot of me to wash!" he said, slapping her on the back.

"DAD," she said. "OUCH." But it hadn't really hurt.

Nat went back to her room. It was so nice in there, tidy and cool and spacious. So spacious! Their whole trailer could fit in there. Also, there was something about air-conditioning that made the room feel as though it were holding its breath.

She sighed and sat down on the bed. She picked up her phone. The cool air made the phone feel extra cool, too. She pressed it against her cheek, and then she tried the Bird's number again. This time, she *knew* that the Bird wasn't going to answer, so she wasn't surprised when she didn't. Nat felt empty, like the unanswered ring was echoing inside her, even after she shut it off.

Nat stood up and slipped the phone into her pocket, just in case.

The Bird must know her number—she must at least have caller ID, Nat figured.

But the Bird had never ever, not even once, called her.

Nat took that thought and examined it. She tried not to let that hurt her feelings, but it was hard not to. Then she imagined the Bird exclaiming, "My Baleine!" when she called, and the hurt went away.

She hoped the Bird was OK.

Maybe she was on vacation.

Maybe she was at a beach, watching whales.

Better yet, maybe she was diving, like she had told Nat she used to do, with her camera in her hand, filming a humpback whale, twisting in the sun's rays.

Nat swallowed. She felt like crying, but she didn't know why she felt like crying.

Stop it, she told herself.

Nat went downstairs. Her dad was already there, waiting for her, wearing her backpack, which was so tiny on him, it looked like a toy. He smiled when he saw her. She could swear that when he smiled, she could see every single one of his teeth.

He really had a massive amount of teeth. Like more teeth than most people, probably. It was probably some kind of medical condition.

"Do you think you have more than the normal amount of teeth?" she asked him. "Has a dentist ever mentioned anything?"

"Nope. But I don't know! Want to count?"

"No! I was joking! I do not want to count your teeth! Just stop showing them to me. It's, like, *aggressively* happy."

Her dad laughed. "Yep yep," he said. "Will do, Natters. Mental note: *No smiling*. Check." He grinned again. "Oh, sorry, my bad."

"Give me my backpack, at least. You look pretty ridiculous, Dad. Ridiculous *and* aggressively happy, both."

"No way, kiddo," he said. "It's heavy. I brought"—he held up his fingers and started counting on them—"one, two, three, four, five bottles of water. In case we get thirsty. We gotta stay hydrated in this heat! And two of the World's Best Sandwiches, made by yours truly."

"And that means I can't carry the backpack?" she said.

"It means the backpack is heavy," he said. "I don't have all these muscles for nothing. That would be a waste."

"Fine," she said. Then she mumbled, "I can't help it if you want to look ridic."

"Oh, I look *ridic*? How about now?" He put on her hot pink baseball cap, the one with a sprinkle of purple glitter on the brim. "Do I still look *ridic*?"

"Dad! Give me my hat! Yes, you do!" He held it up out of reach. "I'm not jumping for that hat!" she said, jumping. She feinted with her right fist, then jabbed his abs with her left. He folded over and she grabbed the hat, triumphant. "Ha!" she said.

"Ha yourself," he said. "I'm still carrying the pack."

"I didn't want to carry it anyway," Nat told him.

She liked this part, when it was just her and her dad.

This felt right.

This felt normal.

She hadn't seen Harry yet that morning. He must have

gotten up and moved downstairs sometime in the night, because he was gone when she woke up. Maybe he was sleeping in. He sometimes did that.

Harry, like Nat, wasn't a morning person.

Thinking about Harry made Nat remember the night before, and how her heart had whistled. She wanted to unfeel that feeling.

And she wanted to feel it again.

THE TALK

Nat and her dad started walking toward the beach.

Just like at home, it was at the bottom of a sloping piece of property, but here there were no ancient Douglas firs or salal to wade through. "Look!" Nat's dad grabbed her shoulder. He pointed. Through the fronds of a palm tree, the sun's rays were splayed out like an outstretched hand.

"*Komorebi*!" she told him. *Komorebi* was a Japanese word for exactly what they could see: the sunlight streaming through the trees.

"Kohlrabi," he said. "Man, I never thought kohlrabi was that beautiful."

"DAD, kohlrabi is a vegetable. *Komorebi* is when the sun does that in the trees. It's Japanese," she added.

"Interesting," he said, pretending to write it down.

"Dad! I won't tell you stuff like this if you're going to be goofy about it!"

"I'm just kidding with you, Natter-Bat. You know that."

Nat swatted him on the back.

"Hey! Watch the sandwiches!" He ran on his tiptoes a few feet, then ducked behind the palm tree, just like he did in the blockbuster dinosaur movie *T-REX: WRATH OF THE KING.*

"Dad!" she yelled. "Watch out for dinosaurs! You are in no way hidden by that skinny tree!"

He stuck his arms out on both sides of the trunk and did the wave with them. "I'm invisible!" he yelled.

Nat giggled and kept walking. All along the slope, small purple flowers were growing. "Wild disarray," she murmured. She could hear her dad thumping down the hill behind her.

"BOO!"

"Dad! What are you *doing*?"

"Well, kiddo, I'm glad you asked. What we're doing is that we're birthdaying! Plus, exploring. Looking for ways to find ourselves in this new place! This is amazing! Amazing! Right?" He took a deep lungful of air. "Smell that!"

She sniffed. "It smells like the sea. And whatever these flowers are."

"How did you get so wise?" He shook his head in wonder. "MY DAUGHTER IS A GENIUS!" he shouted into the trees. He sniffed deeply. "It also smells like sweat, kiddo. Did you shower today?"

"Ha ha," she said.

"Did you?"

"Shut up, Dad!"

"*You* shut up," he said. He lowered his voice. "Seriously, Nat-a-Tat," he said. "I know I'm not good at talking about, you know, girl things, but I got you some deodorant. It's natural. Now that you're thirteen. Well, you know. I don't want you using none of that aluminum stuff. I was going to wrap it up, but I don't want to embarrass you in front of your friend. It's just that when you get close to puberty, it's like your body—"

"OK! ENOUGH! DAD! Stop! I get it. Fine, I stink. I'll use the deodorant. Thank you. Now *please* shut up."

He was wrong about what it smelled like out here, anyway.

To Nat, it smelled like *secrets*—oceany and fresh and salty.

They were on the beach now. The sand was burning, even through her sneakers. Nat could hear her pulse and the sound of her feet thumping down on the gravelly sand. Off to the right, she could see the Brasches on their beach chairs. Mr. Brasch was reading a book under a huge umbrella. Mrs. Brasch looked like she'd dipped her whole body in oil, and she was working on her tan. The last thing that Nat wanted to do was make conversation with the Brasches.

"Let's go that way!" She steered her dad in the opposite direction.

"Sure thing, kiddo," he said. He seemed a little nervous. Maybe even jumpy. She wondered why. Had he seen a paparazzo? He kept looking over his shoulder, like he was expecting to see someone following them.

Nat started to run. He ran along with her.

Basically, the only thing that ever scared her dad were the paps.

And for good reason.

Nat stopped running when she ran out of breath and sat down in the sand. It was hot, but she didn't care.

"What are you doing?" said her dad. He wasn't even

slightly winded. Well, duh. The man worked out for six hours a day. His lungs were the size of bathtubs probably.

"This seemed like a good place," she gasped.

"Nah, too exposed. Let's move into the shade, at least." He pointed toward some palm trees.

"Fine, have it your way."

They trudged silently toward the spot. "Come on, Dad. What is this big talk about? You're making me nervous," she said, when she could breathe again.

"Sandwiches first! Like they say, you should never have a talk on an empty stomach!"

Nat stopped walking, and her dad crashed right into her from behind. "Who?" she said. "Who says that?"

"Everyone!" He laughed his gigantic, booming laugh.

Nat rolled her eyes. "Here?" she said.

"Sure," he answered.

Nat flopped down in the shade and took one of the water bottles that he held out. She unscrewed the lid and gulped three times without stopping. Then she hiccupped.

"Dad," she said, when the hiccups stopped.

"Yeah?" he said.

"I'm really sorry about San Francisco," she said.

"It's OK," he said. "You couldn't have known. I do *not* blame you for it. Not even a little. *None* of it was your fault, Natters. I hope you know that. But man, that must've hurt. Turns out Solly wasn't such a good friend, selling you out like that. You didn't deserve that! That's gotta be a hard thing to deal with when you're a kid."

Nat swallowed. "She *is* a good friend. I think she did it for her mom. I think they just needed—"

"You should never have been in that position! I hate that these guys prey on you. It won't happen again." Nat could tell he was getting worked up. He was doing that thing with his jaw.

"Calm down, Dad! I'm sorry, that's all. I was thinking about it and I wanted to say that."

"Uh-huh."

"I guess maybe I've got to forgive Solly," she said. "Remember how you said that staying mad at someone was like holding on to a hot coal and hoping that the other person got burned?"

"Did I say that? It sounds really wise. Man, I'm good."

"Ha ha."

"Forgiveness is a big part about feeling OK with yourself. I get that."

"So I should forgive her?"

"Yep yep."

Nat took a bite of her sandwich. It was delicious, layers of avocado and tomato and thick bacon. Her dad ate his in about two bites. "You done?"

"Dad! I've taken, like, one bite. I don't have a huge mouth like you."

"Oh." He got up and stretched his arms and legs. "I'll be right back." He bounded down to the place where the water was breaking. Before she knew it, he was in up to his knees and splashing around. He waved at her and then leaned backward, disappearing into a wave.

"You're getting your clothes wet!" Nat shouted. Sometimes she wondered who was the parent. She was torn between feeling annoyed with him and wanting to jump in there with him.

"Wait up!" she yelled. But she still didn't get up.

He threw his hands into the air. "The water here is AMAZING!" he shouted.

"Amazing" made her think of mazes cut perfectly out of topiary hedges, like one that she and her dad had gotten lost in somewhere in England the previous summer. When they finally, laughing, stumbled on the statue in the middle, a photographer leapt out from behind the hedgerow and nearly scared her to death. She'd actually peed her pants, and then she'd cried. The picture of her crying showed up on a magazine under the headline, "XAN THE MAN: SHOUTS ABUSE AT SICK DAUGHTER, PASSERSBY EXPRESS CONCERN." The photo zoomed in on the wet patch on her jeans. That wet patch photo made her want to die.

It was kind of amazing that she'd made any friends at all after that, actually, she thought.

Nat dropped her shoulders a little. The weight of remembering stuff like that was sometimes as heavy as an actual thing on her back. She took a deep breath in and held it. Her dad was walking back toward her, water pouring off his jean shorts. He looked ridiculous. Then he turned and galloped into the waves again like a demented pony. She took another bite of her sandwich and chewed.

Maybe she'd go in after she was done.

Maybe she wouldn't.

The thing at the maze in England was nothing compared to the Thing That Solly Did.

The Thing that Nat was going to forgive her for as soon as she got back to the house. She had bought another pile of postcards in town. She would write on one of them, *I FORGIVE YOU.*

She wondered if Solly cared, if she was waiting for forgiveness, or if she really thought everything was fine. Or worse, if she'd forgotten about the whole thing.

The postcard had a picture of a surfing frog on it.

In French, the word for frog was *grenouille.*

There was a lump in her throat that was not sandwich; it was sadness. She swallowed until she felt like she could breathe again.

She thought about the *Thing.*

The Thing that needed forgiving.

The Thing she was going to now (hopefully) forget.

Forgive and forget went together. Everyone knew that.

It had happened behind the Airstream in the director's backyard.

Solly and Nat were in the garden. They went there a lot, after school. Sometimes they played. Sometimes they just sat at the old wrought iron table and talked. It was an uncomfortable table. You couldn't lean on it. It was too lumpy and rusty.

They were sitting at the table when Solly reached into her backpack and took out the pack of cigarettes. She did it so casually that Nat at first didn't realize what it even was. Then she did a double take.

"Whoa," she said. "What is *that*?"

"Duh," said Solly. "You know."

"Cigarettes?" whispered Nat. "Why do you have those?"

"Why are we whispering?" whispered Solly. "Yes!" she added in her normal voice. "Cigarettes." She looked at Nat and laughed. "Don't look so worried! They're clove. Cloves are plants, right?"

"Lots of things are plants. That doesn't mean we should smoke them."

"*You* don't have to. But I'm going to."

Nat hesitated. "But . . . why?" She looked around the garden at all the stuff they usually did. Right behind them was the fort they had built partway up the huge Japanese maple tree, hidden in the leaves. Over by the fountain was the huge chalk drawing that they had started on Tuesday. "I don't really want to."

Solly rolled her eyes. "They're my mom's. Would Mom smoke them if they were bad?"

The girls both stared at the cigarettes.

"Probably," said Nat, breaking the silence. "I think she would."

"You think you're so great," said Solly. "I should just go." But she didn't move, she just kept looking at Nat.

"I have asthma," Nat lied.

"Liar." Solly had recently added dark blue and green highlights to her hair. It glittered like a mermaid's tail. She lowered her voice. "I think you're chicken."

"So what if I am?"

"I should have known you wouldn't. Hailey said—"

"Hailey said something about me? I'm sure it was dumb. Hailey hates me."

"Hailey's OK," said Solly. "Look, you're leaving, right? So I have to have someone to be friends with."

"But Hailey? Ugh! You can do way better, Sol."

"Sometimes I don't know why you and me are even friends," said Solly. "You're so square."

Solly had never talked to her like that before. Square! Did people even say that anymore? It sounded like something Solly's mom would say. Nat didn't really understand what was happening.

"Fine!" Nat said. She grabbed the cigarette box and held it up. It was surprisingly light. "I'll smoke your stupid cigarette! What is wrong with you?"

"Nothing." Solly smiled. "I was kidding."

Solly reached across the table and took the box out of Nat's hand. Nat felt like she was in a bad movie. "Smoking is dumb!" was obviously the moral of this one, but she reached her hand out and took out a cigarette. It felt funny in her fingers, like a featherlight, papery pen. She put it between her lips. It smelled like tea. Not so bad. She inhaled deeply.

Solly laughed. "It's not even lit!" she said. "You're ridic!"

"*You're* ridic!" said Nat. "I was just practicing."

Solly rolled her eyes. "I don't think it's a hard thing to learn." She reached into her pocket and pulled out a lighter.

"Where did you get *that*?" The lighter somehow made the whole thing real. Real *and* terrible.

Nat thought about all the things that could happen. She could imagine the whole garden burning to the ground. What then? Or her dad appearing and seeing her smoking. Then his face would get that devastated, sad look and her heart would literally break into a million pieces.

"I don't . . ." she started.

But Solly had that look on her face, and Nat knew better than to chicken out now. She was lucky Solly was her friend. Solly was crazy, for sure, but she was fun and interesting, at least. And she never acted like XAN GALLAGHER was a big deal. That was a huge plus.

"Hey!" Solly snapped her fingers. "Wake up!"

"I was just thinking, that, um . . ."

"Were you holding your breath?" said Solly.

"No!"

"OK, I'm lighting it," said Solly. She leaned forward with the lighter lit. "Put it between your lips! Then inhale when the flame touches it! Do I have to teach you everything?"

Nat giggled. She didn't think it was funny—she was just nervous.

Solly touched the lighter to the cigarette and Nat inhaled.

Click-click-click, the camera went from somewhere in the bushes.

Click-click-click.

Nat dropped the cigarette and started to choke. She couldn't remember to breathe in or to breathe out. Her throat was closing.

"Oh my gosh," Solly said. She was pounding Nat on the back. "I'm sorry, Nat. Are you OK? Please be OK! I didn't mean to!"

Then she ran away, leaving Nat with the pack of cigarettes, coughing so hard she thought she was going to die.

Even thinking about it now made her want to cry:

How the Lion jumped out of the shrubbery.

How her dad saw the photos on the Internet.

Right after that, her dad told her they were moving to Canada. He said that wasn't why, but she knew it was.

It was Solly's fault.

And the Lion's.

Maybe more the Lion's than Solly's, actually. He must have offered her a deal. All Solly did was to go through with it.

"I forgive you, Solly," Nat said out loud, with a mouthful of sandwich. "But I will never forgive the Lion."

She put the sandwich down in the sand. It would be wrecked, but she didn't care. Suddenly, she wasn't even a little bit hungry anymore.

"So, Natters, are you done? Why didn't you come in? Man, that water is great, by the way." He paused. "Warm! Amazing!"

"Great, Dad. I'm glad to hear it."

"Soooooooooooo," he said. He sat down right next to her, his gigantic wet leg pressing against hers.

"DAD."

"What? I just want to sit next to my girl, is that so wrong?"

"You're wet!"

He shook his head like a dog, spraying her sandy sandwich.

"I guess I'm done," she said.

"Hey," he said. "Come on. We need to talk. I know you don't like them talks. But I promise I'll make it painless! We've got this!"

"DAD." The sandwich in Nat's stomach turned to stone. She leaned over, pressing on her belly. "It's *those* talks," she said, flatly, facing the sand. She picked up some sand and ran it through her hands. It was silky smooth and unbelievably warm. She wanted to crawl into it, like it was blankets on a bed. "About what?"

"Things!" said her dad. "Stuff! You know, life!"

Nat thought about how when people are going to die, their whole life flashes in front of their eyes. This was like that, only different.

He's going to tell me about my mother, she thought. She held her breath.

Her dad cleared his throat. *Grak, grak.* It sounded like a spoon stuck in a garbage disposal. *Grak.* "I know I'm not a woman," he started.

"Thank goodness," interrupted Nat. "You're way too hairy."

"Hey now," he said. "I'd make a gorgeous woman."

"You'd make a hairy woman."

Her dad stared at her soulfully, and then sighed and gazed thoughtfully out to sea. He put his hand on her shoulder.

"Stop being so actory," she told him. "You're driving me crazy!"

He *grak*ed again. "You're thirteen today," he said. "Man, it goes by fast. I can't believe it! Thirteen! People are right, you know. Everyone says that it goes by so fast and you're like, 'I don't believe you!' But they're right! They were all right!"

"DAD," she said. "What were you saying?"

"I'm saying it! This is it! Are you listening, Nat-a-Tat?"

"DAD, yes. I wish you'd just say whatever. Do you have cancer?"

"No! I'm so sorry you thought that. Were you worried? That sucks! I should have phrased it differently!" He took a deep breath. "The thing is," he said, "now that you're a teen, things are going to start happening. Changes, I mean. To your body." He took a huge gulp of water. Then another one, which took care of the entire liter. He put the lid back on. "Your body is gonna start to—"

Nat interrupted. "*Dad*, it's fine. We've had that talk at school. Every year, for the last three years. I know all the stuff. Please don't. Please, please, please."

He ignored her. He framed his hands in the air. "I think of it like a great *blossoming*, like your body is born in winter and then, BAM, you start growin' up and then it's SPRING! Spring! Think of it!"

"DAD," Nat shouted. She picked up an entire handful of sand and dumped it onto her dad's head.

Unbelievably, he just shook it off and kept talking. "—and one of these days, you're going to get your period," he said.

Nat's blood ran cold. "Dad," she said, quietly. "Don't."

He forged ahead like she hadn't said anything at all. "I bought you some supplies at home, but I didn't bring them to Mexico. Of course, this isn't all going to happen tomorrow or anything. But you gotta figure out which thing is going to—"

Nat felt herself starting to cry. "Dad, if you even say the word 'tampon' out loud, I'm going to run into the sea and swim away forever, I swear to you. Please stop. Please. I know all this stuff! I don't want to talk about it!"

Nat was seeing spots around her vision. She thought that maybe she was going to faint.

"Dad," she said. "Dad." Her ears were roaring. She was crying. She couldn't stand it, and she didn't know what specifically it was that she couldn't stand: Was it just *him* trying to tell her about her own body or that her own body was going to change and she wasn't ready and this was what moms were for, right?

Then something broke through the white noise.

Click-click-click.

Click-click-click.

That something was the sound of a camera clicking.

Both Nat and her dad swiveled toward the sound. Nat was crying so hard that snot was pouring down her face. Actual snot!

The camera kept clicking.

She blinked. It was the Lion.

"No," she shouted. "NO!"

Her dad was on his feet and he was running in his wet shorts, glistening like a weird, shiny superhero, and then he was *on* the Lion and Nat knew he wasn't going to hug him.

Her dad was so *huge*, and the Lion was so small.

"Dad," she screamed, but nothing came out of her mouth. It was like a nightmare.

It was happening in slow motion.

"Stop, you'll kill him," she mouthed.

"WHAT ARE YOU DOING?" Nat heard her dad shouting. "WHY ARE YOU DOING THIS TO US? WHO DO YOU THINK YOU ARE?"

She had never heard her dad so angry before. She had once plugged the blender into a faulty outlet, and she felt exactly like she did at that moment: stuck to the current, scared, and like she might die.

Her dad grabbed the Lion's camera. The Lion's mouth was open. He was as pale as her dad's terrible favorite white cheese.

Then Nat's dad threw the camera toward the sea. They all watched as the camera hit the crest of a wave and disappeared.

The Lion made a belching sound. Nat wondered if he was going to throw up.

Nat said, "Holy cow." She didn't think she'd ever said that before in her whole life.

"Oh man," said XAN GALLAGHER. "Lion, I'm sorry, man. You *know* my kid is off-limits. My kid! Me and Natters, we were having a moment. A *private* moment." Her dad slumped down on the sand and dropped his gigantic head into his gigantic hands. "I shouldn't have done that. Man, I am so sorry."

The Lion made another noise in his throat, like he'd been

so scared that he'd swallowed his voice and was now choking on it. He sat down next to her dad. Nat got up. She couldn't feel her legs. Somehow she stumbled over to her dad and sat on his other side. A crab scuttled over Nat's foot, over the hearts that Solly drew.

"What the heck," the Lion mumbled, finally. "That camera was five thousand dollars!"

"I'll buy you another one," said Nat's dad.

The Lion got a sour look on his face. He looked from Nat to her dad and back again. "So," he said, "you finally tellin' her the truth about her mom?"

Nat's legs surged with strength. She stood up.

She stood right over the Lion.

She took a deep breath.

"I will never forgive you," she said. "Not ever."

Then she turned and started to run.

THE AMAZING RACE

There was a German word, *mutterseelinallein*, which meant intense loneliness, but what it really translated to directly was "your mother's soul has left you."

"*Mutterseelinallein*," Nat said out loud.

She was back in her air-conditioned, cavernous room. Her shoes were full of sand. She took them off and dumped them on the floor, where they made a small, slippery sandpile.

She wanted to know what the Lion had been about to say, but the last person she wanted to hear it from was the Lion.

Nat wanted to hear it from her *dad*. She made a decision. She was going to ask him.

Nat had been *mutterseelinallein* for her whole life.

Nat's mother's soul left when she was born.

She didn't want to be *mutterseelinallein* anymore.

The magazine she had taken from Harry's bathroom was in her suitcase. She had packed it, just in case, but she didn't take it out. She could picture the cover: her dad's huge grin and her own red face, scrunched up in the turquoise baby carrier.

But Nat didn't want to read the truth in a magazine.

She wanted to hear it from his own mouth.

That's what she wanted for her birthday. More than seeing the whales. More than anything.

She wanted the *truth*.

I'm thirteen now, she told herself. *I am old enough for this*. She felt excited, and also like she might throw up.

Someone was her mother.

"I have a right to know," she said out loud. Her voice sounded wobbly, even alone in her room.

Nat got off the bed and looked in the mirror. She looked the same as she did the day before. Her boobs were still . . . there. "Boobida," she whispered, and stuck out her tongue.

She looked at her body sideways. Maybe she was getting used to them.

She knew everyone was waiting for her downstairs.

She knew she wanted to talk to her dad before they went to see the whales.

She also knew she had to write the postcard.

She found the pen and the frog postcard and held them both in her hand.

She imagined Solly rolling her eyes. She saw Solly lighting the cigarette.

Nat pictured her friendship with Solly like a piece of melting plastic, being pulled from two sides. The plastic was a long long thread stretching from her heart to Solly's heart, but now it was broken. She didn't want to fix it, but she wanted to say goodbye.

Goodbye and thank you.

Anyway, she was still a little bit mad.

Dear Solly, Nat wrote.

I forgive you. (You know what for.)

I don't have my period yet.

I have not kissed a boy.

Love and goodbye,

Nat(alia)

It seemed to Nat there was a lot to say that she couldn't say, but it was right there in between the words if Solly wanted to read it closely enough.

It was complicated.

Solly, of all people, should get that.

Nat put the postcard in her pocket. She could mail it from the SUPERMARKET MERCADO.

Nat got changed into a clean T-shirt and jeans and put her sneakers back on. They were a bit tight. Like everything else, her feet were suddenly growing.

She washed her face and brushed her hair and her teeth. She sniffed her armpits, which didn't smell, but she put on the natural deodorant her dad had left on her bathroom counter with a bow on the top.

"Ha ha, Dad," she said. She sniffed the deodorant. It smelled like Creamsicles.

"Amazing," she said.

DOWNSTAIRS, EVERYONE—HARRY AND HER dad and Harry's parents—was sitting around the big table in the dining room. There were balloons all over the ceiling.

"Where did you get balloons?" she asked, just as they all shouted, "HAPPY BIRTHDAY!"

In the middle of the table, there was a huge cake. *Happy*

Birthday, Nat! it said. Then, under that, it said, *Feliz cumpleaños!* There was a whale made out of icing diving between the words.

"I love it!" she said. "Thank you!"

She blew out the thirteen candles. *I wish I could meet my mom,* she wished silently. *Just once.*

"Did you wish about whales?" Harry whispered.

"No," she whispered back.

"I love you more than cod," her dad said.

"You don't even like cod," Nat said.

"I love *you*, Nat-a-Tat," he said. "Happy birthday!"

"Yeah, you do," she said.

Mr. Brasch stood up and clapped his hands, just like Mr. Hajeezi did at school. "We're going to be late!" he said.

Outside, the sky was crowded with clouds of all different shades of white and gray. In between, there were tiny bits of blue, struggling to be seen. It made Nat want to blow really hard so that the clouds would part and let the blue out.

She used to do that, when she was a kid.

She used to believe that would work.

They drove past the closed restaurant and the T-shirt stand, then the post office, bank, and 7-Eleven. Everything seemed much closer to the house now that they were driving and not riding ill-fitting bikes. When they passed the no-bus bus station, Harry whispered, "*Hanyauku!*" and Nat giggled. There was something about Mr. Brasch being in the car that made her want to be quiet though.

"What's that, Harry?" Mrs. Brasch asked Harry.

"Nothing, Mom," said Harry.

"Oh, an inside joke!" said Mrs. Brasch. "That's nice."

"MOM," he said. He sounded happier than he ever did at home. Maybe his dad was intimidated by XAN THE MAN, because he wasn't correcting everyone who called Harry "Harry." Maybe XAN GALLAGHER had even said something to him, something like, "Hey, li'l buddy"—that's what he called Mr. Brasch—"you must be so proud of Harry for just being who he is, even when the whole world might not be so cool with it. You're cool for doing that!"

Nat could practically hear him saying exactly that.

She could imagine Mr. Brasch nodding uncomfortably and making a calibration in his closed mind, shifting the dial from "Closed" to "Slightly Open." She imagined the name "Harry" sneaking in through that open door.

This was good.

At least, it was better.

It really, truly, suddenly felt like they were on vacation from themselves and everything that had been so awkward and clunky about their lives in Sooke.

Nat wasn't the least bit lonely here.

They were on vacation from loneliness.

They were on vacation from complications.

Or, at least, they had been. Until this morning.

Nat's dad turned on the car stereo, and music blasted over them. "Man, I *love* this song. You like?" He turned to look at the kids.

"Dad!" said Nat. "Eyes on the road!"

"Mr. Gallagher!" shouted Harry.

Then there was a terrible thump.

"DAD!" Nat screamed.

The car had stopped in a cloud of dust.

"What the heck was that?" said Nat's dad.

Nat was already out of the car. There, practically invisible in the dust, was the dust-colored dog.

"TUFTY!" shouted Nat.

Tufty got up, barked at Nat once, twice, three times, and then ran off into the brush.

"I thought you killed him!" Nat said, getting back into the car. "That was Tufty. He's a stray."

"You hit that dog, Xan," said Mr. Brasch. "Gosh. Maybe keep your eyes on the road." He reached over and turned off the radio just as Nat's dad was starting to hum. He stopped abruptly, midnote. "'Little Lion Man,'" he said. "Huh. I used to like that song. But now it reminds me of someone." He sighed and then shook his head. "The Lion won't be back, Nat-a-Tat, not this time."

"I know, Dad," Nat said. "Let's not talk about it. Seriously."

"Are you speaking in code?" said Mrs. Brasch. "I love your relationship with each other. It's so cute."

"Yep yep," Nat's dad said. "We're not speaking in code."

"So you *are?*" Mrs. Brasch asked.

"He means nope," said Nat, helpfully.

"It's like 'yeah, no,'" supplied Harry. "Or 'no, yeah.'"

"None of you are making sense," said Mr. Brasch. "I'm feeling a little carsick."

The car swooped along, past the SUPERMARKET MER-CADO. The parking lot was still empty. Nat wondered if the pretty cashier was through the book yet, or if she'd started a new one. She wondered if the dancing old lady was still mad. She wanted to ask if they could stop but couldn't think of a reason, except for the postcard. When she remembered the postcard, she felt a bit lighter. But it was too late to stop then. They were past it. She would mail it later.

After a few minutes the road they were on joined a much busier road. It was like a real highway, with traffic.

"What time are we supposed to be there?" said Mr. Brasch. "I don't want to be late."

"I'm hungry," said Harry.

"Let's have tacos," said Nat.

"Do we have time?" said Mrs. Brasch.

Nat's dad winked at Nat in the mirror. It was a wink that said, "Traveling with other people is hard!"

"You know it," said Nat.

"I don't want you to get seasick on Hugh's boat," said her dad. "You can eat after."

"That's a fine idea," said Mr. Brasch. "Are you sure you know where you're going?"

"More or less," said Nat's dad. "Is any way really the wrong way?"

Mr. Brasch gave him a funny look. "Yes," he said. "If you end up in the wrong place, you've gone the wrong way."

"Right you are, my man." Nat's dad clapped Mr. Brasch on the back. Nat wondered when Mr. Brasch was going to start bracing himself for that. Not yet, apparently.

Nat's dad slammed on the brakes and pulled the car over to the side of the road. "I've got to check the map," he said.

"We're in traffic!" said Mrs. Brasch. "Shouldn't you wait until we're in a parking lot?"

"Nah, we're good," said Nat's dad, unfolding a huge map.

Nat and Harry made eye contact. Nat blushed and looked out the window.

"Nat?" said Harry. "Are you OK?"

She nodded. "Hot," she mumbled.

"If you end up in the wrong place, you've gone the wrong way," Nat's dad repeated. "Man, that's a good one."

"Will you put it on the Twitter?" asked Mr. Brasch. "I've heard of that."

Nat's dad chuckled. "Good man," he said.

"Thank you," said Mr. Brasch, stiffly.

"Des," said Mrs. Brasch. "Twitter is social media."

"I know what it is!" said Mr. Brasch. "I pay attention."

Harry rolled his eyes.

Nat's dad pulled the car back into traffic with a screech of tires, but after only a few seconds he wheeled off down an exit.

"Are you sure this is the right turn?" said Mr. Brasch. "On the map, it looked like you should go straight for at least another mile."

"Shortcut. I have a keen sense of direction," Nat's dad told him. He tapped his temple. "It's all up here. Yep yep."

"Have you ever been here before?" Mrs. Brasch asked.

"Not technically," said Nat's dad. He winked at Nat in the mirror again.

Harry giggled. Mrs. Brasch didn't answer directly. "Men," she muttered, under her breath.

They were in an empty parking lot at the top of a set of stairs that led down to a beach.

"Here we are!" said Nat's dad. He unfolded himself and got out of the car. He was so gigantic that he made every car look tiny. He definitely made Mr. Brasch look tiny. "For you." Nat's dad handed her a piece of paper from his pocket.

WHALE EXPERIENCE FACTORY! was written on the

paper. Then in parentheses, it said, (*Just kidding, go down the stairs, your clue is at the bottom of the steps*).

"Like *The Amazing Race*!" he said. "You get it? Man, I love that show."

"It's very produced," said Mr. Brasch. "Scripted."

"Nah," said Nat's dad. "Anyway, me and Natters have a thing where we do clues when we travel."

"Right," said Nat, even though it wasn't quite true.

They did it *once* before.

That was last time they were in Mexico, right before the fan pushed her down the stairs on the pyramid. That clue had said, *A gift awaits at the top of the stairs!* At the top of the stairs, though, someone had stolen the gift.

"I can't believe it!" said her dad. She could tell he was genuinely upset. She wondered now what it was. She had never asked, because of the whole falling-down-the-stairs thing. She frowned. He probably wouldn't even remember.

"Go!" Nat's dad said. "Harry's getting ahead of you!"

Nat looked. Harry was already disappearing from view.

"Wait up!" she called. "Hang on! Harry!"

Harry had already found the next clue by the time she caught up to him on the sand.

"When did your dad even *do* all this?"

Nat shrugged. "I have no idea! He gets really into stuff like this. He's a little *duende*."

"I don't know what that means," said Harry.

"It's like magic," she said. "He's a magical elf."

"He's way too big to be an elf. He must have people," said Harry. "Does he have a secret staff? Where did he get the cake? And the balloons?"

"I don't know! The SUPERMARKET ᴍᴇʀᴄᴀᴅᴏ?"

"That just doesn't seem like a place where you can get cake and helium balloons!"

"He probably just drove to Costco or whatever."

"Maybe." He looked dubious. "But when? Being a movie star is weird. It's like, 'Your wish is our command!' stuff."

"Are you going to read the clue?" She peered over his shoulder. He smelled like toothpaste and sunscreen. There was a tiny ladybug sitting on the back of his T-shirt. She decided not to tell him. It was good luck. He needed it, probably.

"OK, OK. *You* read it. It's *your* birthday."

Nat took the clue out of Harry's hand. It looked like a real *Amazing Race* clue. It was yellow and black. It said, *Go back up to the top of the steps and find your bikes. Get on them and ride downhill until you see the flag.*

"Isn't that dangerous?" said Harry. "That's a terrible clue."

"It's fine!" said Nat. "We wouldn't do it if it wasn't fine!" But the idea of riding that falling-apart bike again didn't sound fun to her, either. She looked up to the top of the stairs. Down the end of the beach, a man beside a tiny red boat waved at them. Nat waved back.

"Why are you waving?" said Harry. "Who is that?"

"I'm being friendly! I have no idea who it is. A friendly fisherman." She didn't feel like going all the way back up the stairs. It was hot. She was starting to sweat. "*Dépit*," she muttered. "De Pits."

"What?"

"*Dépit*," she repeated. "It's a French word for . . . never mind. It's too hard to explain. Let's go find the bikes, I guess."

"This doesn't seem fun," he said.

She shrugged. "You don't have to come."

"I want to! It's not that."

"Whatever."

"Let me look at it," he said.

"What are you looking for? A part that says 'just kidding'?"

Harry took the clue out of her hand. He flipped it over.

On the back, it said, *Just kidding! That's your ride at the end of the beach. Happy birthday!*

"Oh, ha ha," said Nat. "He's hilarious." She looked up at the top of the stairs. "VERY FUNNY, DAD!" she yelled.

Harry laughed. "It is *sort of* funny," he said. He punched her in the arm.

"You're getting more like my dad every day. Don't do that. Don't punch me!"

"Sorry! Jeez."

"It's my birthday! I just don't want to be punched!"

"Fine! What is the untranslatable word for 'settle down'?"

"It's just 'settle down'! It's English!"

"Fine!" He started tiptoeing down the beach. "*Hanyauku!*" he yelled.

"Funny," she said, sarcastically, but she laughed, too.

It was sort of funny, after all.

Besides, having fun with Harry was a lot better than being mad at Harry. Nat had a choice. And she chose fun.

"It IS my birthday," she said.

"Yeah," said Harry. "I know. *Duh.*"

"Duh yourself," she said.

THE WHALE

The beach was sandy and soft and the water was a gorgeous aquamarine. Nat could tell Harry was happy now. "This is great," he said. "I feel like we're inside a postcard or something."

"Yep yep," Nat said. They passed a family with a big, colorful beach umbrella and two little kids who were fighting over a bucket. "Gimme the shovel!" the bigger kid said, and he bonked the littler one on the head. The littler one screamed. The dad yelled at the bigger kid. The mom yelled at the dad. The whole family was yelling by the time they walked past.

"Well," said Nat, "*that* escalated quickly." She shook her head. "Tourists are the worst."

"We're tourists," Harry pointed out.

"It's different," she said, but she hoped he wouldn't ask in what way it was different, because she didn't know. Maybe, like her dad, she existed on a different plane. Everything was different when you were famous. She had always thought she hated being famous, but maybe she didn't hate it so much after all.

Complicated, she thought. She took the word "complicated" apart in her head. It looked like sharp colorful triangles cut from plastic that you were meant to arrange into a pattern. If you held up one of the triangles to the light, you could see through it.

They were close enough to the man with the red boat now to see his hat. On the brim were two words. "Yep yep."

"Where did he get the hat?" Harry said.

"XAN GALLAGHER is everywhere," Nat answered. "There is no escape. Anyway, I think that's our clue."

"Oh!" said Harry. "Dude."

As they got closer, they could see that the paint on the boat was badly chipped. "I have a sinking feeling," said Nat.

"You'll probably have more of one soon," said Harry. "That boat is two hundred years old." Then, louder, he said, "*HOLA, SEÑOR.*"

The man in the hat smiled slowly and nodded.

"HARRY," said Harry, pointing at himself. "NAT."

"Harry, don't," said Nat. "He probably speaks English! Do you speak English?" she said to the fisherman.

The fisherman shook his head. "*Lo siento*," he said.

"He doesn't understand," Nat told Harry.

"This feels dangerous," said Harry, in his normal voice.

"Harry!" mouthed Nat. "He'll hear you!"

"So what? He doesn't understand! What if this is the wrong guy?"

"He's wearing the hat," Nat pointed out. "Dad must have given him the hat."

The fisherman tapped the hat. "Hugh," he said. He smiled again.

"*HOLA*, HUGH," said Harry.

"I don't think Hugh is a Mexican name," said Nat. "That might not be his name."

Hugh pointed at the boat and then at the kids. Nat and Harry looked at each other. "It's my birthday," said Nat. "Being kidnapped on your birthday would be terrible."

"We'll probably see some really cool whales," said Harry, but neither of them moved.

The fisherman said something in Spanish and pointed to the boat again.

"Is this a good idea?" said Harry.

"No," said Nat. She looked at Hugh from the side. He didn't look like a kidnapper. But what did kidnappers look like? She suspected successful kidnappers didn't look like kidnappers at all. They looked like regular guys. Regular guys who drove windowless vans and could throw kids into them without being caught.

"HEY, GUYS!" Nat turned around. Her dad was sitting cross-legged in a lean-to of logs that he'd built above the tide line. He winked hugely and then closed his eyes as though he were meditating.

"Get on the boat!" he yelled. "You're gonna love it! Authentic!" He raised his hands in some kind of victory salute.

Harry rolled his eyes, but he waded into the water and got into the boat. Nat followed him, forgetting about her sneakers, which got wet. "My sneakers!" she said. "I hope the hearts don't wash off."

"Why didn't you take them off?"

"I don't know!" Nat swallowed her tears. She didn't want to be *dépit* on her birthday. She didn't want to be plain, old-fashioned sad either. She tried to concentrate on the whales. The *potential* whales. "Potential whales are everywhere," she said out loud. "Mostly sunny, with a possibility of whales." At some point, the clouds had begun fading from the sky. Only a few white wisps remained, like someone had swiped a paintbrush across the blue that had some white left on it from something else.

"Duh," said Harry. He'd put his sunglasses on. In the reflection on the lenses, she could see the stripe of zinc sunscreen on her nose. Harry's whole face was covered in it, but he had that thin kind of white skin that burned like crazy.

The fisherman said something else to Nat in Spanish. "*Lo siento*," she said. "*No hablo español.*"

He gave her a quizzical look. "I'm not Mexican!" she said in English. "American! Me!"

The boat smelled like seaweed and gasoline. The engine roared to life.

Nat waved to her dad. He waved back.

She wondered where the Brasches had gone. Maybe he had dropped them off at one of those places that sold tourist stuff. They seemed like the kind of people who would want to buy a sombrero to take home and hang on the wall next to the creepy deer head.

Nat rolled her eyes.

The Airstream did not have wall space for hanging huge Mexican hats, or anything else, for that matter. They only had one thing on the wall, which was a map of the world. It had a lot of pins in it from places they'd been. It had even more pins in it of places they wanted to go. Nat had stuck pins in the Arctic and the Antarctic and also Vietnam and New Orleans.

Hugh had one wandering eye and a short beard that Nat could see skin through, and that skin was puckered and shiny white, like scar tissue. Her dad always assumed that people who had crummy jobs were good people. "Salt of the Earth," he'd say. "Every one of 'em!" But Nat didn't know why her dad thought that. There was *always* a possibility that someone was bad.

There was always a possibility they were kidnappers, or worse, paparazzi.

"What kind of car do you drive?" she wanted to ask him. "Is it a windowless van?" She tried to arrange the Spanish words she knew in the right order. "What" was *que*. "Car" was probably *auto*, she reasoned. "*Que auto?*" she tried.

Hugh held his hand to his ear like he couldn't hear her.

"QUE AUTO?" she said, more loudly. She thought that if it was a van of any kind, she might dive right off the boat. The water was turquoise and looked warm and deep. She peered over the side. She couldn't see the bottom, but she did see a school of colorful fish.

"Look!" Nat poked Harry.

His hair had come out of its fastener and was blowing toward her. He turned around. "WHAT?" His hair whipped into his mouth and eyes.

"Nothing," she said. "Do you see any whales?"

But he'd turned around again and he didn't hear her. The little boat pounded up and down on the chop of the sea, and the bench she was sitting on vibrated. The whole boat felt very *splintery*. She ran her finger along the edge, and flakes of paint came off.

Hugh caught her eye and winked at her. When her dad winked, that was one thing, but when other people did it, it made her nervous. She wished she'd worn sunglasses to have something to hide behind. Her dad wore sunglasses all the time, even inside, when they were in public. "Eyes are the windows to the soul," he'd said when she asked him about it. "You don't want just anybody stealin' yours."

"My eyes?" she'd said.

"Your soul, Natters," he'd said.

The sun glinted and glimmered off the waves in sharp dots. The Whale Experience Factory boat in the brochure looked like it had a roof. Nat guessed that the Whale Experience Factory boat probably also didn't have an inch of water in the bottom. She turned sideways and put her feet up on the bench to protect her shoes, even though they were already soaked. The hearts were definitely getting blurry. She wished Solly had used a Sharpie so it wouldn't have come off like this.

Then the boat hit a wave and she nearly fell, grabbing the side with both hands.

Harry turned to look at her. "This is awesome!"

Nat gave him a thumbs-up, even though she was surprised. That wasn't exactly what she was thinking, but she felt like she should be. It *was* awesome. Right? There were going to be whales! She didn't understand *why* she didn't feel happy. Lately, it felt like her moods were skidding in the opposite direction of her thoughts, making her feel as pulled apart as a whole roasted chicken being prepped for dinner.

Her stomach growled.

"Did you bring any food?" she said to Harry, but he'd turned away again. She patted the pockets of her jeans just to see if anything was hiding in there, like a granola bar or even a pack of gum.

Her phone.

Her phone wasn't in her pocket.

For a second, she panicked. Then she realized that she must have left it in her room. She hoped she wouldn't have a reason to need to call 911. Without her phone in her pocket, she felt untethered, unsafe, alone.

She waved at the dot on the beach, which she knew to be her dad. The wave meant, "GOODBYE FOREVER PROBABLY."

Nat breathed in through her nose and out through her mouth. Then she decided to hold her breath instead. *One*, she counted. *Two, three, four, five.* She was on one hundred and fourteen when she heard the long, slow, familiar huffing exhalation of a whale.

The whale was right beside the boat.

Hugh cut the engine.

"Whale!" yelled Harry, who was in charge of saying obvious stuff.

Nat smiled at Hugh. "*Gracias*," she said, pointing, as though Hugh himself were responsible for this whale. She liked him better all of a sudden. She felt like they were friends.

The whale was so close that Nat could taste the air it just exhaled. It tasted like rotten fish and rubber tires.

"This is *real*," shouted Harry.

"I know!" Nat said. "Don't shout. You'll scare it."

The whale was enormous.

It started to sink down next to them. Nat couldn't see its tail unless she turned her head. The whale was about four times longer than the boat.

"It's a humpback!" she said. She had been expecting gray whales. All the humpbacks were in South Africa. Well, not *in* South Africa, but off the coast. Last time she talked to the Bird, before they left for Mexico, the Bird told her that for some reason, the whole world's population of humpback whales seemed to be gathering there, and nobody knew why.

"It's a mystery," she'd said.

"But you're an expert," Nat had said. "Why do you think they are going there?"

"I think it's probably a message," said the Bird. "I think they are trying to tell us something."

"But what?" Nat asked. "What could the whales want to tell us?"

"I hope they aren't telling us that it's the end of the world," the Bird chirped, and then she laughed.

"That isn't very funny," Nat said.

"I know it isn't, my little prank caller, my Baleine," the Bird said, softly. "I just think maybe it is."

"The end of the world?" Nat asked. Her mouth tasted funny, tinny and strange. "You think the world is ending?" Her head was whirling. What if the world *was* ending? She didn't know who her mother was! She couldn't die before she knew!

Then the Bird laughed. "Of course not," she said. "I'm sorry, I was joking. It didn't come across like a joke, did it? No one knows why they are gathering there. It's probably just a party though. A whale party."

"Whales don't have parties!" Nat said. She was so *dépit*, she wanted to cry. "Why can't you answer seriously?"

"I'm sorry, my little friend," the Bird said. "The truth is that no one knows. Humpbacks mostly travel alone. This is very unusual. Who knows what it could mean? Maybe we aren't meant to know. We don't always need to have answers to our questions, you know."

"We don't?" said Nat. "Yes, we do." She thought about all of her own questions. She had a lot of them.

She wanted to know everything. She wanted all of the answers.

"Ah, but that's not how it works, is it? Sometimes we live our whole lives and never know."

"Do you have a question you want to know the answer to?" Nat asked. She was holding her breath, waiting for the Bird to answer. She felt like the answer the Bird needed was going to be the answer she needed, too.

"I suppose I just want to know the point of it all," the Bird said. She sounded sad.

"Oh," said Nat. Her heart beat in a wobbly way that reminded her of a water balloon. She didn't like how that felt. "I have to go now."

Then Nat had hung up.

That was the last time she'd talked to the Bird.

Tears welled up in Nat's eyes. The whale blew again.

"It's huge!" said Harry. "I know that's an obvious thing to say, but look at it!"

"*Ballena jorobada*!" said Hugh.

"*Ballena*!" said Nat. "*Si*!"

The boat rocked and rolled. The whale surfaced again and huffed another huge cloud of misty water. Its skin was covered with deep grooves and scratches and barnacles that looked like a beautiful and intentional pattern, like someone had drawn them on. Like how Solly had drawn the hearts on her shoes.

You're beautiful, Nat told the whale, telepathically. *Can you slap your tail?*

The whale dove down. All three of them leaned to one side of the boat to watch. The boat tipped to that side precipitously.

"*Ten cuidado*!" Hugh shouted, pushing Nat backward.

"Hey," she said.

The whale was surfacing again.

Then it did it.

It slapped its tail.

A huge rainbow rose up in the splash.

Then Hugh reached into a cooler that he had near his feet. When he opened it up, Nat saw a camera.

It looked expensive.

It looked like a paparazzi camera.

"Hey," she said, "that . . ."

Hugh did not take a photo of the whale. He took a photo of Nat.

"Harry," said Nat. Her voice wasn't coming out right.

It was more like a whisper.

"Paparazzi," she said.

Harry didn't answer.

Nat turned back to the whale. She didn't know what to do. She couldn't exactly jump off the side of the boat and swim to safety.

But she wanted the whale to flip the boat.

She wanted the whale to toss "Hugh" into the water.

The whale started to swim away. Then it slapped its tail again, harder, like it was angry. The wave was so big that the boat nearly tipped again.

Click-click-click, she heard from behind her.

The whale turned back toward them and slapped its front fins, rolling slightly from side to side. A wave sluiced over the edge of the boat, cold and salty and startling. Nat reached over the side and she touched the whale's head. The whale's skin was smooth and cool and rubbery. The whale's gigantic eye stared into Nat's much smaller one. *I love you*, Nat thought.

The whale slowly lowered its eyelid and opened it again.

"That whale winked at me!" Nat said. The skin on the back of her neck was prickling. She knew the camera was there, but she didn't want to think about how it was there. The camera was ruining everything.

She wanted Harry to save her.

She wanted her dad to be there, so he could throw the camera into the water.

But she was on her own.

Harry was still looking away from her. He was following the whale with his eyes.

It seemed to be moving away again, its back making a slow arch in the water.

It felt holy, the slow rise of it and then the disappearing. Spiritual.

Nat had never liked church very much, but suddenly she had the same feeling that she knew she was supposed to get in church.

She felt *connected*.

She held out her hands toward the departing whale.

She closed her eyes.

"I can't believe that happened!" said Harry, swinging around again, his eyes shining. "We didn't bring a camera! Why didn't we bring a camera? Oh, good, Hugh has one!"

He didn't see Hugh for what Hugh was because he was Harry and he didn't know. But Nat still felt furious with him.

"Pose!" said Harry. He put his arm around her and gave Hugh a thumbs-up.

Click-click-click.

"That's a nice camera," said Harry.

"No," Nat shook her head. "He's a—" she started to say, but then suddenly—SUDDENLY—the whale reappeared.

It was swimming fast and upward from below.

Nat could see it, below the surface, the idea of a whale more than the whale itself. It was a blur.

And then it was breaching.

The whale breached all the way out of the water.

Harry made a sound in his throat like gargling. His eyes were wide.

That's weird, Nat thought. *He seems scared.*

The only other time she'd heard the sound Harry just made was when her dad threw the Lion's camera into the waves.

That morning.

Which felt like a lifetime ago.

"I—" Nat didn't have time to finish her sentence.

The whale began to *unbreach*, which was to say, what goes up, must come down. It landed abruptly and directly on top of the boat, all hugeness and slippery rough skin and splinters and sounds and *water water water* everywhere and Nat was screaming "*Ayúdeme!*" and Harry was yelling "Help!" and Hugh was just shouting in general, mostly in Spanish, mostly words that Nat and Harry would probably never be allowed to use.

And then Nat and Hugh and Harry were all in the ocean feeling like they came apart in a million pieces and were glued back together to form themselves again, and their seats weren't flotation devices like on airplanes, they were just wooden benches. They were swimming or treading water or floating and the bits of the boat were all around them, and Nat thought loudly to the whale, *What did you do* that *for?* and the whale didn't say anything back at all.

IN THE WATER

Nat would have thought she'd be more scared.

She was a little bit scared, but she was also calm.

She reached out and touched the skin of the whale, which was still there, still with them. It was like touching a feeling. That feeling was love.

She thought about what the Bird had said, the thing about wanting to know the point.

Love was obviously the point.

"Duh," she said out loud.

"What?" Harry said. He seemed dazed. "Are we going to die?"

Nat shook her head. She wished that she'd been able to reach the Bird this morning. She wished she'd known then the answer to the question "What is the point?"

She would have said, "Thank you for everything. I love you."

She would have said, "Goodbye," and meant it.

Then maybe she wouldn't need the Bird anymore, at least not in the same way.

Anyway, if today had gone as it was meant to go, by the end of it she would know who her *real* mother was.

But today was not going how it was meant to go. Nat kicked her legs in the water. Her jeans felt heavy. Her legs felt too slow.

The whale was swimming around them in tight circles—or as tight as a twenty-foot-long whale could circle—while they clutched broken pieces of the wooden boat. The swimming was creating a whirlpool, which was making it easier for them to float.

Nat didn't want to *die* on her thirteenth birthday.

She thought of all the things that were going to happen next, now that she was thirteen.

She was going to get bigger boobs. She was going to get her period. She was probably going to start having crushes on boys. Maybe she'd even kiss one.

She didn't really want all that stuff. All of it made her want to cry. But she didn't want to *miss* them either.

"We can't die," said Nat, out loud. "It's my birthday." It seemed strange to be talking to Harry normally, their legs kicking to keep them afloat, amid the wreckage of the boat, a paparazzo, and a whale.

"Dude," he said. "I don't think that's how it works." He looked like he was going to cry. "I haven't even had my real life yet. I've just had the hard part. That's not fair."

"Life isn't really fair," Nat said.

"Don't say stuff like that," he said. "Not now."

His sunglasses had fallen off. Nat reached for his hand.

"I'm sorry," she said, and then she leaned as close to him

as she could and kissed him right on the lips. His lips felt like whale skin: smooth and bumpy at the same time.

"Hey!" Harry yelped. He spit in the water. "Gross."

"Sorry," she said, and then she was crying for real, the snotty kind of crying with tears.

"Forget it," said Harry. "I'll just pretend you were giving me CPR."

And then, suddenly, they were both laughing. "I can't laugh and float at the same time," gasped Nat.

Hugh was lying down on a bigger piece of the side of the boat. Nat hoped he was regretting his life choices. Mostly, he was probably regretting dropping the camera. Nat wondered how many expensive cameras were at the bottom of the sea, held down by seaweed and coral, little fish swimming around their useless lenses.

The whale was still making slow circles.

"What is going to happen?" Nat wondered out loud. "Is someone going to rescue us?"

"I think we're going to die," said Harry. "I love you."

"I love you, too," said Nat. "Not in *that* way, though."

"Yeah, I know," he said. "Duh. I didn't mean *that*."

Then suddenly, Nat wasn't floating. She was under the water looking up at the surface, which was like glass flecked with pieces of wood, big and small. She could see that *Harry* was still floating, holding on to a long red board. His feet were above her, and she was sinking and sinking. She felt happy that he was floating. She felt mostly confused about why she was not.

Weird, Nat thought, but she didn't *do* anything about it.

She started to count. Four and a half minutes was the same as two hundred and seventy seconds and she knew she could hold her breath for that long. It was her record. She had two hundred and seventy seconds to figure out how to get back to the surface. She tried kicking her legs but they were really seriously too heavy in her jeans. She kicked off her sneakers. The surface looked really far away. She could see Harry's legs kicking frantically.

It's OK, Harry, she told him telepathically. *Don't panic. Stop kicking.*

Harry stopped kicking.

Nat peeled off her jeans. It was hard. She sank even more. Deeper and deeper. Impossibly deep.

Then Nat was kicking, bare-legged, rising up again, like a whale. She thought she would make it to the surface.

But she couldn't do it.

She couldn't reach it.

Then Hugh was diving toward her. He was reaching for her. She let him grab her hand.

And then—SUDDENLY—the whale was underneath them.

The whale was underneath them, pushing them to the surface.

They were *on* the whale.

It couldn't be true, but it was true.

Sometimes things are like that.

Some things happen that are *unbelievable.*

"Unbelievable" was another perfect English word. If you rearranged some of the letters, Nat realized, you could spell "be alive." Which seemed like a crazy thing to be thinking at that moment, but there it was: *Be alive.*

They burst through the surface, gasping.

The sky was clear of clouds now—blown clean by the

collective breath of all of them, maybe—and relentlessly, postcard-perfect blue. The sun was huge and fierce on her face.

Nat wanted to ask, "Did that really just happen?"

But she knew that it did.

The whale groaned audibly and then sank down again.

That was when Nat saw the other whales.

There were whales all around them.

They were swimming in a huge circle around the remains of the boat, around Harry and Nat, around Hugh.

Hugh had saved her.

Well, she thought.

There were bubbles everywhere.

All three of them were floating on their backs now, clinging to the boards like monkeys, arms and legs wrapped around them. *Stick monkey*, thought Nat. *Monkey umbrellas.* She was strangely sleepy. She closed her eyes and dreamed about a postcard.

Dear Mom, she wrote. *Why didn't you want me? What did I do wrong?*

It's not that I didn't want you, a woman's voice said. *It's that he wanted you more.*

"*Te amo*," Nat said out loud. "You sound like Dad."

Te amo, *you too*, said her mom.

"I can speak Spanish?" Nat said.

"You speak a little bit of everything," said Harry. "Remember? Your weird word collection?"

"I was dreaming," said Nat. She closed her eyes again, but the dream was gone.

"Don't fall asleep!" Harry said. "Then you'll drown! I'm tired, too. But, like, we can't. We'll die."

"Me, too." Nat couldn't feel her arms and legs, but she could see them. "Tired."

Hugh was still muttering.

Harry and Nat were holding hands.

Then Harry and Nat's hands were suddenly not holding each other.

There was red in the water.

The red was blood.

Nat considered fainting. Her vision dimmed, but then it brightened again. She stopped herself. If she fainted, she would drown for sure.

Then, suddenly, between them, rising out of the depths, was the whale.

And a baby.

The whale had had a *baby*.

"Wow," said Nat.

"Look," said Harry, at the same time.

"*Bebé*," mumbled Hugh.

The mother whale was so close that Nat could see the white paper folds of the skin under her chin. She could see her baleen.

Te amo, said the whale in the Bird's voice. *Baleine*.

Then Nat heard a sound like a helicopter. Was it her heart? It was scaring her. It was like a vibration in the water but it was moving her, and then the whales were gone—all of them were gone—and something orange appeared.

Something huge and loud and orange.

The orange thing was a boat.

WHALE EXPERIENCE FACTORY was painted on the side of the boat in big letters. Nat wanted to laugh, but she was too tired, and then she was being scooped out of the water and so were Harry and, she supposed, Hugh, but she was too tired to make sure.

Nat was pretty sure that it was ironic to be rescued by the Whale Experience Factory, though.

She smiled.

CHANGES

Nat woke up the next morning with a stomachache and a headache. It was almost a headache but not quite a headache. It was a feeling that was mirroring the feeling in her stomach. She pictured something gray and fuzzy pushing at her from all directions.

Her room in the house was the same, but it felt completely different from before. Everything looked different. She held up her hand and looked at it.

That looked the same.

"I am still me," she said. "I look like myself."

Nat got up to go to the bathroom. She felt a little dizzy. She used the toilet, same as usual.

"Hola, fish," she said, same as usual. "What's new?"

The fish in the tank swam around behind the plants, avoiding her, same as usual.

"Be that way," Nat told them. "But I would have told you a really good story if you'd wanted to hear it."

Her head was buzzing with everything that had happened. It was so surreal. She suddenly liked the word "surreal." English actually had a lot to offer, if you looked at it closely.

She got off the toilet and went to flush, and then she saw it. Blood.

She sat down. She looked in her underwear.

Definitely blood.

Stars floated down around her.

Her vision tunneled.

"Uh-oh," Nat said. She put her head between her knees so that she wouldn't faint. She had to think. Thinking was hard, because she didn't feel well. What should she do?

She looked in the cabinet under the sink, but there was nothing in there except toilet paper rolls. She took a bunch of toilet paper and folded it and folded it and folded it. Then she put that in her underwear and stood up. She had to deal with this. She didn't have a choice.

Nat went back into her room and put on some clean jeans. It was freezing in there. She felt too hot and too cold at the same time, which was impossible but also true. She remembered kicking off her shoes and jeans under the water. Her heart sneakers were now at the bottom of the sea. She thought about that for a second. It was like poking a bruise, but it hurt less than she would have thought. She could get new sneakers. She could draw hearts on them. But maybe she wouldn't. Maybe she could ask Harry to draw orcas.

"Tattorca," she said out loud, and she laughed.

The tattorca seemed like forever ago. Like it happened in a completely different life.

Nat picked up the phone from the desk. She pressed it against her cheek. It felt cool and solid. She looked at the display: 9:19 a.m., it said. There was a picture of a sun. For some reason, the sun had a smiley face on it. She'd never noticed that before. She flipped the phone open and closed a few times. It made a satisfying *snap snap snap* sound.

She sat down on the unmade bed. She dialed the Bird's number.

"Hello?"

"Where *were* you yesterday?" said Nat. "I was calling!"

"Who is this?"

"Who is *this*?"

"Who is this? Oh! I know who you are. You're the prank caller, right?"

"You aren't the Bird," said Nat. Her voice sounded funny. Maybe it was just the echo in this big room.

"Is that what you call her? The Bird? That's so . . . well, it's so accurate. She did look like a bird, didn't she?"

"Did she?" said Nat. There was something in her stomach that was hard as a rock. It hurt so badly. Something terrible was happening inside her. It wasn't just her period. It was something else. Something more terrible than she had ever imagined.

"Hang on, Prank Caller. She left a letter. She wanted me to read it to you."

"OK," said Nat. She tried to rearrange the person's voice so they were not saying what she knew they were saying. "Something has happened to the Bird," she whispered to the origami bra frog that was on her bedside table. "I think the Bird is dead."

"Are you still there?" said the voice.

"Yes," said Nat, although she wondered if it were true.

She felt like she was floating upward, separating into layers.

She felt like she was on the ceiling looking down at herself, cross-legged on the bed, talking on the phone.

"OK, I'm just going to read it." The person cleared her throat. "Sorry, I'm a bit emotional. I don't want to cry."

"It's OK," said Nat.

"I'm reading it now. This is what it says." The person took a big breath in and let it out. It sounded like a gust of wind. "'Dear one,'" she read. Her voice was as wavy as the sea. "'I've been meaning to tell you that I think we put so much importance on mothers because mothers are our first loves. But they aren't everything. You love your father. I loved my father, too. And then I loved my stepmother. And I love my own daughter. I said I'd tell you which situation was worse, yours or mine, and then I realized that both of them were the same and neither of them were terrible. They just shone a light on . . .'" The woman's voice cracked. "I'm sorry," she said. "She was my mom."

"*I'm* sorry," said Nat. She was crying, too, but the eye-leaking kind of crying, not the noisy kind.

"I'll read the end, I just have to . . ." Nat heard the person blowing her nose. "'They just shone a light on love for us. They made us look for it more and better than we would have if it had just been handed to us. That's what I think, anyway. Thank you for prank calling me. I love you. Goodbye, little Baleine.'"

The voice pronounced *Baleine* wrong.

Maybe no one would ever get it right again.

"Oh no," said Nat. She was still on the ceiling. She was on the ceiling but she could feel her heart beating in her body. It was beating really hard. Her face was soaking wet. "Thank you. I'm really sorry about your mom." She swallowed. She watched herself lie back on the pillows. "She was great. She was the best. She was . . ." Nat didn't know what to say. "The Bird," she finished. "She was *my* Bird."

"Me, too," said the woman. "I'm sorry, too. But she was sick for a long time. She'd been really sick. She had been in bed for a year. A whole year. Can you imagine?"

Nat *could* imagine. Nat imagined the Bird, lying on a perfectly made bed, her ankles crossed, her phone beside her. She imagined the Bird looking out the window while she spoke to Nat, while she made everything OK for Nat, every time she called.

"Peanut butter sandwich," Nat said, desperately.

Then she pressed the "end" button on the phone.

It was too late to ask what the Bird's name was.

It was too late to know who she really was.

Nat felt something terrible. That something was anger.

How dare the Bird leave without saying goodbye? She wouldn't do that! But she *did* do that. How could she not tell Nat she was dying? How could she let Nat believe that she'd just always be there for her, on the other end of the phone? How could she die without knowing what happened to Nat and Harry with the whale?

But maybe, Nat thought, *the whale was the Bird, coming to say goodbye.*

She liked that idea, so she decided to keep it.

Nat wasn't sure she understood the love parts of what the Bird had said in her note, so she quickly wrote down the words she remembered so she could look at it later.

Missing mothers make us look harder for love, she wrote. Then she crossed out *harder* and changed it to *better*. She remembered the *better*.

Then she also remembered that she was bleeding.

"This is so *complicated*," Nat said.

QUINCEAÑERA

Nat had two choices.

Her choices were Harry. Or her dad.

Would Harry want to talk about periods?

She was pretty sure not.

On the other hand, she'd rather die than talk to her dad again about periods.

But her dad could drive.

And she *had* to go to the store.

And the last thing Harry wanted to talk about, she knew, was *girl* stuff.

"This is not that complicated," she said out loud. "I can do this." She wasn't really sure what she meant by "this," but whatever it was, she could handle it.

After the previous day, she could handle anything.

Nothing felt quite right. It was all like a dream. A terrible dream in which the Bird was dead. Her heart shuffled strangely.

Do not think about that right now, she told herself firmly. *Just don't.*

Nat went to put on her shoes, but they weren't there. They were at the bottom of the ocean. "Surreal," she said out loud. "Surreal" was a word that made her think of seals and of round rubber inner tubes floating in the current.

She stepped out into the hallway barefoot. "DAD!" she yelled. "I need a ride to the SUPERMARKET MERCADO!"

"Where are you going?" said Harry, popping his head out of his door. "I want to come, too. Do you feel terrible? I feel *terrible*. Like I have the flu."

"You don't have the flu," said Nat. "You just have an I-almost-died-but-didn't feeling. It's good, not bad."

"Why are you so happy?"

"I'm not happy. I'm sad. I just found out that . . . and I got . . . Never mind. I'm not just one thing. People can be more than one thing, you know."

"Can you get me some Fruity Pebbles?" he said. "If you won't let me come?"

"Sure," said Nat. "Whatever."

"Sheesh," he said. Then, under his breath, "Testy."

"I am not!" said Nat. "I'm happy, sad, and testy, all at once."

"Crazy," he mouthed.

"What?" said Nat, and laughed.

Harry laughed, too.

"Bye then," he said. "*Hasta la vista.*"

"*Hasta la vista* yourself," she said.

"What's the emergency?" said her dad, appearing at the bottom of the stairs. He bounded up them two at a time. "Man, I'm glad you two are alive. Come here." He lifted them both straight off the ground in a hug. He smelled terrible, like armpit sweat. He must have found a gym, or created one. It didn't matter where they were, he could find a way to work out. He was probably bench-pressing the furniture. Doing chin-ups on the plumbing. Carrying Mr. Brasch up and down the hill while doing lunges. Nat giggled.

"I love you, Dad," she said.

"Yeah, you DO!" he shouted.

"Put me down!" yelled Harry.

"*Dad*," said Nat, remembering. She wriggled free. "No time for this. We have to go to the store. It's an emergency."

Then she winked.

"Ohhhh," said her dad. "I like mysteries. Can we guess?" He was still holding Harry. It looked weird, like Santa carrying an elf. Like you knew it was *possible*, you just couldn't imagine why it would ever happen.

"Put him down, Dad!" Nat said. "*Don't* guess. I mean, it's private. *Really* private."

"What could be so private that you can't tell your dad and your bestie?"

"*Dad.*"

"You tell us everything, right?" Nat's dad put Harry down and then gave him a fist bump. "My man," he said.

"It's a girl thing," said Nat. She gave him a look. *YOU KNOW WHAT I MEAN*, she shouted telepathically.

She watched her dad receive her message. His eyes shut and then opened and then shut again.

"Dad," she said. "Stop blinking."

"Natters! Is it? Did you? Are you?"

"*Dad*," she said.

"I'm getting the keys," he said.

WHERE THE ROAD CURVED closer to the sea, Nat could see the surf curling in, the water blue and perfect and calm, like nothing dramatic had ever happened there, like it had already forgotten the day before.

Did the sea remember things?

Was that how it worked?

The whale would remember—she was sure of that.

"A lot of opposite things can happen at the same time," she said to her dad. He'd probably get it.

"Yep yep," he said. "Coexistence of Opposites. That's a thing. Man, that would be a great title for something. Maybe a song."

"Sure," Nat agreed.

Her dad looked over at her and smiled his too-toothy smile.

"So many teeth!" she said.

There was a song playing on the radio. It was Gracie.

"Whoa," said her dad. "What is *this*? It's fantastic!" He started thumping the wheel in time to the music. "I *love* this song!"

"Dad!" said Nat. "It's Gracie. Solly's mom."

"It is? Man, she's really good! I love this! *Good* for her!"

"It's OK, I guess," said Nat. She couldn't explain how the song made her think about the Cigarette Incident. She didn't want to say that now that Solly and her mom weren't desperate for money anymore, maybe they wouldn't sell photo ops to paparazzi. She sort of wanted to scream. Instead, she just reached over and turned it off.

"Hey!" said her dad. But then he seemed to remember. "Nah," he said. "You know what? It's not *that* great."

"Nope nope," said Nat.

"I'm really proud of you," he added. "Is that the right thing to say? Congratulations? Should we have a cake?"

"We had a cake yesterday! Please don't make this a big deal. Just, *shhhh*."

"Want me to come in with you?"

"Dad! No! I'll do it."

They were nearly at the turnoff for the SUPERMARKET MERCADO when Nat spotted a dog lying on the side of the road. She knew before she really understood what she was seeing. "TUFTY!" she screamed. "Dad! Stop! Someone has run over Tufty!"

"That dog from yesterday? Again?" he said. "That dog has a death wish!"

But he slammed on the brakes, and even before the car stopped, Nat was opening the door and getting out. "Tufty!" she yelled. "Tufty!"

"This is like déjà vu," her dad was saying. "How many times can this dog get run over?"

The dust was stinging Nat's eyes. *Don't you dare be dead*, she said, using telepathy. She flat-out couldn't handle anyone else being dead, even though the Bird being dead felt mostly like a dream.

The Bird wasn't anything but a voice, she thought. But that wasn't true. The Bird was so much more than that.

She was a mom.

She just wasn't Nat's mom.

Nat heard a whimper and then she was on her knees, gathering the dog into her arms. He was all fur and bones. He licked her hand frantically.

"OMG!" she said. "He's hurt this time! He's really hurt, Dad!"

She stood up, still holding tightly to the dog. He was loose and floppy in her arms.

"Oh man." Nat's dad was beside her now. "Poor little guy."

He gently lifted the dog from Nat's arms. In her dad's gigantic hands, Tufty looked tiny, like a toy. "Don't hurt him, Dad!"

"I'm not hurting him." He lifted the dog closer to his face and whispered something into his ear. Tufty tilted his head to the side, as though he were listening. Then he made a small yipping sound.

"See?" said her dad. "He's not dead. He's not even dying."

He whispered something else. Then he raised his eyebrow at Nat. "You didn't know I was the dog whisperer, did you? I might be your dad, but there's lots of stuff about me that you don't know."

He put the dog carefully down on the road. Tufty sneezed once, twice, three times. He shook himself vigorously, like her dad emerging from the surf.

Tufty barked and ran off up the hill.

"Aw," said Nat. "I hoped we could keep him."

"We don't do pets, remember? We're minimalists! We want to be able to fly away on a moment's notice! We might need to go to Peru! Or New Zealand! Or Detroit!"

Nat laughed. "I know, I know. Forget it. But you have to teach me how to be a dog whisperer, too."

"Oh, you already know." He made a gesture with his fingers, pointing at her, then at his own eyes. "I see you."

Nat grinned.

"To the SUPERMARKET MERCADO?" he said.

"To the SUPERMARKET MERCADO," she agreed.

It already felt like a hundred years since she rode the green bike to the SUPERMARKET MERCADO with Harry. She was a different person then. She was a person who rode a tiny green bike and had never kissed a boy and didn't have her period and hadn't been nearly drowned in the Sea of Cortez and hadn't forgiven Solly and hadn't lost one Bird (Mom) and maybe found (one day) another.

"Wait here," Nat said. She got out.

Things were feeling less than good, down there. She needed something, stat. She took a deep breath in and held it.

Nat counted to twenty-nine before she got to the door. She pushed it open. The cold air rushed over her like water.

The bored-looking girl was behind the counter. She was still reading, but it was a different book. "Air-conditioner is fixed," she said. She was wearing another *Imagine Unicorns* shirt. This one was neon green. The unicorn had one rainbow-colored eye.

Nat cleared her throat.

The girl looked up. She raised her eyebrows.

"Um, do you sell . . ." Nat started. Then she stopped.

The girl looked back at her book.

Nat opened her mouth and then closed it again. Why was it so hard to say "pads" out loud? Or "tampons"? Not that she thought she wanted to try those. She definitely didn't feel ready for that. "I like your shirt," she said instead.

The cashier looked down at her shirt. "Oh, hey, thanks. It's my band," she said. "I play the guitar."

"Cool," said Nat. "I like guitars. I don't play one though."

"Uh-huh," said the girl. She looked down at her book, then back at Nat. She sighed. "Are you *sure* I can't help you find something?"

"I . . ." started Nat. Then she burst into tears. The tears surprised even her. She didn't know why she was crying. "The Bird died!" she said.

"What bird?" said the girl. She put the book down on the counter. She came around the counter to where Nat was standing and patted her awkwardly on the shoulder. "Are you OK?"

"Not a bird," said Nat. "A person named the Bird. And that's not even her name! I don't even know her name! And then the whale had a baby!" She was crying really hard now. It was embarrassing, but she couldn't stop.

"Oh, that was *you*! I heard about that," said the girl. "Boy, you must have a really weird life."

"It's pretty weird," said Nat. "But that was extra bad. And then I got my period!" She was crying so hard now, she could hardly get the words out.

"What?" said the cashier. "You need to calm down, girl. Your dad is XAN GALLAGHER? He was so *amazing* in that earthquake movie."

Nat nodded and shrugged at the same time. She couldn't answer, because she was crying. She tried hard to swallow. Of course the cashier loved her dad. *Everyone* loved her dad. But she didn't want to talk about her dad.

She needed help. She wanted the girl to help her.

"Help," she whispered. "*Ayúdeme.*"

"What?" said the girl. "Hang on." She had picked up her phone. She was texting someone. Nat knew she was probably texting her friends about XAN GALLAGHER. She wiped her nose on her arm. That was gross, because her T-shirt didn't have long sleeves. She hid her arm behind her back. She tried to take a deep breath, to get control of herself. When that didn't work, she tried holding her breath instead. She knew she could hold her breath for at least two hundred and seventy seconds. She started to count.

The cashier kept typing.

By the time Nat got to two hundred and six, she had stopped needing to cry so much. She stood up straighter. "I've got my period," she said.

The girl looked up. "So?" she said.

"It's my first one and I don't have anything. I need to buy something. I need . . ." She stopped. She had almost said, "I need my mom," which was also true.

The girl stared at her. She tapped her perfect nails on the cash register. "Oh," she said. She shrugged her shoulders, like she was giving up on something, and put down her phone. "First time, huh."

"First time," said Nat.

"We have stuff," said the cashier. "I can show you. Are you by yourself?"

Nat nodded.

"Aw," said the girl.

"My dad is in the car," said Nat, just so the girl didn't feel sorry for her.

Nat had to swallow again. The lump in her throat felt permanent.

"Come with me," said the girl. "I'll show you. I'm María, by the way."

"Nat," said Nat. "Natalia."

"Nice to meet you, Natalia," said María. She reached out and shook Nat's hand. "How old are you, anyway?"

"I'm thirteen," said Nat. "I'm a late bloomer."

María laughed. "I was fourteen!" she said. "You aren't

late. Everyone is different. Maybe those other people are just too early. Where's your mama? Why isn't she helping you?"

"Oh," said Nat. "I don't really have one."

"Ah, I think I read about that somewhere! Your dad got full custody of you because Melina Martinez, well, everyone knows that she's—"

"Don't tell me!" Nat held up her hand.

Melina Martinez?

Melina Martinez was an actress.

She was not French.

She was not a makeup artist.

She was the woman in the magazine. Nat closed her eyes, and she could still see the image. The black hair. The sunglasses. *Duh*, she thought.

Something inside Nat collapsed, like a sand castle being disintegrated by a rising tide. She held on to her stomach, just to have something to hold on to. She bent over. The tears were leaking again. "I don't know her," she managed.

"Are you OK? Do you have cramps?"

"I guess," said Nat.

"Cramps are the worst. You need a hot water bottle. You need to go lie down."

"I will," said Nat, still bending over.

"How can you not know your own mother?" said María.

"I just don't," said Nat. "Everyone is different. Some people have mothers. I have a dad."

"You have XAN GALLAGHER! You are SO lucky."

"I'm lucky," said Nat. "He's great." She thought about Harry's parents. "Maybe everyone gets one good parent."

"My parents are OK," María said. "Both of them."

"Maybe you're just super lucky?"

"Yeah, maybe." María had stopped walking. They were in aisle seven. There were rows and rows of deodorant and razors. There were shelves of "feminine hygiene products." There were so many of them. Nat felt light-headed.

María reached up to the shelf and she got down a package. It had little flowers all over it and it was pink. She rolled her eyes. "I know, right? Nothing says 'bleeding from your uterus' like a few pink flowers, right? So dumb. Probably designed by a man." She laughed.

Nat tried to smile. The packaging looked the same as the ones Nat had seen at home. She was relieved. She didn't think she wanted to deal with vintage period supplies. Vintage cereal was one thing, but vintage maxi pads? No, thanks. She had read *Are You There God? It's Me, Margaret.* All of *that* sounded terrible, with pins and belts.

Thank goodness for technology, she thought.

"Are you OK?" said María.

"Not really. Sort of. My stomach hurts," confessed Nat.

"It's not really so much fun," said María. She smiled. "But you're a woman now!" She handed Nat the package of pads. "Go into the bathroom here, OK? You just stick it in your underwear. It's easy."

"I can figure it out," said Nat. "Thanks."

Nat went into the bathroom and closed the door behind her. Then she clicked the lock into place. In the mirror, she was herself, but pale, or at least her version of pale. She never really got pale-pale. Still, her freckles were standing out like constellations. Her hair was a mess.

Melina Martinez, she mouthed to herself. *Melina Martinez is my mother.*

Of course, she *knew* that.

She already knew that.

She must have recognized her from the picture. Melina was recognizable.

Nat had even met her once at a party at the director's house the year before. She remembered it because Melina had called her dad "Alex."

No one called her dad "Alex" except for Grandma Gallagher. Nat's heart made a solid *click* of recognition, with the certainty of a padlock snapping shut. "Melina Martinez is my mother," she repeated out loud.

She tried to figure out what she was feeling, but she couldn't. It wasn't even a feeling without an English word. It was just no feeling at all.

She felt nothing.

Melina seemed like an OK sort of normal person.

But she obviously *wasn't* a normal person.

She was a person who left her baby with XAN GALLAGHER.

She was a person who could later be at a party with *that very baby* and not say to that baby, "I am your mother."

Or, "I'm sorry."

Or anything.

Nothing that Nat could remember, anyway.

Nat looked in the mirror again, then she slowly raised her middle finger. That was for Melina Martinez.

Nat opened the package of pads and replaced the toilet tissue with a real pad. It had wings that she folded down over the sides of her underwear. When she pulled her pants up again, it felt fine. The pad was so thin, like paper. It was thinner than the wad of toilet paper.

Then Nat realized she had forgotten to bring money.

She'd have to go to the car and ask her dad. She hoped María didn't think she was trying to steal the pads. Maybe she should just leave the rest of the package behind.

But she'd need them.

"Duh," she said out loud.

She went back out to the front of the store. "I just have to get money from my dad. He's in the car," she told María.

María smiled. She seemed so much nicer now than she'd seemed before. "Nah, it's a present from me to you. OK? I also want to give you this." She handed Nat a box of tea and a huge bar of chocolate. The tea was peppermint.

"What's this for?" Nat said.

"I just like peppermint tea for my cramps," she said. "And chocolate. Well, chocolate is always good, right?"

"Right," said Nat. "Thank you." She couldn't explain about the sugar and how she didn't like it. Maybe it would be OK this time. With the peppermint tea, it might almost be like mint chocolate chip ice cream.

María walked around the counter and gave Nat an awkward hug. "I am happy for you," she said. "Congratulations."

"I don't think *I'm* happy for me. But thanks. Thanks for being nice to me."

"Why not?" asked María. "Why aren't you happy?"

"I'm just . . . I don't know. I just don't feel like . . . I can't explain." Nat swallowed. She didn't want to cry again. "Anyway, thanks."

"You're welcome," said María. "Tell your boyfriend hi." She winked. "Tell him that cereal isn't old—the packaging is just different because of marketing. It's different in different countries."

"He's not my boyfriend!" said Nat. She thought about

explaining but it seemed too complicated. Or maybe it wasn't complicated at all. "He's my *best* friend, actually."

"Good. It is good to have cute boys as best friends. You have your period now. Your dad is XAN GALLAGHER. You have a cute boy friend. You have lots to be happy about, right?"

Nat shrugged. "*Saudade*," she mouthed.

"What?" said María. "I didn't hear you."

Nat *really* wanted to tell María.

To explain it to someone.

Anyone. So that it would make sense to her, too.

But it was hard. "I sort of feel like I'm not really . . . ready," Nat whispered, finally. She couldn't understand why she was still standing there. Her arms were covered with goose bumps. It was really cold in the store. The car would be warm. Her dad would understand all of this better than this stranger in a grocery store! But she kept standing there.

"Ready for what?"

Nat looked down at her feet. They were bare.

"Ready to be, you know, a *woman*."

"Why do you have bare feet?" said María.

"Oh, um, I lost my shoes. Yesterday. When . . ." She made a gesture with her hand that she hoped meant "a whale sank the boat," because the words had left her.

María laughed. "You need shoes!" She went over to a rack near the postcards at the front of the store. It was covered in flip-flops. "These are all the same size," she said. "Stupid. Too big for you, but you can have them, OK?"

"Thanks," said Nat. She took the flip-flops from María

and tried to pull them apart. They were attached with a plastic tag. María reached over and snipped it with scissors.

Nat put the flip-flops on. They were huge and silver. She smiled.

María patted the counter next to her. "Sit," she said.

Nat hoisted herself up and sat, holding the flip-flops on her feet by curling her toes. María sat next to her. Their backs were to the door. Nat could see a whole pile of books under the counter. María must read a lot.

"You're thirteen, right?"

"Yes."

"OK, here is the thing, Natalia. In Mexico, we have a celebration, it is called *quinceañera*. Do you know what that is?"

Nat shook her head. "No."

"It is when you turn fifteen years old. You go to church and there is a big Mass, and then there is a huge party. You get to wear an amazing dress. People spend so much money on their *quinceañera* dress! It is as big as a *piñata*! It is crazy, but also it is so much fun. Anyway, this party, this *quinceañera*, it is to celebrate when you go from being a *niña*, like a child, to being a *señorita*! Which is a woman, but like a young woman. You have two whole years more of being a *niña*!" She looked seriously at Nat. "Do you think you'll be ready in two years to be a *señorita*?"

Nat nodded. "Two years sounds like a long time. Long enough."

María smiled. "It *is* a long time."

"I have to go!" Nat said, suddenly. "My dad is in the car!"

"Go!" said María. "And Natalia?"

"Yes?"

"You're welcome."

"Oh," said Nat. "Sorry. I mean, thank you."

María picked up her book. She held up her hand. "Bye, *niña*," she said.

"Bye, *señorita*," said Nat. She stood by the door, waiting for something more, but María was already reading again, she was already done with Nat.

"Melina Martinez," Nat murmured. "Melina Martinez is my mother." The more she said it out loud, the less strange it seemed.

"I thought you were leaving," said María.

"Bye," said Nat. "I mean, I am. I'm leaving now. Thank you."

"You already said that."

"I'm saying it twice," said Nat, pushing the door. "Three times, even. THANK YOU!" she shouted, over her shoulder.

"BYE," said María. "Seriously. Bye."

The door closed behind Nat. A wave of heat washed over her. She had the pads clutched in her hand. She sort of wished she'd asked for a bag, but bags killed turtles, so it was better this way. She walked over to the car. Her dad was doing his favorite two-thumbs-up hand gesture, which involved his thumbs and his nostrils in a way he found hysterically funny. He had done it at the end of the movie *Hyper Max*, a comedy in which he'd had to join a cheerleading squad. It was one of her absolute favorite movies of his, but at the end, when he'd done *that*, Nat had felt some pretty extreme *myötähäpea*.

"*Why* did you do that?" she'd asked. "You look crazy! My friends might see that!"

He'd tipped his head back and roared with laughter. "Because it was the end!" he'd said, like that was obvious.

Maybe this was it, then.

Maybe this was the end of *this* movie, the movie that was her life *before*.

And the start of the movie that was her life *after*.

HARRY

Harry kept looping through what had happened the day before in his head. He couldn't stop. It just kept starting over. Every time he tried to shake the image from his mind, he could see the whale's huge eye staring at him again, and then the boat in pieces all around him, and then the baby whale, and then Nat's face, sinking into the sea, and then the giant orange boat coming to save them.

He couldn't believe it had happened.

He couldn't believe they didn't die.

He mostly couldn't believe what happened afterward, which was that his dad had hugged him. He had hugged him so hard that Harry thought his ribs might break. He had said, "Harry," in a muffled but clear-enough way into Harry's hair.

Actually, it sounded more like "Hair," but at least it wasn't "Harriet." His dad had stopped before the end.

Harry didn't remember his dad hugging him ever before.

At least, he hadn't done any hugging since Harry had declared his Harry-ness. Definitely not since then.

It felt like a miracle.

All of it.

The whales.

The boat.

Mexico.

And his dad finally saying his name. (Sort of.)

For the first time in a very long time, Harry didn't feel like he should be writing something down. He didn't feel like he should be explaining something to the whole world. He didn't feel responsible for that.

What he felt like doing was learning how to surf.

He looked out the window and there was Nat's dad, XAN GALLAGHER himself, playing a ukulele in the hammock, swinging back and forth, singing with his whole body. Harry laughed. He had never known anyone like XAN GALLAGHER.

He felt lucky.

Quickly, he got changed into his swimsuit. He was going to go down there and ask. He was going to say, "Hey, Xan, what would you say to teaching me how to surf?"

His dad would let him, he was sure of it. His dad would think that was rad.

At least, Harry hoped he would.

THE END OF THE STORY

Up in her room, Nat sat down at the desk for the hundredth time and probably also the last time.

The trip was ending.

This was the last day.

There was a letter that she wanted to write. She just didn't know how to write it. She didn't even know *why* she wanted to write it. She was a postcard person. She wasn't a letter person. Letters were Solly's thing.

Nat thought about the postcard to Solly. It must have gotten ruined, sunk into the sea, along with her jeans that she was wearing the day before. Maybe that was OK.

Maybe it had been for her, and not for Solly at all.

Maybe Solly didn't deserve to know she'd been forgiven. The forgiveness could be a quiet thing that was just for Nat.

Solly probably didn't care. She was rich again. She'd have her own paparazzi. She'd have her own story. She wouldn't need Nat to make herself feel more important.

Nat took a deep breath. She felt fine. She felt good, even. María had been totally right about the peppermint tea.

Nat opened the desk drawer. There was a lot of paper in there, like the owners of this house had anticipated that their guests would be writers-of-letters. She chose a piece of paper and, using her best writing—which was nowhere near as nice as Solly's best—she began to write.

Dear Melina Martinez, she wrote. *I forgive you.*

My name is Natalia Rose Baleine Gallagher, and I am your daughter.

She stopped writing. She wanted to ask about the name Baleine. Why would Melina Martinez, who was American, give her daughter a French name?

That wasn't her main question though. The main one was too hard to ask.

She picked up the pen and spun it between her fingers. Then she put it back down.

"Why did you leave?" she asked, out loud.

She knew she could Google this answer, that someone somewhere would have asked Melina Martinez this question, that she had probably answered it a million times. Maybe her answer even made sense. It probably did. If it didn't, people would hate her, and she wasn't hated, she was famous.

Not for the first time, Nat felt strange to be herself, to be someone who could Google answers to huge personal questions and get answers, right there on the Internet for anyone who wanted to read them to find.

She decided not to ask the question. Her dad said sometimes the better way to get to know people was to give them information about yourself. They would find the questions in your story. She began writing again:

I got my period today. It is the day after my thirteenth birthday. Yesterday, I saw a baby whale being born. The mother whale was right there. She did not swim away.

Nat started to cry. This was harder than she'd thought it would be. Why would a whale stay when a human could leave? A whale would never leave.

She thought about the baby harbor seal.

Some people are whales, she wrote. *Some people are seals.*

She knew Melina Martinez wouldn't know what that meant, that she'd be confused. But maybe that was fair. It was her turn to be confused. It was her turn to feel *something.* Nat had been feeling all of the feelings for thirteen years.

Dad is a whale, she wrote. *Dad is the most majestic of all the whales.*

Nat remembered the Bird telling her once about a whale who was the last of his species. He was called the 52-hertz whale because he sang a song in 52 hertz, which was not the same frequency that was used by any other known whale. She sometimes wondered if her dad was a bit like that 52-hertz whale. He had *her*, Nat, but that was different, because she was his daughter. As far as she knew, he had not had a girlfriend since her mother, Melina Martinez. And Melina Martinez was the wrong kind of whale.

She wasn't a whale at all.

Nat left the part out where she could have written that Melina Martinez was clearly a seal. That was implied.

"Dum-dum," Nat said out loud. That was mean, but she didn't care. Mostly she just felt sad that maybe her dad was the only whale of his kind, singing away at 52 hertz.

She signed her name at the bottom of the page.

She left out the *Baleine.*

Natalia Rose Gallagher, she wrote, in her best writing ever.

Then she folded the letter into the shape of a bird. She made it fly across the desk. It landed awkwardly on the floor. She picked it up.

She put the bird into an envelope. She didn't know what address to write on it. Her dad would know. She'd ask him later.

Maybe not here in Mexico. Maybe at home.

Maybe never.

Maybe it didn't even matter.

Through the window, Nat could see Harry and her dad making their way across the beach to the water. Harry was weaving around a bit under the weight of a surfboard. Nat smiled.

Cute, she thought.

Complicated, she thought.

Nat got up and slipped on the flip-flops. Her heart-faced sneakers were gone forever. That was sad. But it was like so much sad stuff and happy stuff and big stuff and infuriating stuff and great stuff had all happened at once, and all those feelings negated the other ones and left her feeling maybe even the tiniest bit blank.

The flip-flops were ridiculously loose but they slapped the bottom of her feet in a good way. She flip-flopped down the stairs and out the door. Mr. and Mrs. Brasch were sitting on the patio, each reading their own book. Mrs. Brasch looked up. "Are you wearing sunscreen?" she said. "The sun is extra hot today!"

"Yes," lied Nat.

She flip-flopped past the Brasches and past the palm tree and down the slope. The beach was deserted.

The sand was burning her feet.

"*Hanyauku*," she mouthed.

She still loved that word and the shape it made on her tongue.

Nat walked all the way to the water's edge—the tide was way way way out—and she waved to Harry and her dad. The waves lapped softly over her feet, cooling them instantly, and then rolled back out to sea. In one curling wave, she saw a jellyfish with long red tentacles. A crab scuttled over her toes. Her dad shouted something that she didn't hear. She could see his grin though. He fist-bumped the air.

The sun was ferocious on her skin.

Her hair was a black-cat hot again. "What?" she yelled.

Her dad was really gesturing now.

Nat looked out to sea.

There, in the distance, was the huge splash of a whale breaching.

"Whale!" she shouted. "Hello! Hi! Wow! Thank you!"

She felt the prickling on the back of her neck.

Not again, she thought.

She kept her eye on the whale. It looked like a humpback whale. Maybe it was the same humpback whale, come to say goodbye.

The mother.

Maybe the baby was there, too. Of course it was. Whale mothers didn't leave.

It must be just too small to see from here.

"Goodbye!" she called to it. "Goodbye, whale." Then, to herself, "Goodbye, Mom." She wasn't sure what she meant. It was goodbye to the Bird. It was goodbye to the French, whale-loving makeup artist who didn't even exist.

"Goodbye," she said. She traced her silver flip-flop through the sand in a half circle. She blinked so that her eyes didn't start leaking again.

Her dad and Harry disappeared into a wave.

Nat felt the prickle on her neck again, but this time it went all the way down her spine. She could feel her own heartbeat.

"*Tante*," she said out loud. *Tante* was a Chinese word for when you were super anxious and you could hear your own pulse. She *definitely* had that. Right then. At that exact second.

She wished Harry would come back to shore.

She wished her dad would come back to shore.

Click-click-click, Nat heard.

She turned around in slow motion. She felt like she was dreaming, and it was a bad dream and she couldn't wake herself up from it. She sat down, even though it meant that she was sitting on wet sand. The foamy waves surged around her, soaking her, and then tried to pull her out to sea. She felt her body being lifted a tiny bit and then placed back down by the water.

The person holding the camera was walking toward her.

"Hey Nat," he said. "It's me."

The sun was behind the person, so at first she didn't recognize the Lion.

Then she did.

She thought about all the things she could say.

The Lion was wearing flip-flops, too. He shifted from foot to foot. "The sand is so freakin' hot," he said.

"*Hanyauku*," Nat said.

"Yeah, bless you," he said. In the distance, a dog barked.

The barking got closer. And closer.

Tufty! said Nat, telepathically. *Bite him.*

Tufty growled low in his throat. Then he launched himself at the Lion's leg.

"Get your stupid dog off me!"

Nat shook her head.

The Lion ran into the water. "I hate dogs."

"They don't seem to like you much either," Nat muttered.

"I can't hear you," said the Lion.

"I said, 'MY DAD IS GOING TO KILL YOU,'" she said.

"I hear you were on a boat that sank yesterday," the Lion said. He was knee-deep in the water. Every wave that landed looked like it was going to knock him sideways. Him and his expensive camera.

Karma, Nat thought.

"I thought that Hugh was a friend of mine. I don't know what he was thinking. Everyone knows you guys are mine."

Nat made a sound that wasn't a sound. She rolled her eyes.

"Aw, come on, kid," he said. "Your dad used to be nice to me. He was always hugging me and stuff. We're on the same side. We're all making money, right? How about we do a trade. I have something you want. And you have something I want. So can we trade?"

"You don't have anything I want," said Nat.

Tufty pressed his body into Nat's legs. She picked the dog up and buried her nose in the fur on his head, which was wet.

"That dog looks like he has fleas," said the Lion. He lifted his camera and aimed.

"Don't!" said Nat.

"Sorry, kid." He clicked the shutter. "Just one. So are we on?"

"No," she said. "You don't have anything I want, and what happened is private."

He laughed. "Not much," he said. "Your dad doesn't get that right, you know. The right to be private. No way. He's famous. Price you pay and all that. Besides, it's already up on the site. But if I get your side of it, then we'll have a story. Human interest. Your dad let you go out without life jackets? Child Protective Services might be interested in that. You can make it better for him."

"My dad is a good dad. You can write that down."

"He's got a temper. Did you see what he did to my camera? You ever feel scared? Remember at the maze last year?"

"He's a *great* dad."

"Ever wonder why your mom left?" he said. "Ever think about that?"

"Stop talking to me. Please stop, you . . . you . . . you . . . little Lion man."

"Melina Martinez," he said, drawing her name out slowly. "She's a strange one. But I got her info for you. Her address. You could just go there. Show up at her house. Get to know her. You two can compare notes about XAN THE MAN." He thrust a piece of paper into her hand. Tufty growled and snapped at his fingers.

There was a word in Nat's collection from Papua New Guinea. They spoke a language called Kivila. The word was *mokita.*

Mokita is a secret that everyone knows but have implicitly agreed not to talk about.

"*Mokita,*" she said.

"What?" said the Lion.

Nat scrunched the paper into the smallest ball she could. She threw it at the Lion, who caught it reflexively.

"I don't want this," he said. "It's our deal."

"We don't have a deal," said Nat.

"Hey!" Nat heard from a million miles away. "HEY!"

Nat looked up and saw her dad running out of the surf. A surfboard was attached to his ankle and was bouncing after him. Harry was following behind. He was hugging his own board and stumbling in the waves a little. Her dad made it look so easy. Harry, not so much. He tripped and fell down, then bobbed back up again. The Lion lifted his camera and fired off a few shots. Nat could already imagine what they would look like: her dad angrily running at the Lion.

The Lion was running now, too.

The Lion was running away.

Tufty was chasing after him, barking.

Nat's dad lifted her in a huge hug. "You're all wet!" she said. "Put me down!"

"You're all wet, too," he said. "Now." He spun her around and around. She could see the sea, the sky, the house, the dog, Harry, everything.

"I'm going to throw up!" she said. "Put me down."

"Say it!"

"Fine!" she said. "I love you!"

"Yeah, you do," he said, and he put her down.

"Yep yep," she said.

"What did he say to you? You think you know a person. Man, I thought he'd leave us alone, finally. I thought he got it."

Nat shrugged. "Everyone isn't ever all one thing," she reminded him. "But I kind of think he's all bad."

Harry and XAN GALLAGHER headed back toward the water. "One more wave!" Harry called back to her.

"Sure," Nat said. She squinted up at the house. It looked

like the Brasches were still sitting there, reading. Like they lived in their own protected bubble where they didn't have to think about things outside of the bubble. The bubble protected them from complications.

Nat didn't want to be someone who was in a bubble. She didn't like complications, but she wanted to understand them. Once you understood them, they weren't complications anymore. They were just life.

The sun was sinking lower in the sky, and the waves were dying down.

It sure is beautiful, Nat thought. *Like being inside a postcard.*

Nat held up her hands and took a pretend photo. "Insta-perfect," she said.

"I love you," she mouthed at Harry and her dad, both.

She felt lucky that her dad was her dad, and Harry was maybe not her BFF, but she loved him anyway. You could love someone and not have them love you back in exactly the same way, and that was OK, too.

Nat stood on one leg, like a flamingo. Then she stood on her other leg. Her feet were used to the sand now, or maybe it was just cooling off. She did the only yoga stretch she knew, which was the Rising Sun pose. The sun was setting, not rising, but she was pretty sure it wouldn't mind.

Nat's muscles stretched and relaxed. The sky pinked up and turned orange and red, a fiery canvas. It looked not quite real.

She watched her dad and Harry on the wave, then she sat down, still watching, and sifting sand between her fingers. Her fingers brushed against a shell. It was tiny, but she held it up to her ear anyway. The Bird told her once that when you listen to a shell, it's not the ocean that you hear, but your own blood, circulating through your body.

She thought about something Harry said to her the day before, which she didn't get then, but suddenly she did now, all at once. She had said something about his dad, and how it must be really hard when he was a total jerk. And Harry had looked at her and raised one eyebrow—kind of like how her dad did it, come to think of it—and he'd shrugged and said, "You aren't your parents, you know. You're just yourself. You're a separate thing." He paused. "Besides, he's not so bad. I think he's getting better."

Nat hoped that was true.

She listened hard to the shell.

She listened *so* hard, she had to close her eyes. She could hear better when she wasn't looking at the ocean, squinting for fins rising up between the waves.

Nat listened and listened.

Then, finally, over the sound of the wind and surf, she heard a small echo, the tiny ocean of her own beating heart. She looked up. Harry was up on a wave, crouched down like a pro, like someone who was in exactly the right place at the right time. She was pretty sure that her dad was smiling *aggressively*, with all his extra teeth. He waved at her, and she heard him yell, "HEY, NAT!" She stood so she could see him better, just in time to see him doing two big thumbs-up and then bringing his giant thumbs-up to his nose. She rolled her eyes, and then she giggled.

"Because it's the end!" she called, even though she knew he couldn't hear her; her words, instead, were blown back toward the palatial glass house and up into the windy brown hills beyond.

ACKNOWLEDGMENTS

As a writer, I spend a fair amount of time online. I used to feel guilty about this, like I was somehow being lazy or avoiding doing my work. And maybe I was, just a little! But the Internet is also a treasure trove of ideas, and as it happens, over time, it slowly started gifting me with more and more untranslatable words. I started a file where I began collecting my favorites. I didn't know what I was going to do with them, but I knew I would come back to them eventually. And luckily, they were exactly the right collection to share with Natalia Rose as she navigated through seventh grade in Sooke, BC, Canada, with her famous dad in tow.

I would like to acknowledge that both Sooke and French Beach are real places, and very beautiful places, too. (I strongly recommend that you visit them if you can. And maybe, if you're extraordinarily lucky, the orcas will come to shore and pay you a visit. It happens!) However, I did play a little bit with the places in the book. Justin Trudeau Middle School does not exist, for example. Nat and XAN GALLAGHER's trailer, in my imagination, was on a property that is, in real life, parkland. Let's call this "artistic license."

I'm deeply indebted to Dwayne "The Rock" Johnson,

simply for existing, having a sense of humor about himself, and being so great, in general. I have a funny story that I can tell you about the Rock and how I didn't meet him, but I'm still thankful for the positive impact that he's had on my life and the life of my kids, even if he didn't know it was happening. The character of XAN GALLAGHER is a mash-up of my kids' ideal stepdad, the Rock, and maybe a touch of Matthew McConaughey, just in case Dwayne Johnson isn't available to play the part should the movie version of this book ever come into being.

When I began, my goal was to write a modern retake of Judy Blume's book *Are You There God? It's Me, Margaret.* The yellow bathing suit was for Margaret, who got me started on the path of writing this story.

As always, I didn't write this book alone. I had a lot of help, from some amazing people. My agent, Jennifer Laughran, who has a great nickname for this one. My editor, Krestyna Lypen, who understands. My publisher, Elise Howard, who keeps believing in me. The artist who created the magical cover, Julie McLaughlin. The copy editor who helped me perfect the details, Martha Cipolla. And everyone else on the Algonquin team who will hold my hand through the next parts, final polish, the publicity, the reviews, the signing, the public speaking, the awkward air bands, the hectic scheduling, and the parts where I suddenly remember that I'm scared of flying. I feel so very lucky to be taken care of so well. In the book, Nat says that love is when you just *get* someone else, and I've never felt that in my work as strongly as I have with this team of incredible, passionate book people. You all are my book family, and I am so fortunate. <3

I couldn't do any of it without the support of my

family and friends, near and far. My friend Rosy Hernandez Madrigal generously helped me with my Spanish and with all the Mexican aspects of this book. Rob Bittner, who is a super(book)hero, lent me his keen eye and gave me some essential feedback during revisions. That said, any mistakes that I made are mine and not theirs! Thank you, thank you, thank you.

And last but not least, my kids, who taught me everything I know about single parenting: I love you more than everything.

Thank you for reading my book. I hope you enjoyed reading it as much as I enjoyed writing it! I truly loved it. It was all joy, every bit of it.